Pegsy

WADING THROUGH JELLY

All the jelly bestest!

MaryAnn Pledge

WADING THROUGH JELLY

Mary Ann Pledge

ATHENA PRESS
LONDON

ISBN 1 84401 705 2

First Published 2006 by
ATHENA PRESS
Queen's House, 2 Holly Road
Twickenham TW1 4EG
United Kingdom

Apart from Tramp and the warhorse generation,
this is a work of fiction. Any resemblance to real-life in characters
or schools would be entirely coincidental.

Printed for Athena Press

To Bracken (alias Tramp)
who kept my feet warm over the year this book
was written and who died, aged eighteen, soon after its completion.
It is also to my brother, Geoff Pledge, who is always there –
even from half a world away.

Acknowledgements

Many thanks to Miranda, for her superior computer skills, to Georgie Cotton for her great reproductive capabilities, to Bridget Simmons and Dr John Wilson for medical information, to Alison Boyle for her unerring verve, to Bernie and Sarah Wragge Morley for their kind help in data retrieval (when eighteen chapters of this were lost!), and to Matt Chamings, for his authorial knowledge and advice. Thanks, too, to my lovely daughters, Annelisa, Miranda, (aforementioned) and Cissie, for their encouragement, faith and fun – and last, but not least, to Arnold for keeping my feet on the ground and my heart in the sky!

Chapter One

'Good morning, good morning, good morning-ger!' John Lennon's caustic tones reverberated through the plastic cockerel-shaped alarm clock to announce that it was seven o'clock. Connie stretched lazily in its direction as the sound of the telephone began its own competitive assault.

'Shall I get it?' asked a small eager voice from beside her. Connie grunted in grateful assent. There was a pause as Poppy reached for the portable.

'I'm afraid it's for you, Mummy.' She handed over the receiver. 'It's "Oh no, Teaching"!' Poppy confided in a stage whisper. Connie winced.

'Hello, it's "Let's Go Teaching", Matt speaking. Are you free today?'

No – oh no! thought Connie.

'Yes, I believe I am,' she answered brightly, 'and where would this be?' *Not St John's – please not St John's!*

'At St John's school. Year Six. The work isn't set, so could you bring something of your own?'

'No problem. Right – thank you – I'll look forward to it.' *Like a hole in the head!* 'Goodbye!' She put the receiver back and groaned again.

'Why do you do supply teaching if you don't like it?' asked Poppy. *Out of the mouths of babes and sucklings!*

'For dosh, dosh, dosh!' answered Connie, 'and really, of course, it can be very rewarding. At times.' A loud explosive noise rocked the room; something between a sneeze and an expletive, as a large shaggy head peered over the edge of the bed.

The mild round eyes were a myopic milky blue, the ears and most of the coat a raggy rust colour, while the muzzle and whiskers had faded to grey.

'Tramp! Hello old stager! Wag that raggy tail!' chorused Connie and Poppy, rolling to the side where he wavered on flipper-like paws. He allowed them to hold out their hands while he slowly pushed his head and body under them to its full length, before diving around in

9

a circle to repeat the process. After a few turns of this sort, he stretched, extending his flag of a tail and farted. Then, setting his tail at a still jauntier angle and his white whiskered nose in the air, he made his dignified exit, his toenails castanetting a purposeful march, for it was time to receive his dues of adulation from his other three charges.

After a swift and scrappy breakfast, each shambling down in order of breakfast-size and age (teenagers, who ate least, were last), school bags were scooped up and the children ran for the car, mindful of the unrelenting time of the school bus. Tramp, too old now to jump successfully, was bundled into the back with the bags as they scrunched across the gravel and rumbled up the drive, to be dropped at their respective bus stops and schools.

The school run accomplished; Connie made her way to St John's, organising her thoughts for the first lesson as she went. She parked outside the school playground and gave Tramp a hug.

'I may be gone some time,' she breathed into the short soft warm fur on the top of his head, 'but I will be back at lunchtime for our walk,' and with that she shut the door gently as Tramp adjusted himself for his doze. The headmaster was waiting for her anxiously at the top of the school steps, wearing a jaunty pair of joggers and looking as though he might take off at any minute himself, if the going became tougher. Connie assured him that she had plenty of work with her and attempted a confident 'no nonsense' demeanour, calculated to go down well.

'It's quite a *lively* class,' the head warned. Connie shuddered inwardly, for 'lively' was a pedagogical euphemism for pretty much ungovernable, but she nodded reassuringly, as her own role as all-capable Supply demanded.

'All in a day's work!' she answered heartily.

They threaded their way across a riotous playground, between footballs and line dance routines, to a mobile classroom. As Connie was assuring the harassed-looking head that she was sure she would find everything and that there was no need to worry, she felt her mobile phone, which had only just kicked into signal, vibrate against her thigh. She hoped fervently that the head had not also heard the faint buzzing sound, signifying a message, that accompanied the vibration, and wondered what she had in her pocket. His questioning gaze could have signified any number of things, so she simply assured him once more that all would be fine, and thinking, *Dosh, dosh, dosh,* mounted the hazardously slimy wooden steps into the classroom.

The head decided that the funny battery-driven sound really wasn't his problem. The real question was whether this rather scatty-looking woman was going to last the day, as she seemed to think, or whether she would quit at lunchtime, as yesterday's supply had, rendering himself supply understudy again.

It was later than she had thought, but she couldn't resist a quick glance at her mobile before she switched it off. The name Pete lit up the face and she sighed, wondering if any further disaster had happened to him, which would somehow be attributed to her! She knew she should switch it off now, but no one was in yet. She could find out what she was supposed to have done this time, press 'delete' and put the issue behind her, rather than wait until lunchtime. She rang for the message and pressed it to her ear, in an attempt to combat the din from outside, at the same time deftly flipping through her materials on numeracy. As the lengthy message unfolded, however, she froze:

'Don't think badly of me any more –' slurred the voice, 'you just couldn't see how good we were together. And I'm sorry if you're regretting your mistake and missing me now – but you've run out of time. I don't think you realise how much I love you or you wouldn't have been so cruel as to try to finish things…

'What you don't realise is that we'll never be finished! I don't want you blaming yourself because it's my decision. I've got those morphine pills saved from my dad and I have to say they do go down easily as anything with that vodka you gave me when you came back from Amsterdam. You'll probably be feeling really guilty and sad now. I don't want you to be sad – but I hope you realise now what you've thrown away. Better say 'bye – I'm getting sleepy – 'baa.' As she listened, aghast, Connie was too engrossed to notice the ragged stream of children who were coming in for registration, but now she was dimly aware that they were jostling around her. Her naturally tanned complexion had turned sallow as she muttered that she was going to need an ambulance.

As her trembling fingers flexed to dial, the mobile rang.

'Oo – cool ring tone, Miss!'

Here was a dilemma! How could she have any authority remaining if she answered calls in school time? But she couldn't possibly stay now with this news. She should ring for the ambulance and then explain that she had to leave: the children would love that –

and the head would go berserk. Understandably.

'Go on – answer it, Miss!' She glanced at the mobile indecisively and saw Pete's name again!

'Who is it, Miss? *Bet it's her boyfriend!*'

'She 'asn't got one!'

''Ow'd you know?'

'Aw, come on! 'Oo'd go with a teacher, eh?'

The indecision over, Connie grabbed at the mobile and answered, to hear Pete's remarkably normal-sounding voice!

'Pete! What on *earth* were you playing at?'

'*See! I told you she 'ad a boyfriend.*'

'Hello, Connie. How are we?'

'I thought you'd committed suicide!' A reverent hush had descended on the class, but Connie hadn't noticed, due to the relief of hearing Pete, clearly in sound health. Even in these circumstances, she was for once overwhelmingly glad to hear his voice. The next moment, however, she found herself seething at the emotional upheaval he had just dragged her through.

'Ah, well, I *did* drink a lot of that stuff!' he boasted in explanation.

'But the pills! You said…'

'Well, I think I may have taken a few of those too – I can't precisely remember!'

'I was just about to call an ambulance!'

An impressed intake of breath greeted this announcement.

'I say! So you *do* care!'

'Was that all your message was about?' she expostulated. 'To see if I – I can't believe you'd go this far – your self-interest has simply no bounds whatever, has it?'

The children's eyes bulged in awe and admiration.

'*Coo – 'er can really go, can't 'er?*'

'*Don't 'er look better when 'er's 'mazed!*'

'*You'd be 'mazed, too, if you wuz 'er.*'

'I only did it because I love you and you didn't seem to care.' Pete was explaining, 'I shouldn't have, I'll admit, but you have to realise what you drive me to.'

(Ah – here was the blame!)

'Pete, just get off the line – I'm in class – and please don't bother to call back – now or at any time!'

Slowly she returned to focus on the class, who were in stunned and reverential silence! This was a first for St John's. She switched the mobile off and turned to face the children, a blush seeping up from the back of her neck.

The head, hovering outside, ready to sweep in and support the supply teacher over her first onslaught of the day, shook his head in amazed disbelief! There was obviously more to that incompetent-looking Mrs Sharland's teaching abilities than caught the eye: she had Class Six in complete thrall! This promised to be a better day, he thought, as he strode gratefully towards the safety of his computer.

Chapter Two

When it was 'home time', Connie left St John's at what was not meant to look like a sprint. She tousled Tramp's ears (having let him into the front beside her for company) as she revved the old Discovery into life for its exit from the car park. Supply teaching in the more rambunctious schools was certainly not something to which Connie felt cut out: she had only taken the job on because it gave her the freedom to work on her own terms at times when her children were already in school. No other job offered such autonomy and she knew she must be grateful to have found it; but now she sped away, eager to carry on her life where she had left it 'on hold' this morning. This was the time when every moment counted to her, to get home to feed animals, clear breakfast, put on washing and prepare supper, before she fetched her children from their schools and bus stops for the homeward journey. As she bumped into ever-narrower lanes (the amount of grass in their middle being a proportional indication of the infrequency of use), her spirits began to soar; like Moley's in *The Wind in the Willows*, she thought, when he felt the magnetic, beckoning, welcoming finger of home. She gazed out wonderingly, as always, across the expanse of apparently handkerchief-sized fields, which made up the deep red counterpane of North Devon; Dartmoor, dimly blue on her right, and rusty-red Exmoor, closer, to her left. Soon she was rounding the potholes of the drive, having let Tramp out to trot down in his own time and explore his cinema of smells. As the car bumped around the final corner, the house hove into view; a rambling, stone-built Victorian vicarage, the porch of which was shrouded in winding wisteria. It was surrounded by a mixture of deciduous trees, rough-cut lawns, sprawling orchards and vegetable gardens and was the home, not only to the human incumbents and Tramp, but to some very friendly and thoroughly messy Muscovy ducks, a dynasty of hens (too much loved to be eaten) and a motley assembly of rabbits, guinea pigs and hamsters. Connie was not cognisant of the word 'no' where animals were concerned, with the result that they were surrounded by cast-offs from those in search of better time management.

Connie unlocked the blackened oak front door and it swung open, revealing an interior, which exuded the dampish, toasty, polished, churchy smell that was home. The decor had known better days, for the paint up the broad main staircase was striped from trails of sticky fingers, and the rugs were worn threadbare across the middle from numerous games of run-and-slide up the mosaic tiles of the hall. Grubby trainers lined the passage to the kitchen, the door of which Connie kicked open, instantly feeling the rise in temperature from the ancient but faithful Aga, which was set into the terracotta wall. The tall Victorian ceilings and roomy stone-clad walls did little in support of heating elsewhere; but the house radiated its own warmth and comfort through an atmosphere of wellbeing and homeliness, created across the generations of generally contented inmates, both large and small.

Connie's divorce was proving tough, but the one thing she had held out for, having failed miserably in every financial negotiation, was the home. It was the family base, loved, familiar and secure and this, for the sake of the children and for herself, she would not give up without a struggle. None of them deserved the added wrench of having to move from the comfort of their nest, on top of what had happened – here Connie broke off from her reverie, for she did not want to spoil the thrill of the moment with the chill of the thought of what had prompted Stuart to leave, for it still hurt and mortified too much.

I won't think of that today: I'll think about it tomorrow! This was a gambit Connie, a great fan of the resourceful Scarlett O'Hara, had trained herself to adopt at times when she recognised the downward-spiralling anguish concerning the person she had felt she knew best in the world, threaten momentarily to unhinge.

The indoor jobs were hastily accomplished, apart from the ironing, and Connie left the kitchen through the French windows, with a saucepan full of peelings (left over from the soup from the previous night) to take to the ducks and hens. She called the Muscovys and, with the rush of sound created from the air displaced by their wings, they soared over the treetops to land with perfect navigational skill, flippers outspread as brakes, on the pond.

Connie rained the scraps down on them as they snatched and dived greedily. Next there were the hens to feed and clean out, and Bustle, the strawberry hen, to attend to. Bustle managed to fly out of the hen enclosure each day, because she preferred to lay her egg in a little brown nest of brushwood, under the overgrown yew hedge. Once laid, Bustle sat on her speckled egg a while, bragging and complaining, until someone opened the safety of the enclosure for her, before dusk and prowling predators could lay their claims. All the time Bustle was out, her sister, Bashful, would be fussing and clucking and stalking up and down the inside of the enclosure in agitation at Bustle's foolhardiness: Bashful was far too full of nerves to lay eggs!

Connie looked at her watch and realised that it was past time to leave for her school run. She ran to the car, not bothering to lock the house again or to change from her wellies. People only saw the top of her in the car she reasoned: she had dropped children off at school with a jacket thrown over her pyjamas before now, at times when they had slept through the alarm. As she arrived at the little school, jolting over sadistic speed bumps, she saw a host of scurrying Lilliputian-like children, busily swinging bats, shouldering games kits and schoolbags, drinking at the fountain and jumping on and off the low wall surrounding the school. Connie parked and looked expectantly towards the little throng, her eyes searching for just one amongst the mêlée of uniformed children. The crowd parted a little and suddenly there was Poppy, her round pink face lit up by an ear-splitting grin of recognition. Without a thought of resentfulness for her long wait, she was running, a lurching run on account of the large schoolbag she had draped across her inadequate shoulders, her skinny legs moving like pistons in her thick nary tights, which were concertinaed at the ankles. Her dark hair had escaped the confines of its velvet scrunchy, to whip around her face in unruly ringlets. She threw open the car door and flung herself at her mother, the person most dear in her life, and Connie felt her own heart swell with equally measured joy as she hugged her tightly.

Connie received a stream of information regarding Poppy's day as she sped for the bus stop, trying to make up for time lost. She managed to arrive just as the bus was pulling away. The children were waiting under the lychgate to Atherington church, splayed irreverently on the coffin plinth. The little shelter had withstood the rigors of the elements for centuries and hosted as many coffins on their final journey; yet for the Sharland children ectoplasm would always divide for them in this vivid space, which provided their twice daily collection point, spanning their school years, as a refuge, a play area, a limbo between worlds and modes of transport: a place that they would always claim for their own, every ancient stone a familiarity.

Ella was the first to tumble down the bus steps, followed by Demelza and Sophia. They hurled their bags into the back of the car with abandon before arguing over whose turn it was to sit in the front. (Poppy had obligingly moved to the back for them as they drew up.) It was Demelza's turn and she launched into hilarious tales of what had happened on the bus that day, Sophia correcting some of the wilder exaggerations, while Ella punctuated all with disdainful tuts and comments, such as 'How degrading!', 'So?' and 'Whatever!' Demelza continued her monologue good humouredly, completely unfazed by interruption; however, once there was a lull, Poppy clapped a hand over her mouth dramatically.

'Oh my God!' she said.

'Poppy!' remonstrated Connie. 'I think you mean "gosh"!'

'Woopydoo!' sneered Ella.

'Gosh!' corrected Poppy, continuing: 'I've got a maths test tomorrow and I'd completely forgotten!'

'*Woopydoo!*' repeated Ella, yet more derisorily.

'All very well for you!' retorted Poppy, somewhat stung by the lack of importance made of this fact. 'But I get really bad PMT!' Suddenly she had everyone's attention.

'You can't, you're only seven!' laughed Demelza.

'I can: Billy gets it worst – he gets a zero sometimes, even though he's really quite good at maths in class!'

'I don't think boys can get it, can they?' asked Sophia, now rather unsure about it herself.

'Of course they can't: she just doesn't know what it means!' rejoined Ella.

'I do, so *mer!*' Poppy made a grimace. 'It's pre-maths-test tension and lots of people get it!'

There was an explosion of laughter at this from all the other incumbents of the car, including Connie, at which Poppy's small face began to pucker.

'I'm afraid you need a little talk with Mummy about the birds and the bees!' smiled Demelza kindly, before she ruined it by snorting loudly with another convulsion of laughter.

'But it *is* pre-maths tension, isn't it, Mummy?' asked Poppy, a worried look crossing her indignant face.

'It certainly can stand for that as much as anything else,' answered Connie quickly, as Poppy's voice began to wobble, 'and now can we talk about something else, like what we're having for supper?'

'*What are we having for supper?*' they all chorused, and Connie saw in the mirror that Poppy had swallowed her tears.

'Something gastronomically extraordinary, of course!' she replied, wondering herself what it might transpire to be.

When there was a moment on their own, Connie explained the other meaning of PMT and Poppy, no stranger to the concept in a houseful of females, nodded sagely.

'I knew it,' she said.

'Know what?' asked Connie.

'That boys can have PMT!'

'How's that?' asked Connie, bemused by the apparent failure in her explanation.

'Well it's obvious: *men*strual!' Poppy answered triumphantly, 'and Billy is growing up.'

Chapter Three

Connie was preparing to go out, for it was her band practice evening: she fetched her basket containing her flute and microphone and went into her bedroom where the children were trying delaying tactics. These were always successful, since they knew how to make their mother feel guilty about going out: they were proud of their mother being in a band, for it was deemed by their friends to be 'cool', but it was fun to see how long they could keep her too. Ella had agreed to begin, by asking for Connie's help in her science homework, however, a scrunch of tyres on the gravel outside suggested a further delay of its own. Ella ran to the window but withdrew in disgust:

'Oh no! It's Psycho!' she sing-songed and Connie looked out, to see Pete's purple sports car draw up outside, and groaned inwardly. She and Pete had met at a party soon after Stuart had left, and Connie had found herself grateful to have a 'partner' to fill the void, and flattered by his interest. His antics and attentions, however, had quickly grown out of hand and as she found herself uneasy and unequal to these, she had finished their relationship, hoping that they could remain friends. She now realised that going out with him in the first place had shown naïvety and that the children's nickname for him was uncomfortably apt; as had been demonstrated at St John's, for he seemed wildly self-obsessed and quite unable to appreciate any of the complexities of single parenthood, which necessarily occupied Connie first and foremost. She hurried down to speak with him, anxious that the children should remain in ignorance of his latest manoeuvre.

She ran downstairs before he could reach the back door and walk in, when it would be still harder to be rid of him.

'Before you say anything,' he was holding up his fingers in a peace gesture, 'I must apologise for my ridiculous conduct of last night – too many pills, too much booze – I shouldn't have made that phone call, I know I shouldn't. Please forgive.' He got down on one lanky knee, muddying his jeans.

'Oh, for goodness sake get up!' said Connie ungraciously, afraid that the children might think he was proposing, which was another of his habits when he had over-imbibed.

'I shall, only when you say you forgive me!' He smiled charmingly, his lengthy blond hair, still damp from the shower, brushed cherubically from his forehead, his deep blue eyes and dilated irises imploring.

'Forgive? Oh anything. Just please leave us alone – I really can't take much more of this kind of thing, and I'm exhausted from all your calls – *I* have to get up in the morning!' He leapt up instantly.

Pete lived a life of leisure in his own time-span, for he had been left a sizeable inheritance from his stepfather, who had been living on Alderney as a tax exile, after much success as a stockbroker. Pete had been able to rely on handouts and a hefty allowance from his doting but unwise parents, following expulsion from a number of major public schools, to the extent that he had never had to work. He made occasional, and always surprisingly successful, forays to Sri Lanka, where he bought rough-cut gems to sell as they were, or have made up as jewellery, in Britain. His life was without complication and when he suffered from the resultant ennui, he would travel to exotic climes and once he bored of these, he returned home again. Due to all this, he maintained an all-year-round tan, wore the vivid light, bright clothes of the tropics and found it hard to fit in with the strictures of reality, imposed by a less extrovert lifestyle.

'If I have been overdoing it a little,' he admitted, 'it's only because I care – but if you gave me one more chance—'

'Caring doesn't include pretending suicide to get attention! We've been over this so many times – I agreed to stay platonic friends, but nothing more. We simply aren't right for each other. There are plenty of people who will love to go out with you, but I am definitely not the one. I have too many other children to look after.' It was perhaps a good opportunity to say all this again while she was still cross, because she might have sounded too soft in the past for the message to reach home – and maybe she had been at fault for not being more resolute?

'Ouch! If I go now, would you at least *think*—'

'Watch out: you could be moving from feigned suicide to bribery and that would be too much in one day – even for you! I have to go to my practice, so please leave now and *don't* ring again tonight!'

Pete sighed theatrically, but was sensible enough to realise that he was not going to glean any brownie points by pushing the issue just now. He would surprise her and comply!

'I'm going,' he said meekly, as he turned, head down, little boy-like, towards his car, waiting for her to call him back. 'I really just came over to say how sorry I am – and what a fool I've been.' He was trying it on now and Connie knew it, but she felt a pang of guilt all the same, fearing she had been too harsh, when all he had come for was to apologise. She sighed and returned to the children, who were handing around the portable telephone for turns to speak to Grandma. Ah! Here was a voice she was happy to hear! Her mother's voice was warm with concern and interest in Connie's day and Connie basked in the shift of emphasis. Now she herself could be the child for a time and know that whatever she said would take on an importance, where everywhere else it would be too trivial to mention. She spoke of Sophia's imminent visit to the orthodontist.

'Oh dear – how much longer will the poor thing have those dreadful train-tracky things on? Does she mind awfully? Do you think they hurt a lot? I don't suppose even the orthadoodah would know – she's so brave, isn't she?'

Connie gave herself up gratefully to the eager questions, which were of intrinsic interest and not politeness. Her mother told her that she had been at the WRVS office that day and had not only re-clothed an entire family of six but also provided them with every stick of furniture needed in a temporary home, for their own mobile home had been severely flooded in the Cornish floods. She stopped abruptly.

'But enough of me! How is it all going with Mr Unspeakable?' She referred not to Pete, about whom she knew the minimum, but to Connie's soon-to-be-ex-husband, Stuart.

'Well, you know – dosh, dosh, dosh – it's getting pretty difficult when the bills come in. I think he thinks maintenance is his getting another new car, which doesn't even have the capacity for all the children! I'm really trying to stick to my guns with regard to the house, but everything's so…'

'Expensive? Look, darling, I don't think you need worry any more about keeping the house – or maintaining it. I'll make it all right: I'm past my "sell by" date and have too much "dosh", as you call it. It's bothersome and I can't think of a better use for it,' she continued smoothly before Connie could protest, 'so that's one less thing for us both to lie awake worrying about.'

Connie was momentarily lost for words; then she thanked her mother meekly but suggested financial help to her might be unfair on

Jeremy, her brother living in Australia.

'I'll make sure it's all evened out in my will: Jeremy's as anxious as me in wanting to get things straight for you, you know.'

She knew this was true of her generous-hearted older brother and wished so often that he were closer, so that she could share and confide more with her sibling.

'Don't talk about wills: they'd better be highly unnecessary for a good long time to come.'

'But it's such fun making plans and wishes – I have a wonderful wish where Stuart is concerned, I don't mind telling you: to do with Timbuktu!'

'Do you really think that's far enough?' Connie asked innocently, at which they both began to laugh conspiratorially and Connie felt the tensions of the day lift from her shoulders. She thanked her mother again for the offer of financial assistance, but it was firmly brushed aside.

'Let's not think about it any more – I was always told it was vulgar to talk about money and anyway it's so *boring*! But things have been so painful for you: of course we went through some hard times in the War,' she understated, 'but I never had to deal with anything like this – I do wish there was something I could do for you – I feel so useless!'

'Mother, you *are* doing so much for us *all* – just by being there!'

'Ah well – I think it must be time for my snifter and I'm sure it should be yours too! *I looks towards you*!' toasted her mother.

'*I bows accordin'*!' Connie responded, also adopting the rich, purring Devon dialect. '*Yur'z to us!*' Connie continued.

'*None like us!*' came the traditional reply, which never ceased to make them laugh. Full of wellbeing from the old lady's humour and verve, Connie clicked off the portable phone, counting her blessings.

By the time Connie had reached the room under the station that was used for band practice, she could hear, by the assortment of riffs and scales, that the others were already tuned and ready to go. They would be unable to hear her knock, over their own cacophony, so she rang Cake's mobile to get in. He answered the door wearing his customary multi-seasonal T-shirt, sarong and Jesus sandals. His head was shaven, which highlighted his gauntness, for eating was not on his list of priorities. This was due, in part, to his experiences as a trainee Buddhist monk in Thailand, where his begging bowl was not always filled. Living without material goods and from the charity of others had had its difficulties and eventually his grandmother had flown over to check on him and returned him, half-starved, home to Devon. Despite the harshness of the lifestyle, Cake's mind had never totally returned home, for his meditations and his conversation revolved perpetually around his adventures in his beloved Thailand, where the name 'Cake' had been bestowed on him after he admitted that cake was going to be the item most hard to live without.

Classed as psychologically unfit for work, he lived off benefits and such income as the band brought in with their gigs. He was an accomplished drummer, and it was in the world of music that his two existences, past and present, converged into one, where he would play with total absorption and commitment.

The bass player, Andy, smiled shyly as Connie explained some of the catalogue of events leading to her lateness. He was a solicitor during working hours and the band provided his recreational outlet, into which he threw himself with no small degree of manic gusto, happy to shut out the traumas of criminal law and divorce. The latter had complicated itself, as far as the band was concerned, for he was Connie's obvious first choice for a divorce lawyer; however, having willingly taken her on, eschewing normal fees, they had begun seeing each other for extra-curricula supportive chats, which evolved into dates. Connie had found his comments, regarding the criminal world that he inhabited, comically captivating, for he would quietly point out various average-looking people as they entered the bar with: 'Don't look now, but the guy who's just come in was accused of GBH with a poker – I got him off though. Of course he was guilty as *hell*,' or, 'See that woman there, who was looking towards me a minute ago? Well she's got six kids and you won't *believe* what she gets in maintenance!' His company and experience, at this most vulnerable time, had been good for Connie; however, out of the blue he insisted on referring her ongoing divorce to a colleague, for fear of repercussions in the legal brotherhood. Their friendship had necessarily cooled for a while as a result of this, partly because Connie wished she had been let into the full picture before embarking on a relationship; for her own choice would have been to keep the lawyer rather than have the lover: a new solicitor necessitated revisiting the most painful areas of her divorce again, which was a chapter in the public arena of which she had hoped she had closed the lid. The match was not one made in the heavens anyway, since she had found his penchant for nibbling at amorous moments most disconcerting! Water under the bridge and her subsequent relationship with Pete had eased any awkwardness between them and their musical respect for one another remained undiminished.

The guitarist, Nigel, was one of nature's natural musicians: at band functions he remained laconic and seemed to save his feelings for his guitar.

He had a superb ear for melody and tended to play in a lounging stance, without moving his body, saving all his energy for the music, which flowed apparently effortlessly through him. He was strikingly good-looking, with a rare combination of shiny black, wavy hair and piercing blue eyes. He had a natural tan, which set off his piratical, slightly chipped front teeth to greater whiteness and his lean body supported relatively broad shoulders. Perhaps his greatest charm was that he was totally unaware of the effect he had on others, being, apart from work with the band, reclusive. He owned a smallholding near South Molton, where he kept a variety of animals and although a number of girls had attempted to grace the garden path, few had succeeded, for he was thoroughly content with life just as it was, without complication. He grinned and nodded at Connie as she began to assemble her flute, stuck his cigarette in the end of his guitar between the pegs and began to play a riff in repetition. Cake instantly picked up the rhythm and Andy followed with a bass line, hesitantly at first as he watched Nigel's fingers to check the chords, and then more boldly, adding some runs of his own.

Connie huffed into her flute to reach the correct pitch before playing, first in unison with the guitar and then in imitation, in phrases of question and answer. The sound began to take on evenness and the music began to flow, as each extended the musical line a little further until the music appeared to be writing itself. Connie was moving her body in gentle support to the sounds which were moving her fingers, and her breath that was making the sounds.

Gradually, as if speaking in tongues, the musicians moved from cacophony to quieter, gentler climbs before petering out and laughing. Laughing in simple joy at what had been created for those moments, shared, unwitnessed, already gone, a conspiracy of used-up sound. This was how they began most practices. Sometimes the music flowed relatively effortlessly, as at this, and at others it remained more static; but after this release they would be better able to focus their energies to the confines of their gig list and perhaps learn some new songs.

After the practice they were usually just in time for last orders at the pub, to where they would all adjourn, necessarily buying beer for Cake (whose benefits never reached as far as buying a round), and catching up on the miasma of their individual existences. Andy sidled up to Connie.

'Connie, rumour has it you're having a bit of trouble with Pete.' At the name, Connie whirled around automatically, searching the bar and the street outside for the purple sports car.

'I don't think *I've* mentioned it,' she said guardedly, thinking that news travelled simply too fast.

'Oh, don't worry – it's just my observation – after all, you did split up some months ago, didn't you?'

He's fishing, thought Connie.

'We did, as I thought you already knew. But yes – things are still none too easy. He just doesn't seem to accept it and keeps making our friendship into something it never really was. I had hoped that we could stay platonic friends but I'm beginning to feel pretty frazzled.'

'*We* managed the platonic bit all right, didn't we?'

'Oh, Andy, we did – and I'm glad! But with us it was an even shorter space.'

'I'm glad too. But I wish I'd had the chance to get to know you a bit better.'

'Well, you have – I mean here we all are and the band seems to be doing pretty much OK. For myself a few gigs is ideal – I couldn't fit in loads of them because of the children.'

'But I meant that it might be nice to spend some more time together, not with the band. I mean as *well* as the band. On our own. Oh dear – I'm not being very eloquent, am I?' He laughed a little awkwardly, as did Connie.

'I think I'm getting the drift and I do enjoy your company, but...' she looked for inspiration. *How not to offend, but the thought of that nibbling habit of his...* 'The thing is, Andy. Well – once *bitten*...' As she said this she listened in horror to what had slipped out of her mouth and found the nervous giggles, which had never quite deserted her since her school days when in a tight spot, convulse her momentarily; she made a huge effort to pull herself together. Andy didn't take any notice as she fought back the tears of mirth.

'Yes, yes I see. I don't blame you. It was just a thought – probably a rather bad one – it's been one of those days. You see I've always had a bit of a soft spot for you and I just wondered – that's all.'

'Well I'm truly flattered,' gasped Connie. 'It was lovely of you to ask me and I do value your company enormously, but...' She was floundering again, but mercifully he cut in.

'Do you really? That's sweet of you! Then we shall stay the best of company!'

Connie breathed a sigh of relief that this rather mismanaged inquest with someone she valued as a friend was over, without further discomfort for either party, but she then became aware of Andy's eyes, which were narrowing in his efforts to see round a pillar in the bar.

'Yes, I *thought* so! Don't look or anything, but that guy in the black hoodie who's just come in was accused of pinching *twenty-five* DVDs by W H Smith's store detective. I'm defending him but it's going to be tough explaining that he thought they were all free samples.'

Chapter Four

Darling Connie,

I am writing to beg you to be more tolerant about my recent behaviour with the 'suicide' thing.

(I promise you I DID actually think about it, but suicide would have been unfair on you, which is the last thing I want and why ultimately I didn't do it.) I am not trying to make excuses, but you must realise that the way I acted was, in fact, entirely down to YOUR rejection and therefore you are not entirely blameless yourself! Despite my transgressions, what we had – and still might continue to have – was very, very special and you appear so easily to deny this. I hope one day soon you will see its potential. Meantime, I ask you to consider carefully what you would be losing if you continue to reject our love. Please give it a chance to flourish – my impetuousness was only due to my unconditional love, which you seem so prepared to give up. Just remember that none of my more dramatic actions would occur if I had the encouragement and support I perhaps deserve. It's all up, or is it down, to you.

You show kindness to the world in your every movement, so I don't understand why you can't spare some for this miserable fool too?

Loving you to eternity,
Pete

Dear Pete,

Thank you for your letter, but I really don't feel worthy of so much consideration. We split up some time ago now and I think it may be a much happier outcome for us both if we accepted that. Nothing that has happened since has really served to change my mind and I think you may just be fantasising a little about what we shared. It was great fun, I agree; but if you continue to harp in this vein, these positive memories could lose themselves amongst the angst of our very different needs and outlooks. I am so very flattered and touched by your kind thoughts towards me, but I feel they may be rather misdirecting themselves and that there will be someone so very much more special out there for you, who is not getting the chance they deserve, due to the murky cloud surrounding me! I really don't think that I am the right person for you to have those feelings for, since my life is necessarily one which has very little time for the deep sort of relationship you need and deserve.

I am so sorry that I have let you down as you clearly feel and can only say that I was unaware of so doing. My head is always full of muddle and at present more so. However, I have to ask you to give me and my family space, for frequent phone calls block out the computer for homework as well as chat lines! If we say 'Goodbye' on the phone, it is really unacceptable for you to ring back seconds later and then repeatedly throughout the night! And if I take the phone off the hook, which surely shouldn't be necessary, I can't be contacted for work, so then I lose money! You are lucky that your inheritance renders ordinary work unnecessary, but please understand that not everyone shares that privilege! (Green with envy though we may be!)

So please accept my deep regret for not feeling the way you would like me to, but that is me (not wishing to sound like Sharon Osborne or anything!) and my unsuitability is clear. Please go out and have some fun with someone with fewer complications and commitments.

Wishing you wonders,
Connie

Connie read her email through. Pete had been fun, there was no denying it, and to have to come out with all that prior commitment stuff, though true and necessary, made her feel dull, old and somewhat depressed. She hoped it would serve its purpose, however, and that Pete would cease to harass her to the extent that he had. She decided that this would have to be added to the list of things not to think about today but tomorrow; however, before she had fully managed to bring this maxim into play, her inbox was pinging with a new missive:

Dearest Connie,
I so completely understand. I must back off and give you space, for if I don't, I see I am in fear of losing you and this would be more tragic than anything. Perhaps I must accept, for the moment, that you don't have time for me in your crowded existence. I really would like to help

you, and not hinder, so if I promise to ease the apparent bombardment of calls – I see I may have been a little over-zealous there, but you didn't seem to understand – could we continue to see one another sometimes, simply as friends?

There's the James Bond ball coming up, remember, and I still have the tickets: would you do me the great honour of still accompanying me as JB's moll? (Only a platonic one, which I doubt is in any script for JB, but poetic licence and all that!) Do say yes: whatever you say I will try to behave with more decorum, for I see you seem to think I was being a might self-centred (when indeed I was actually only being YOU centred.) But let that pass. (You see? I'm being reasonable as Hell.) I value your friendship and good karma towards me more than anything – DO come!

Fingers and toes, crossed and double-crossed,
Pete

Connie cogitated for a while over this. She, too, had been looking forward to the James Bond ball for a while and if Pete really could be a partner to her, without threatening involvement, this might be ideal; for his hurt would ease and she wouldn't feel as vulnerable as she did when going to parties alone. Furthermore, it might also serve to assuage the guilt, which she found herself surrounded by where Pete was concerned, for his contradictory accusations never ceased to move her in their sway. It might be fun to have Pete's company, as it had been before it all became so complex, for his sense of fun was of the ridiculous and infectious.

Dear Pete,
If our friendship can really be uncomplicatedly platonic, then I can't think of anything nicer than going with you to the ball. I do value your friendship, as long as there can be no further ifs and buts – AND that you'll allow us to sleep without the barrage of calls!

I'll look forward to it,
Yours, Moll

———⟨⟩———

Wonderful Molly!
Cool!
Love, James ~~Banned~~ Bond!

Chapter Five

Pete kept his distance over the next few weeks, making only the odd conciliatory phone call, and Connie was able to sleep better, with one of her problems apparently erased. Her supply work continued erratically: often there was no work when she felt available and ready to cope, after which there might be incessant offers on overload from the agency. These she dare not turn down for fear of a resultant dearth of offers, which, in turn, 'dominoed' financial pressure. On this particular morning she had landed a picturesque village school in which she was relatively well known. There was the undeniable advantage of familiarity with the day's format and with most of the children's names, and Connie set out, happy in the knowledge of what was expected.

As the white wooden gate swung open to admit her, announcing her arrival by the grating of its rusty hinges, the children looked up from their play and, calling her name excitedly, ran towards her, winding their arms about her. Although all teachers' handbooks decreed complete lack of physical contact with children – from disallowing the application of sun block without special written permission, to not comforting the injured or confused youngster with a cuddle – all such communicative restraint was ignored here and Connie returned the welcomed hugs with pleasure.

One of the difficulties inherent in the village school system was the perpetual struggle against governmental pressure to close, made more acute by the economies, which sometimes had to be met through staffing cuts. Thus there were often three different year groups to a classroom, which were taught by the head teacher, who had a hundred other administrative jobs to do. Connie was often called in to cover a head's class, when they had meetings or were completely snowed under with paperwork. Preparation from Connie's viewpoint had to involve topics which encompassed three levels and these, in turn, were made more complicated by anxiously scribbled memos from the class teacher to explain that Kevin and Charlie would not be capable of work set for Year Two standard (in spite of it being their age group) while Samantha should do Year

Three work, since she was too bright for her own year and if she became bored she could be troublesome.

On this occasion Connie's topic was Elizabeth the First and she began by pretending they were in a time capsule and talking generally about the Elizabethans, the clothes, the housing, the contrasts between rich and poor and the appalling smells they would have encountered, connected with Queen Elizabeth's penchant for strewing her floors with sweet-smelling meadowsweet to combat the odour of her courtiers. This never failed to provoke interest across the spectrum, as the children wrinkled their noses in mock horror, shuffling around on the carpet and proclaiming, 'Pwoorh!'

'Did they *really* just chuck their rubbish right out in the street?'

'Cool!'

'You done that round your farm with all they tractor tyres: my Mum says you're just like the Grundys!'

'Tyres never stink – n'anyway we don't know no Grundys.'

'Tiz on *The Archers*, brains for bindertwine!'

Connie felt that the chafing was in danger of becoming a little too personal between Winston, a brick red-faced blond, his large chubby body crammed into a shiny inadequate pair of shorts, out of which his dimpled, pink legs stuck uncomfortably, and Samantha, whose bright freckled face peered from behind steel-rimmed spectacles, the ear pieces of which tangled with the tawny thick bunches, stuck at right-angles to her face in bottle-brush style.

Connie scratched her head and began to make non-verbal sounds commensurate with moving back to the subject, when her glance happened to land briefly on her nail, from which waved a pair of dark bristling pincers!

She stared at these in revulsion, attempting to dislodge them surreptitiously for better inspection: this was not difficult and there, waving from the palm of her hand, was a nit!

The psychological impact was intense and she was instantly ravaged by itches spanning her entire head.

'Of course, the Elizabethans would also have suffered from being louse-ridden all over,' Connie continued, 'on account, of course, of having no running water at home; no basins, no baths and no loos. Can you imagine that?'

'Miss, they would have itched!'

'And *scratched*!'

'*And* stunk and *farted*!' called out Denzil happily: he was the oldest in the class and was completely disinterested in any formal education beyond drawing large faces with smiling lips and red noses, covering the entire page. He was especially fond of Connie because her presence generally took life away from the norm, which was less boring, and he liked the way her eyes smiled, like in his pictures, even when, as now, he had said something that he felt was naughty.

By now the entire class had taken on their own interpretation of the Elizabethans, which consisted of dramatic scratches and raspberry blowing.

Connie had intended to take the lesson on through Sir Walter Raleigh's gallantry, wars with Spain, and further intricacies of Elizabeth's long reign; however, her mind became numb to anything beyond the desire to scratch, which she was doing gently as she feigned the children's exaggerated impromptu dramatisation of the Elizabethan populace. She began to mention Elizabeth the First's auburn wig, under which she was reputed to be bald, but this led to further speculation.

'I bet 'er itched under that like crazy!' Denzil was rolling on the carpet like a puppy, in convulsions of laughter: this was indeed proving to be the best school day in ages.

The point of heralding poor Queen Elizabeth had truly passed and Connie hurriedly issued the children off to their different tables to write and illustrate their impressions of Elizabeth thus far, while she escaped to the confines of the walk-in resources cupboard, in which she indulged in the most rigorous scratch, paralleling that of Balloo in *The Jungle Book*. Scratching gave her the same intense pleasure, but the moment she stopped in one place, with a view to rejoining the class, the agony of itches began afresh in another and she felt she had to indulge in just one more delicious scraping head-massage.

The headmaster had taken the afternoon to interview some prospective parents. It was important to keep the numbers to a maximum for fear of closure. The government being based in Westminster didn't bode well in terms of understanding the necessary expenses for a school like this, such as school buses, which had to go further to supply the wider catchment area. He wanted the catchment area to be as wide as possible in order to garner more children, and more children could mean the extra classroom that they so badly needed – and perhaps an extra teacher too. It was all a matter of PR and balance. The family he had this afternoon were from Brigstow, but the parents felt that their children might benefit more from the greater nurture of a village school. The head was fairly confident that the school spoke for itself and began his usual tour around the classrooms, being careful to take them the long way around the boys' lavatories, which tended to block rather easily and could reek a little at this time of day. At the door of Connie's classroom he paused, explaining that they had a supply in today, but that she was well tested and approved by the school. He opened the door and the sound of organised chaos dipped to a more sensible level at his entrance, in reverence and respect for his station. (This was something which still engendered a secret buzz!) He stared around the classroom beatifically and then looked again more carefully.

'Uhm – where's Mrs Sharland?' he asked, taking in with satisfaction the neat heading of 'Queen Elizabeth the First' on the board.

''Er'z in the cupboard, Zur!' answered half a dozen helpful voices.

'Ah! Our *resources* cupboard,' he explained eagerly to the visitors as he swiftly and deftly positioned himself between them and Denzil's picture, which he had noticed to be one of Denzil's infamous large portraits, this time of someone who was bald with what looked like tarantulas on their head. It was labelled in Winston's round unpractised hand 'Queen Pongy!'

Connie heard the interruption and pulled herself together instantly. She picked up an armful of A3 paper and some coloured pencils and emerged from the cupboard with that apologetic smile the head had begun to like.

What was most unfortunate, however, thought the head, was that Mrs Sharland had clearly had some sort of major bad hair day, or had she been walking that dog of hers in a force ten gale? Whichever, she should have allowed time to check in the mirror at *some* point, he thought. Her tawny hair was standing out fantastically from every angle of her head, indeed every hair seemed to be separated from its neighbour and bushed from the next; and there seemed to be about as much of it standing above her head as there was to the sides and below!

'Everything all right, Mrs Sharland?'

'Absolutely fine, Mr Smith. We are just getting to grips with the reign of Elizabeth the First!' smiled Connie, glad that he was not venturing further into the room to view some of the more imaginative and graphic accounts of Elizabethan olfaction.

'Good, good: well, they look most absorbed!' responded Mr Smith from his place beside Denzil as he expertly gauged the expressions of the visitors, noticing with relief that they seemed more amused than disgruntled. 'Well, well, we'll leave you to it.' He ushered the visitors out, thinking that although Mrs Sharland might *look* and behave a little eccentrically, the children – even the normally vacant Denzil – seemed comfortable with her, and perhaps that was the main thing.

Once the door had closed behind the head and Connie had inwardly heaved a sigh of relief, Denzil looked at her rooks' nest hair and drew a loud intake of breath.

'Miss! You'm lookin' *boodiful*!' he sighed admiringly.

On the way home Connie visited the chemist, where she bought a quantity of de-lousing shampoo and then explained to her children the necessity for them all to treat themselves on the same evening. This was met with sighs and moans.

'Not again! Poppy! Why can't you keep your head clear from your little preppy friends!'

'I do!' cried Poppy indignantly. 'And anyway why pick on me? We could just as easily have got them through you, Demelza!'

'Oo, not *me*! You wouldn't catch *me* fraternising with *nit-heads*!' said Demelza, quelling the strong desire to scratch her own head.

'*Saw you* scratch anyway!' defended Sophia loyally.

'You did not!'

'She who scratched it batched it!' rejoined Ella.

'Then you *all* batched it!' said Poppy gleefully, for as she looked around, there appeared to be no holds barred any more. Each individual had given way to the most thorough, nail-digging ploughs through their scalps, as they itched uncontrollably. The banter and mockery continued in tandem throughout the rest of the journey and each felt relief as they arrived at the house and spilled out of the car, their dishevelled hair taking on cartoon proportions.

'I rather suspect,' said Connie, as she heaved open the front door, 'that you all contracted the nits through *me* and one of my schools, probably St John's.

'Which means,' she added, as she thundered up the stairs, 'that I get first crack with the shampoo!' This had never occurred to them, but their cries of disgust were drowned by the rushing of the taps, under which Connie had already placed her tortured head!

Chapter Six

It was the evening of the James Bond ball and the children were sprawled over Connie's bed giving advice, painting her nails and straightening her super shiny (thanks to the nit shampoo) unruly, hair. She had borrowed a shimmering mini dress from Clara, which she wore with Ella's high-heeled boots and was feeling faintly ridiculous at all the fuss. Demelza and Ella had overdone her make-up hugely and she was determined to somehow scrape some of it off surreptitiously before she went out. The phone rang and four arms lunged towards it: it was Grandma, and Ella managed first grab.

'I've just had a phone call from Fish!' an excited Grandma whistled down the earpiece. Fish was a friend who was in the same sector of Intelligence as her during the War. 'She says she's coming to Cornwall to stay, so I shall have to get the sherries in!'

'You certainly will – and dust the cobwebs from the *Scrabble* board!'

'Oh yes, I am looking forward to it: it's so lovely when you're so well matched and you can try your best, you know!'

'You mean you're both as brainy as each other!'

'I don't mean that at all – just well matched!' she repeated good-naturedly.

Demelza snatched the phone from Ella.

'You will bring Fish to see us, won't you, Grandma? She's so cool.'

'Well, if we're invited, then yes, *please!*'

'She says "yes",' stage-whispered Demelza regally.

'And what is your good mother up to?' inquired Grandma.

'My good mother is about to be very bad!'

'Oh? How's that?' asked Grandma, unperturbed.

'She's going to get very, very drunk – she's going out tonight, and I feel it in my bones—'

Connie took over and enthused with her mother over the proposed visit with Fish.

'Well, I'd better leave you to get ready – and if Demelza's right, I think I'll get a start on you with my snifter!'

'*I looks towards you* then!'

'*I bows accordin'. Yur'z to us!*'

'*None like us!*' they all chorused, as Connie returned the phone and there was the sound of scrunching gravel outside. Sophia ran to the window:

'Uh oh! Psycho!' she called, as she looked down on the purple sports car.

Connie hushed them all and sent Poppy down to let him in, as the thrum of a four-by-four announced another arrival, that of Max and Clara, who were giving them a lift to the venue. Max, a wine merchant, was looking suave and debonair in a dinner jacket with white tie, his dark hair straightened through gloops of hair gel. Clara, an accountant, was visibly pregnant, which was why she was offering to do the driving for all. A figure-hugging fluffy cat suit, complete with tail, boasted her state to its most feminine advantage.

'Thought I'd make the most of the cleavage!' she announced proudly as she patted a bursting bosom, bedecked with diamonds. Pete rushed ahead of Poppy to the front door, throwing it open welcomingly in the gesture of mine host. He was dressed gangster-style, in a dark suit, under which was a black roll-neck sweater. A black knitted balaclava hid much of his floppy blond hair, and from which his china blue eyes, curiously dilated, shone with excitement. His top pocket bulged with a water pistol, which he whipped out at Ella, telling her to 'stick 'em up!'

'Never point guns, even in fun,' said Ella, witheringly.

Max and Clara were aware of the tensions between Connie and Pete and had arrived equipped with a bottle of Bollinger to convivialise the atmosphere, which Max wasted no time in opening expertly with barely a pop.

'It's straight from the fridge so I don't think it's had time to warm,' he explained as he tilted back his head, letting the liquid roll over his tongue appraisingly. Pete took a gulp and nodded sagely.

'I told you everyone was going to get very, *verra* drunk!' called Demelza excitedly from her vantage point on the stairs.

'Here's hoping!' answered Pete.

Ella raised her eyes to the ceiling and Connie glared at her, but fortunately Pete had not noticed.

'Mum, why are you giving me evils?' Ella asked innocently. Connie pretended not to hear and instead admired Clara's outfit.

'You don't think it's a bit over the top?' asked Clara anxiously.

'A bit?' chortled Pete.

'Isn't it meant to be, darling?' countered Max.

'On anyone else, yes!' soothed Connie. 'But you can carry it off with pizzazz even when pregnant and I really don't think it's fair on the rest of the human race.'

'Absolutely!' echoed Pete gallantly, not completely sure by now to what they were referring, but wishing to be in positive agreement whatever it might be.

Max looked at his watch and drained his glass. 'Well – we'd better be heading off, our carriage awaits.'

'Absolutely!' returned Pete again, at which Sophia and Demelza burst into suppressed coughs and snorts, which turned into giggles.

'What did I tell you?' beamed the triumphant Demelza to her sisters. '*Very*, very, verra…'

'Nobody gets drunk on just a glassful,' sneered Ella knowledgably, but Demelza was unquenchable and continued to chant 'very, *verra* dunk!' at her mother as she hugged her goodbye.

'Do lots of things we couldn't do!' she called out after them as, waving, they climbed into the car, Max feigning a drunken stagger for Demelza's benefit.

Once in the car Pete called out 'stick 'em up!' again, reaching into his bulging top pocket for what they expected to be the water pistol, but this time, conjurer like, he produced a large spliff, sprouting from a veritable cache, before opening an inside pocket to display more of the same.

'Anyone for a pre-match shot?' he laughed delightedly in his James Bond voice, pointing the spliff pistol-like at the others and producing a lighter from another pocket: 'Boy Scout's motto, don't you know, "Be prepared" – and I am!'

'I'm driving,' answered Max.

'I'm pregnant,' excused Clara.

'No, thank you,' replied Connie, groaning inwardly as he began to light up.

'Pete! Neither Max nor Clara smoke, plus Clara's just reminded you she's pregnant!' Connie hissed indignantly.

'Oops, sorry! Just thought it might be fun to make things a little woopydoo!' Pete explained good naturedly, as he put it out, returning it to his pocket.

'Not at all,' soothed Clara, feeling for Connie.

Chapter Seven

They drew up, without further incident, at the George Hotel at Instow amongst a maelstrom of James Bonds and sassy-looking ladies in every variety of shape and guise, who were all spilling out of taxis before the door to the foyer. The hotel stood starkly white against a backdrop of palms and tropical flowers, overlooking an empty expanse of ocean with Lundy Island a distant smudge on the horizon. Connie need not have worried at the shortness of her dress, for some of the women were dressed in stylish swimming costumes with high heels and feather boas, while others wore full evening fig, set off by jewel-encrusted tiaras. Pete had made a beeline for the bar and Connie was suddenly seized by an overwhelming shyness, seeing so many smiling couples, comfortable in their familiarity with one another. She felt gauche and absurd in her sparkly dress, with her token ex-partner already propping up the bar. Clara and Max stood sensitively at her side as she gratefully accepted a cocktail from a dinner-jacketed waiter, whom Connie recognised as a friend of Ella's. His hair was slicked and moulded into a number of peaks, which had the undesired effect of emphasising his youth.

Connie sensed that he was feeling about as awkward as she.

'Hello, Henry!' she smiled, raising her glass towards him, and then, in an undertone: '*Isn't this ghastly?*' Henry, realising that he had been rumbled, broke into a cheeky grin.

'Never mind, Mrs Sharland,' he whispered conspiratorially, '*it'll all be over before you can say 007!* Would you like to get another of these down you?'

Connie had been sipping at top speed, her most unfortunate trait when nervous. 'Good idea – but shaken not stirred. I feel better already!' she exclaimed bravely, as she replaced her glass on Henry's tray and gratefully exchanged it for a full one. 'That's the spirit – ha ha!' punned Henry gallantly, as he moved away to attend to other glasses and Connie began to relax cautiously and soak up the rarefied atmosphere of the evening, admiring costumes and chatting to those whom she knew.

A bell was brandished in the air, followed by a shrieked announcement that dinner was served in the dining room and would they all take their seats at their allotted tables. Connie found her table, where Pete was already waiting. In front of him stood eight bottles of Spanish sparkling wine, which he had generously bought for the table.

'Thought we should keep the bubbly bubbling!' he called heartily, for the noise of the assembled company was mounting. He picked up a bottle and yanked at the cork, cheering at the loud pop, as the contents of the bottle spilled over the table and into Connie's hastily proffered glass. He filled the glasses of the other members of the table, stopping at Clara.

'Oops! I remember – *baby*! Bad luck!' Connie winced, but Clara giggled and stretched for the water jug. At this point Max ambled over, but stopped short as he saw the wine.

'Fancy the hotel providing such crap wine!' he exclaimed. 'Especially considering the price of the tickets. How cheapskate can they get?' He decided to take command of the situation; after all, it would be bad business to be spotted drinking this stuff. 'I'll take the rest of these up to the bar and see if they'll exchange them for fewer bottles of something more drinkable.' He looked around the table, anticipating approval, but instead he saw Clara looking cringingly at him and wrinkling her pretty freckled nose, while no one else met his eye at all. Misreading the situation again, he clapped his hand to his mouth.

'Sorry, darling! I'm being a wine bore again, aren't I? But I'm sure you must all agree that this is mouthwash?' No one contradicted him so he went on. 'OK. Pete? D'you want to give me a hand with this little pile of pooh?'

With this, Max swept up as many of the unopened bottles as he could and Pete, quite affably, followed after with the rest, muttering to Connie, 'We had bubbles earlier – I just thought…'

'Yes, quite,' answered Connie, 'it was sweet of you. Just wires crossed I think.'

As soon as they had gone, there was an outburst of laughter. Clara was apologising for Max's lack of tact, explaining that he was so used to evaluating wine that he wouldn't have *thought*, but that she would tick him off later. Connie was excusing Pete's lack of taste: 'He spends so much time in Sri Lanka where booze is just booze.' Connie was blushing for Pete, for she realised he was truly doing his best to be charming and, as with everything else, his eagerness was having hypergolic results.

Soon Max and Pete returned, armed with a tasteful selection of Merlot and Chardonnay and they all began their starters of scallops in champagne sauce.

'I bet the sauce is made with that filthy stuff they landed us with earlier!' put in Max affably and was pleased and quite surprised at the amount of amusement clearly derived from this remark. Fortunately Pete missed this quip, due to a visit to the gents. A cabaret accompanied the main course, consisting of a Shirley Bassey lookalike, dressed in white fur and jewels from head to foot. She teetered around the tables on a pair of towering stilettos, which must have taken little short of a crane to put on, crooning 'Diamonds are Forever'.

'That's meant to be *my* song!' reminded Clara, with a swish of her cat's tail and a purr well capable of rivalling that of even Edith Pillaff, let alone this Shirley! After the dessert the band could be heard tuning up. Pete had disappeared to the gents again and everyone was getting up to dance.

Clara asked Connie if she wanted to join in with them, but Connie answered absently that she was fine, for she was tuning herself into the band. She sat alone at the table, wrapped in the opening song, comparing it with her own band's version and seeing if there were any embellishments that they might garner from it. Pete appeared and swept her off to dance, his eyes suspiciously dilated and his pocket bulging somewhat less. He began singing along to the lyrics of The Pretenders' song, 'I'm Special', as though they were his own thoughts, his hand clutching an imagined mike while the other rent the air:

> "Cause I! Am gonna make you *see*
> Nobody else here
> Nobody like me-hee
> I'm special – so special
> I'm gonna get some of your attention
> Give it to me!'

He danced the dance of an animated spider, his hands, when not gesturing, depicting circles in the air; the clever part being that the circles of each hand turned in diametrically opposite directions. Of this feat he was immensely proud, being convinced that he was alone in possessing this ability and as he circled he beamed the beatific beam of the conqueror. Now the song had moved on to the all-familiar, graphic refrain:

'*Gonna use my arms*' – here his arms stretched the circles larger. '*Gonna use my legs*' – Oops! Could he do the same with his legs without falling over? It seemed he could! '*Gonna use my fingers*' – a digital breeze! '*Gonna use my senses*' – here the circles Catherine-wheeled at incredible speed! '*Gonna use my, my, my imagination!*'

His dancing had created a wide space on the crowded dance floor, partly through the other guests' interest in their own safety and partly because Pete's dancing was so much more entertaining than their own: however at the mention of 'imagination', his vigorous pelvic thrusts, graphically executed, had Connie backing hastily away from contact – as she had seen the 'Fool' back from the 'Oss' at Padstow's May Day – while the gathering crowd clapped and laughed at the spectacle. Pete lapped up his success and reminded Connie that he didn't know why, but he had always been good at dancing, before he deserted her again for another trip to the lavatories.

As Connie was returning to her seat, Matthew, who told her not to sit down for he was claiming the next dance, grasped her hand. He was the husband of Sue, both of whom were Connie's close friends and who worked for the hospice, for which the ball was a money raiser. He twisted her expertly in a sprightly jive, which Connie enjoyed enormously. However, as she leant her weight backwards in response to Matthew's complicated manoeuvre, she found herself leading instead of following, which resulted in a loud click and Matthew's face contorting with pain.

'It's OK,' (clearly it wasn't) 'it's just my shoulder again,' he explained to Sue, who was also a nurse. She had been proudly watching her husband's jiving prowess with Connie when the accident occurred and had immediately sped over. Seeing the awkward angle of his arm, she knew what to do.

'It's dislocated again,' explained Sue, 'but I'm going to sort it right now this time rather than wait hours for those paramedics.' At this she hitched back her satin sleeves, grasped Matthew's hand and elbow, and turning her back, gave one sharp, hard pull. There was a scrunch and a cry of pain from Matthew and then his arm was back in place and he was massaging his shoulder. Connie apologised and said she thought it was all because she had always had to take the boy's part in school dancing lessons because she was tall. They assured her that Matthew would be fine and that it was his fault anyway, at which point another friend's husband emerged and asked her if she would do it to him! She danced with one partner after another, realising this to be a conspiracy amongst her friends to keep her dancing and from being a wallflower amongst Pete's repeated trips to the lavatory. However, by this time she didn't mind: she had felt it pertinent to finish off Pete's bubbly bottles that had been started and which everyone else had discarded, and these, on top of the cocktails, had served to send her into a hazy, spinning state of euphoria, cushioned by the care of thoughtful friends.

The band announced a break, for it was time for the Auction of Promises, and everyone returned to their tables. The items to be auctioned showed extreme generosity (rivalled only by the competitiveness of the bidding), the proceeds of which were in the good cause of the hospice. Items auctioned ranged from romantic weekend breaks for two, offered in the off-season by local hoteliers, to 'Viewing Devon's private parts' by helicopter.

Connie glanced anxiously towards Pete, whose eyes were glazed and dilated to cartoon proportions by this time, but he had pushed back his chair majestically and was striding towards the stage. She saw him reappear from behind the stage curtain and whistle at the auctioneers. They ignored him good-naturedly for a time, but as his calls became more urgent one of them went over to him. They had a discussion: Pete was nodding his head while the auctioneer appeared to be shaking his. After this they both smiled and Pete seemed to slip something in a handkerchief into the auctioneer's hand and return to his seat, where he sat alert, his head slightly on one side, apparently straining to catch every nuance of the bidding.

All items on the list had been handsomely sold and the auction appeared to be over. The jovial babble of voices began to mount again, relieved that the 'working' part of the evening was finished; however, the auctioneer held up his hand.

'Ladies and gentlemen, I have received another generous donation for auction at this eleventh hour!'

Here Pete leaned forward more intently still, hushing at the general populace. The auctioneer continued.

'I have here a thirty-carat uncut emerald. I understand emeralds are appreciating in value even as we speak! Now, who will start me off?' There was a silence, while Pete craned his neck, parrot-like, around a series of angles, searching eagerly for prospective bidders.

'Come on, ladies and gentlemen, what am I bid for this, um, most unusual and beautiful gemstone? Shall we say fifty pounds?'

Pete looked appalled at the meagreness of the opening amount, after which there was another pause and Pete began to shake his head dramatically.

'What would you say to forty?' continued the auctioneer, clearly ready to have done.

'Outrageous!' expostulated Pete in fury. Connie could feel the blush rising uncomfortably into the roots of her hair, suffusing with perspiration, while she lowered her eyes to evade sympathy or – even worse – amusement at Pete's loud mutterings.

'Got it in Sri Lanka – in spite of the Tsunami – not that anyone here seems to have a clue about decent jewellery!' He stared pointedly at some of the tiara wearers. 'I suppose *they* think that gems grow in jewellery like milk's made in bottles!' After another query from the auctioneer and more exasperated huffing from Pete, a loud and familiar voice called out.

'Two hundred!'

'Three hundred!' countered Matthew's voice, stridently.

'That's more like it!' enthused Pete, restored instantly to his original state of bonhomie.

The auctioneer caught the drift and asked if anyone would offer him three-fifty and after another decent pause he called, 'At three hundred pounds I am bid then, ladies and gentlemen. Going, going, gone!' And he slapped his gavel on the makeshift table with obvious relief.

'Anything for a worthwhile cause!' Pete was saying loudly, confident of deserved praise and admiration.

Connie was extremely conscious that the bids had been put-up jobs by her friends, to save her embarrassment and the evening from further unwanted histrionics from Pete. She felt mortified that she had provided the means for anyone to have to put themselves on the line in this way, but grateful too, that they had saved Pete's face, if he did but know it. She wished he would stop behaving so insufferably smugly though, for he was now making mock bows at everyone as if he had been the only contributor to the auction.

The band was playing again with freshened vigour, but Connie was anxious to find Jack, and Matthew (who was now nursing a very bruised shoulder), to thank them for their prompt bids. They shrugged off her thanks.

'It was all down to Sue,' Matthew answered vicariously, as Sue patted Connie on the back saying that it didn't matter, it all added to the drama! Connie felt overwhelmed by their kindness and hugged her friends, except Matthew, who was putting a brave face on things but was clearly in extreme discomfort from his shoulder.

'Well, I'm not dancing with you again after what you did to me!' he quipped.

They looked towards the dance floor to see Pete on his own, limbo dancing beneath a decorative paper chain, which had fluttered from the ceiling, but Max and Clara had come over.

'Sorry, I'm exhausted and really ready to go home,' said Clara. 'Do you want to come with us, or...'

'I'll get Pete and we'll come now!' said Connie gratefully, as she dodged across the room to fetch him.

'We're not going now! The party's just getting started!' protested Pete, swaying gently and gazing at her from his huge irises, but Connie insisted that they needed their lift and he left the dance floor reluctantly, waving cheerily at the band.

Pete snatched a bottle off the table as they left the room and carried it out to the car park, where he tipped the contents down his throat in several loud glugs.

'Good stuff!' he nodded approvingly. 'Knows a thing or two about wine, does our Max.' At this he deposited the bottle into a decorative tub of flowers, into which he placed the remains of the spliff he had smoked, while they waited for Clara's car to emerge from the car park.

'God bless this steamer and all who sail in her!' he called into the bottle, his voice reverberating thickly and making him giggle. He sucked at the neck of the bottle, from which a thin stream of smoke was still rising, commenting, 'Mmm... jolly good steamship too, though I say it myself!'

'Get in the car!' insisted Connie, and Pete lurched over obediently. In the fug of the car Connie fell instantly asleep, only coming to as they jolted over the cattle grid at the top of the drive.

'*Will you be OK?*' whispered the ever-sensitive Clara anxiously, as Connie and Pete got out.

Connie assured her that she was going to be just fine, thinking, *Why wouldn't I be?*

She waved them off and looked around for Pete, but he was nowhere behind her. She called his name but there was no reply, so, with a sigh of relief at reaching her home and hearing Tramp's feet pounding down from the landing from which he awaited her return, she heaved the heavy front door to. She hugged Tramp, telling him that she was in quite a state, and tottered upstairs, checking the children before repairing gratefully to bed. Tramp lollopped loyally along behind her, ready to flop onto his rug at last.

The sleep that Connie returned to was of the sort where the slumberer falls through floating feathery layers of sleep, deeper and deeper, until the most blissful state of relaxation is achieved. From the depths of this, Connie was aware of a sort of scattering noise. She fell still sumptuously farther.

The sound wasn't so much scattering really, it was more of a thumping, crashing; she began to bubble upwards towards consciousness, reversing the nap of all the kind layers of feathers. At last she was aware of the sharp crack of stones on wall and window. She ran to the window to look out, which she might have thought better of, had she not been so heavily asleep moments earlier: the moon was bright and she had no trouble in picking out Pete, his jacket torn and mud-bespattered, standing on the roof of his purple sports car, lobbing an armful of stones.

'Pete! What are you doing?'

'You shut me out!' he wined reproachfully.

'But you weren't there after we got out of the car...'

'I only went for a pee and then I overbalanced down your ha-ha – not very ha, I must say – and I think I must have been out of it for a bit.'

Connie couldn't help laughing for he sounded so very Eeyore-ish. 'I see. Well, why don't you go home now?' she asked gently.

'I'm in no state to drive anywhere,' answered Pete, and Connie realised that in her befuddled state she hadn't thought of this.

'Why are you standing up there on the roof of your car?'

'I thought I might get a better aim at your bedroom window from here: it was too difficult from the ground.' He looked down and lurched dangerously, tottering to all fours.

'Well, you can come down now,' replied Connie from her vantage point, a wave of sleep claiming her once more as she shut the window and crawled back to the warmth of her bed.

Her head had only been back on the pillow for what seemed a

moment before she heard a hollering sound from outside. This time she knew exactly what it was and rushed back to the window to find out what was irking Pete this time. His body was now spreadeagled across the roof of his purple sports car, the remains of his jacket flapping in time with his flailing fists, which were drumming a tattoo.

'How could you leave me!' he was shouting.

'Shhh! We've been through all this loads of times,' soothed Connie, wearily.

'No, I mean *here*! How could you leave me – and how could you leave me *here*?'

'*Please* keep your voice down – what if the children woke up?'

'What if, what if? I don't care about your wretched children, about whom you fuss far too much. I'm stuck! It's a long way to the ground!'

'But it isn't!' insisted Connie. 'And you must have got yourself up there all right.'

'I may have got myself up – but that doesn't necessarily mean I can get down!'

'So you mean you're unable to get down or up?' Connie clarified at last, catching his drift through the layers of befuddled, heady fatigue.

'If you *cared* about me at all you would have searched for me...'

'Please let's not get into all that again – you know I care, but not in the way you mean. And I'm sorry I didn't search: I was half-asleep and not a little tipsy myself – I just supposed you'd sort of gone!' she added lamely, wondering slightly at herself as she said it. All this time Pete was on his hands and knees on the roof of his car, his knuckles whitened from his tight grip on the edge of the roof. He started to shake.

'Connie, I'm scared! I know you don't love me at all but get me off this thing!'

Connie began to understand through her own fog that he was in earnest and truly in difficulty – from his own perspective at least.

'Tell you what, I'll come down and *guide* you off!' She stepped over the recumbent Tramp, grabbed a dressing gown and, still barefoot, ran down the stairs. Heaving back the heavy iron bolts on the front door, she moved to the car, its purpleness gloomy-dark in the moonlight. Pete's face shone down at her, white and wet with sweat, his shaking uncontrollable.

'It'll be all right, I'm here,' Connie said gently, in the reassuring voice she normally reserved for the children when they had nightmares. 'Now, move your foot backwards in the windscreen direction.'

'I can't move!' Pete answered, meekly miserable. 'Connie, I'm so scared!'

'That's ridiculous!' scoffed Connie, attempting a girl guide heartiness. 'It's just mind over matter!'

'My mind is numb. I do not matter. This is all because of you!'

'It's all because of your junky diet, more like! Look, you're going to be fine: I'm coming up to get you.'

With this Connie stepped onto the front bumper, from whence she raised her knees, one after the other, onto the long smooth bonnet and crawled to the windscreen. Supporting herself by the roof, she managed to stand on the bonnet and edge her hands gingerly along the roof until she was able to catch Pete's foot. He screamed and kicked out and Connie moved backwards involuntarily, making a grab for whatever came to hand. She found herself clutching a windscreen wiper, which had come adrift as she had seized at it.

'What was that for?' Connie asked incredulously from her new position of comparative safety. 'This is *me* coming to rescue you.'

'Sorry, I didn't realise it was you,' whimpered Pete.

'I'm going to take your foot again and move it backwards to safety – and try to keep *quiet*,' commanded Connie. She threw the windscreen blade to the ground and edged back up the windscreen again to take his foot, meeting no resistance this time. She then took the other and, gently and gingerly, pulled them slowly backwards over the edge of the windscreen, heaving herself groundwards all the time but never letting go. In this fashion she negotiated his legs across the long, smooth bonnet, his body a lead weight, flopping after:

'It's hurting my balls!' he complained in a resigned voice as his trunk slid over the remaining windscreen wiper. Finally, Connie was standing on terra firma and with the last heave, gravity assisted her with sliding the lanky body to a crumpled heap at her feet. This final exertion caught her off balance and she toppled backwards into a soft bed of anemones.

The absurdity of the situation and the relief that it was accomplished caught her unawares, and she found herself laughing hysterically, remembering, for no good reason, Clara's anxious parting words: 'Will you be OK?'

'I think, in retrospect, the answer to that may have been *no*!' she blurted out aloud.

Gradually Connie became aware that Pete was not joining in or even complaining. She sat up and looked at the tangle of humanity that was Pete and poked him gently. He let out a loud snore and curled himself further into a ball. Connie found herself looking on his now peaceful face maternally.

'*Now* what am I to do with you?' she asked aloud. She tried to shake him awake, but to no avail.

I don't want Ella to know about this, so I can't ask her to help me, she thought.

She pondered putting him into his car but she couldn't lift him or fold him into the shape necessary to enter it. Eventually, she succeeded in lugging and shoving his recumbent weight onto the smooth tiles of the porch, after which she went in search of some covers, half-vexed and half-laughing at the ridiculousness of the situation in which she had found herself this time!

Returning with an assortment of sleeping bags and cushions, she manoeuvred them around him as best she could, reasoning that it was May, after all, which was supposed to count as summer and he was 'camping'.

She hoped fervently that he might awaken before the village postman did his rounds, for his snores and snuffles rivalled those of Tramp and told their own story. Circumspectly, she dropped her ripped and grubby dressing gown into the wheelie bin under some other rubbish, before, still giggling, she returned to the sanctity of her bed.

Chapter Eight

A steaming cup of tea was being waved beneath Connie's nostrils by an attendant Sophia.

'Mummy, how was your ball? Did everyone like your costume?' Connie rallied herself and attempted to sit up, as an acute pain crept up her neck and into the base of her skull. She winced involuntarily as the pain thrummed a smart blow across her temples.

'Did you...?'

Connie cut in: 'Actually yes, I did, Sophia! Very verra and I don't want to talk any more about that.' She managed a weak smile, thinking of *Forrest Gump*. 'But it was a lovely evening – and so is this.' She indicated to the tea. 'You are the best doctor in the world!' Sophia's shiny cheeks turned a rosier pink as she grinned, baring the lurid green and purple beads of her brace.

'Also Grandma rang and said you were to remember that she and Fish are coming today. I said you couldn't speak because you were still asleep and she said you probably had a Hanover. Mummy, what exactly is a Hanover?'

'A hangover is a pain in the head from drinking too much alcohol... what I have,' answered Connie wearily, easing herself cautiously into the density of the soft feather pillows, 'which may be somewhat dissipated by having gallons of tea made for the sufferer.'

Poppy trotted in, brandishing what, on first inspection, seemed to be a steel rod.

'Mummy what is this?'

Connie scrutinised it more closely, recognising it to be a windscreen wiper. The previous night's excursions returned to her in a rush.

'Where did you find it?'

'On the drive – and there are all these sleeping bags and things in the porch. D'you think we've had a vagrant?' This was Demelza, who had joined the populace in the bedroom. With this news Connie knew, with relief, that Pete must have left before he had been spotted.

'I lent them to Pete for bedding.' Connie felt safe in the

knowledge that no one could possibly have guessed what had taken place – indeed, it now seemed somewhat incredible to her. To change the subject quickly, she asked what time Grandma and Fish were expected and was told that they had mentioned lunchtime. Glancing painfully at her watch, Connie realised it was already midday and sprang up, resulting in a punishing wave of nausea, which she ignored, thinking 'mind over matter'. This phrase struck a familiar chord, as she pieced together the kaleidoscope of events from the previous evening.

They prepared a salad for Fish and Grandma, after which Connie inquired after Ella, whom she hadn't yet seen, but no one seemed to have noticed her about the house for some time. Connie went outside to feed the animals and clear her head, hoping she might find her. Fresh air began to work its usual magic and she began to revive, before long being able to bend down to pick up Bustle's egg without so much as a hint of the swingeing sensation of missing a beat that she had experienced earlier. As she went into the stables in search of 'Layers' pellets' from the loft, she noticed a tiny column of blue smoke rising through the floorboards above one of the stalls.

Fearing fire, she hastened down the loft ladder and into the stall in question. Here she found Ella, sitting comfortably and apparently innocently in a mound of hay, surrounded by the unmistakable smell of nicotine.

'Ella! Are you smoking?' asked Connie.

'No – of course not!' snapped Ella. 'You know I don't!' Unprepared for lies, Connie accepted this for a moment – but then logic told her otherwise.

'But, Ella, I can smell it.'

'Oh that's right, blame me before thinking about asking your other perfect daughters!' Connie received the force of this jibe with hurt, for she always strove to treat them all equally. Ella was aware of this, which was why she invariably used this tack at any accusation, because she knew it provoked indignation in her mother. Realising she had the upper hand for a moment, even if unfairly, she pressed it further home: 'For instance, you have no idea,' she went on nastily, 'of what your dear little Demelza's really like – all my year at school hate her!' Connie immediately began to worry in case this were true, wondering if Demelza had provoked others, with her insatiable sense of fun, or whether this was unfair and it had, in its turn, made Demelza secretly unhappy.

'Then you should stand up for your sister. But this isn't about her, is it?' Connie returned to the original subject, from which crafty Ella had begun to draw her. 'Ella, I saw the smoke, and you're the only one in here!' Ella shrugged. 'Oh come on! The air is thick with it and if this was nothing to do with you you'd show me your pockets.' Ella shrugged again.

'*Whatever*,' she answered. This was her stock, non-committal response which, when adopted, was closest to acknowledging that she had been caught out.

'But you lied about it point blank and tried to put the blame on your sisters!' returned the exasperated Connie.

'So?' shrugged Ella again, in exaggerated rising tone, apparently unrepentant or concerned about the moral issue.

'What a waste of pocket money, Ella, when there are so many things you want…' attempted Connie, trying another tack that might appeal to Ella's wavelength, aware that it would be a fruitless exercise to pronounce on the health aspects of smoking to a teenager.

'I was given them actually,' sneered Ella, oblivious or uncaring that now she had completely admitted to guilt on all counts.

'Who by?'

'A *friend*.'

'Which friend?'

'Like I'm going to tell you!' Connie was taken aback and a little afraid at the contempt in Ella's voice. She was used to in-fighting and bickering, but this was new. This was teenage, she supposed, and she felt more at a loss to know how to proceed than Ella apparently did; but she was resolved not to show it if she could help it.

'Ella, is there a need to speak to me in this horrible manner?'

'*Whatever*.'

'Your intellectual skills are far too good for constant repetition.' The attempt at flattery was a mistake.

'Whatever!' Ella snapped again angrily, smug at having scored a rise out of her mother, who had given away that this line was effective.

'If you're not going to discuss this like an adult then there's no point in my trying to treat you like one.' Connie was trying an old chestnut here, but why not? Nothing else was working. 'Buying cigarettes is illegal until you're sixteen and you're only fourteen, so hand them over!' Connie was quaking: what if Ella refused?

'You can't make me!' responded Ella, reading her thoughts.

'I can't, but I'm asking you, as an adult to a minor – before you set this stable and all rabbits and guinea pigs who live in it alight!' To Connie's surprise and relief, Ella put her hand in her pocket, bringing out a battered packet of Embassy. Ella was secretly relieved, too, for the mention of their pets gave an excuse to hand over the cigarettes without losing face, which, she felt inwardly, she'd lost pretty badly over the lies and the whole thing. Ella threw the packet on the cobbled floor at Connie's feet and stalked out.

'I'm going to see Carl!' she said over her shoulder. Carl was her boyfriend from a neighbouring village.

'If you're asking if you may see Carl, then you can – that's fine,' Connie called after her, 'but ask him to come here rather than you go to him, because Grandma's coming.'

'Whatever,' was the ungracious reply, but it meant that Ella was agreeing and at least Carl would improve her mood. Connie didn't relish her mother seeing Ella treat her like this. She bent down wearily to retrieve the remainder of the cigarettes.

Connie felt depressed. It wasn't so much the smoking itself – she knew that all teenagers needed proof of rebellion against the strands of parental control, and she had done the same herself at that age – it was the lies and the accompanying attitude of hostility and contempt! She would have liked to cuddle and make up, as in previous years, but Ella's teenage-hood seemed to render this beneath her dignity. Ella was in a world where children, by whom she was surrounded, were at best an annoyance while adults, into which state she was rapidly reaching and claiming to have attained, were contemptuous, for they, of course, had no concept of the thrilling, teenage world that Ella inhabited. Connie was glad that there would be the company of her mother's generation, where she could be a child again herself; for at the moment she felt the responsibilities of motherhood weighing on her in an unfamiliar, lonely way. There was Pete's drug-crazed performance last night – was that really her fault too? She remained in the stable, the cigarette packet scrunched tightly in her hand, and gave way to the tears, which were pricking her eyelids.

The welcome interruption of Poppy into Connie's melancholic reverie brought her to and she looked away, hurriedly blinking back the tears. Poppy mustn't know the depths she fell into sometimes – and these troughs always seemed to concern some aspect of her children.

'Mummy, are you all right?'

'I'm all right,' echoed Connie, smiling sadly. Poppy's big and sensitive heart felt the untruth.

'I think you need hugs!' she said correctly. 'And here they come, loving you!' Poppy stretched up to cuddle her mother, her animal instinct answering the need for comfort. Connie lifted the little figure off the ground and danced her slowly round and around until one of Poppy's wellie boots fell off and they were laughing.

'Grandma's still not here,' Poppy announced, remembering what she had originally come to say, 'and we were thinking we'd better eat the salad.'

'Good idea,' answered Connie, her sense of proportion restored, but now wondering, uneasily, what had happened to the older generation?

An hour later, with Connie trying to disguise her mounting anxiety at her mother's absence (for she had said they were leaving south Cornwall after breakfast, and the journey generally took an hour and a half at most), Ella was to be seen sauntering down the drive hand in hand with Carl. She waved a casual hand, all differences apparently forgotten, Connie noted gratefully.

Carl cut a deliberately imposing figure, for his hair, which was dyed Barbie-pink, was parted into a patchwork of tufts, each of which had been twisted, gelled and wound by a rubber band. These stood out from his head at every conceivable angle. Rings hung from his eyebrow, his nose and a number around his ears; but most arresting was the pair of what appeared to be bone tusks, which stuck, warthog-like from either side of his mouth. Tattoos emblazoned his body, snaking up his neck from out of his Eminem T-shirt. His skinny hips protruded from his jeans, which hung so low that the crutch was close on his knees, which, he complained, hampered walking.

Carl had attended school as little as he could get away with because he didn't approve of 'enforced bureaucracy', ('no offence or anything, Connie!') and now, at sixteen – though he did look older – he had opted to do A levels at evening classes, which he supported through doing odd jobs and babysitting. Wherever he went, heads would turn, giving him the welcomed opportunity to return a suitably animal grimace or gesture. His personality was entirely contrary to his demeanour however, for he was outgoing, charming and courteous. He was easy with adult company and his anarchic views on society were well supported, showing a wealth of balanced reading. Connie privately hoped that his friendship with Ella would be longer lasting than most and that his indifference to gaps between generations might rub off on her. He was interested to know how Fish came by such a 'cool' name.

'It's because she drinks like a fish!' answered Ella.

'It's because she bubbles like a fish,' suggested Demelza.

'Don't listen to them,' answered Connie. 'It's only because her maiden name was Ships and she got that nickname way back during the War and it just seems to have stuck.'

'It has *swum* with her over the ages!' suggested Demelza.

'Fish n' ships… cool,' said Carl again, approvingly, and while Ella frowned jealously at the beaming Demelza, Connie remained grateful to Carl for breaking the mounting tension from her mother's continued absence.

Carl suggested that he and Ella went to the top of the drive to meet Grandma and Fish, because they felt they needed to take some action, while Demelza said she would make some rock cakes because it was now more like teatime than lunch. Connie decided to try to become occupied with some deadheading, telling herself that if there had been an accident, the police would surely have contacted them by now. She cursed her mother's independence, for she stalwartly refused to have a mobile phone, reasoning that she had lived all these years without them, so what had happened for one to suddenly be imperative now?

As Connie began to consider calling the police, a high-pitched tooting sound and much laughter assailed Connie's grateful ears and her mother's Mini hove slowly into view around the final bend in the drive. Carl was sitting precariously on the roof (*What is this fixation with mounting car roofs?* wondered Connie) and Ella was jogging alongside. Each time Grandma beeped the horn, Carl shot up from his perch in mock alarm.

The two incumbents of the car emerged stiffly, straightening themselves slowly, their heads two jaunty identical pompoms of baby-soft white hair, their faces showing a patchworked pattern of life and times. Each wore a worn tweed skirt and quilted jacket. Everyone rushed up to be hugged and admired.

'Steady on!' called Grandma delightedly, as one by one the children hurled themselves at them. Fish looked up appealingly at Connie from the mêlée, shaping her hands into the letter 'T', which Connie interpreted, asking Sophia to run ahead and put the kettle on. Hearing this, Fish nodded vigorously and gave Sophia the thumbs up. Fish, a sufferer from osteoporosis, had hunched a few degrees further south, Connie noted uncomfortably, since they had last seen her, although this never seemed to dampen her spirits.

'By my great age *everyone* has something wrong with them, but I'm so lucky because this doesn't hurt!' she would say from the height of Poppy.

'What on earth happened to you?' asked Connie as she greeted the old ladies joyfully, ushering them in with the rest.

'We were making such good headway that before we knew it we'd overshot the turning and were entering South Molton!' explained Fish.

'By that time we didn't think we'd risk going any further without spending a penny, so we went into that nice old coaching inn,' put in Mary, Connie's mother.

'We didn't think it would be right to use the facilities without so much as buying a little sherry, so we did. Then such a nice young man asked us if we were ordering lunch and there we were, so we thought we'd better!'

'I do hope you weren't worried or anything, darling?' her mother asked anxiously.

'Oh no! We knew you old veterans would be up to something,' interposed Connie quickly, before any of the others had time to say anything different.

Demelza's rock cakes proved to be just ready for lashings of butter to melt into them and Fish was revived by the long-awaited tea, after which Grandma said she must go out for 'a gasper' making a purposeful face for Connie to follow.

'Can I come for a gasper?' asked Poppy. 'What's a gasper?'

'A fag, Dodo!' sneered Ella.

'Well, can I come for a fag then?'

'Certainly not: please don't ever adopt my ghastly gasping habits!' admonished her grandmother.

'They say smoking is dangerous for everyone, but it hasn't killed you, has it, Grandma?' continued Poppy. Fish made an explosive noise into her tea.

'In my case not,' said Grandma, and seeing Sophia's anxious face she added, 'because I shall live to a hundred, like all our other relatives.'

'So if we're all destined to live so long we might as well all smoke,' said Ella, shooting a triumphant look at Connie.

'I'm afraid the immunity runs out at my generation: you're all so much more mollycoddled!' Before anyone could ask who Molly Coddle was, Grandma was out of the French windows and scrabbling in her handbag for her cigarettes and lighter.

Fish scraped back her chair as everyone made to follow.

'Would anyone care for a game of *Beggar my Neighbour*?' she asked imposingly. The younger children chorused that they would, while Ella raised an eyebrow at Carl, wondering if it would be beneath them to play cards with an old lady.

'Oh, how rude!' chortled Carl. 'I'm definitely game on!'

'Aren't you coming, Mummy?' asked Poppy, as she saw Connie preparing to follow Mary's summons outside.

'Give your mummy a chance to be on her own with *her* mummy,' answered Fish, as she went in search of cards.

Connie took advantage of the opportunity that Fish had presented and slipped out of the French windows after her mother, just in time to catch her feeding the ducks with the remains of Demelza's rock cake.

'They really were delicious but I couldn't manage another one after the lunch we had,' Mary explained rather guiltily, as she puffed at her cigarette, 'and now that we have a moment to ourselves tell me how things are really.' She looked at Connie with her piercing perceptive blue eyes, magnified and rounded by her spectacles. Connie made an attempt at being stoical.

'Things are fine: you've been so helpful with everything,' she said in a bright voice.

'My dear, you know very well I've done nothing myself... Connie?' This was the voice her mother had always used to signal questioning disbelief, under which scrutiny Connie felt herself to be five years old again and unable to meet the gaze. After a pause, during which Mary's rasping breath punctuated the silence, Connie blurted it out in a rush.

'Well, it's just the school fees: Stuart says he can only afford one lot of school fees and I have to find the rest. He says they can all change to state schools, which would have been all very well, but by now they've each developed their own friends and routine at school –

and it doesn't seem fair to make them suffer any more changes.'

'Quite. *Does* he indeed? Do you think he means it, or could it be plain bluff?'

'How can I tell? He has had to buy himself a new house, but I'm supposed to be the one who knows him and I realise now I haven't had a clue about him over so many things. Not that I want to know any more,' she added, dolefully.

'Well it sounds as though the sooner you can *agree* over things, the sooner you won't have to think about the perfidious monster – and the happier you'll be.' This sounded annoyingly logical.

'Easier said than done…'

'Look, I told you I'd help with the house, but I should have been clearer. What I *really* meant was that I'd help with anything I could, *including* school fees if necessary: let me visit my solicitor and get something drawn up to the tune that I will cover any shortfall, such as school fees, or indeed anything else that may crop up and I've been too short-sighted to think of.'

'But you can't do that: they're ridiculously expensive!' Connie wailed.

'My darling, since my own mother died I seem to be blessed with a ridiculous amount of money and little use for it these days. As long as I have enough to visit Jeremy in Australia when I need to, there really isn't anything else I want.'

'But I feel so pathetic to be in this sort of fix.'

'Pathetic you are not!' answered Mary sharply. 'You are managing to keep those children happy and healthy and that's an admirable thing.'

'But I had a real falling out with Ella only today,' continued Connie, determined to illustrate her incapability.

'My dear, she's a teenager: need we say more? When I was young we had the War and it took up all our energies. I think it made life far easier because we were all pulling in one direction: I didn't even have time to get married, let alone divorced, but I'm sure if I had, I would have accepted a great deal more from my mother than you get from me. Please simply accept what I'm suggesting and make your old ma happy.' Mary and Fish had been in the signals section of Intelligence, which had involved the crucial job of picking up the intentions of German fighter planes and 'U' boats through the use of radar; but in spite of the responsibility, the difficulties and the danger, their stories, emergent from those days, were fraught with the hilarious and the bizarre.

'But you were so brave and able, it seems, and here am I, spineless and inept!'

'Nonsense! Cease this self-defeating twaddle instantly and take some of what lies mouldering in the bank – do it for your children.' (Here was a crafty master stroke.) 'You said yourself that they deserved it.' At this Connie realised she had been outflanked and gave in gratefully.

'Put like that, all I can say is OK and thank you,' she said simply, demonstrating her feelings with a hug and realising that another weight had been lifted from her shoulders.

Her mother reciprocated the hug, drew a final puff on her cigarette and suggested they found the others; the old lady was as relieved as her daughter, for she had felt that there were further difficulties, through tone of voice and things Connie didn't say, and had been rehearsing inwardly how she might persuade her to accept further help without a blow to Connie's pride. It had all gone rather well, she thought, as she searched for the sherry that she had brought, humming one of her favourites: *Pack up your troubles in your old kit bag and smile, smile, smile!*

On entering the sitting room they found the children and Fish down on the floor playing cards.

'We played *Beggar my Neighbour* and Demelza won!' called out Poppy.

'Yes, I buggered my neighbours,' bragged Demelza with a twinkle.

'And now we're playing *Old Maid* and I've already been old maid once!' put in Carl. 'It didn't feel any different.' Fish, Carl and Sophia were still in, and the old maid, the queen of hearts, was moving around the three amidst squeals of anguish, as further pairs were discarded. Finally Fish was left with the queen.

'I'm an old maid!' she squealed, infected by the boisterous spirits of the young. There was a dramatic pause before Grandma brandished the sherry bottle.

'My dear, who more fitting to wind up with the queen of farts!' she told Fish haughtily.

'Look who's talking – you've heard of the pot and the kettle!' retorted Fish in mock indignation, as the others rocked with delighted laughter at the elderly 'talking rude'! Carl's eyes rounded.

'You are two of the coolest ladies I've ever met!' he marvelled and Ella felt a glow of pride. Mary and Fish smiled delightedly at one another and made mock nods and curtsies of acknowledgement, while Connie doled out the sherry.

'I looks towards you!' she said, as the two old ladies 'bowed accordin'.

'Yur'z to us,' they went on.

'None like us!'

'You're not kidding!' muttered Carl, in admiration.

When Connie was tucking Poppy in that evening, Poppy turned to her earnestly, 'Mummy – I want to ask you something – do grown-ups always cry without making a noise?'

'Not necessarily.'

'How do they do it?' she persisted.

'I think maybe they do it because they don't want anyone to hear,' Connie answered, somewhat inadequately.

'I see – you didn't mind me asking?'

'Not a bit. But it's not something for you to dwell on – they're usually better for it.'

'Good.'

'Are you all right?'

'I think I am now. Hug?'

'Hugs coming over,' and Connie made an aeroplane of her arms as she hummed towards the little figure in the large bed, realising that she needed the ensuing cuddles quite as much as her daughter.

Chapter Nine

The house was still and silent. Fish and Grandma had left the following afternoon in a frivolous haze of toots and cheers and Connie had dropped the children off that morning at their father's house, where they were staying for the weekend. Each child carried a hastily packed bag, bulging with weekend clothes and their personal items. Somehow the teddies, without whom the children could not sleep, sticking out at rakish angles from their baggage, contributed the most to the lump in Connie's throat; for these representatives of solace were travelling away from their home to provide comfort where she could not, in that 'otherness', the existence about which she didn't want to think, and which it was not her right to share. She would be purposefully jolly all the way to Stuart's house, trying to keep both the children's minds and her own from the imminent moment where her responsibility for them was handed over. The children would grow uncomfortably silent in the car, feeling their mother's floundering courage and wishing that she would stop trying so hard. Poppy's little hand would somehow have snaked over from the confines of the back seat to stroke her mother's shoulder, illustrating, in her tactility, her depth of understanding over what was about to take place.

Once their mother had left, they had to undergo the same procedure in reverse, this time with their father: they would remain glum with shyness at the unfamiliarity that had grown between him and them, and it would be his turn to demonstrate the jollity that he felt he should feel at having his family restored. After a while the awkwardness between both parties would wear off and he would take them on exciting outings, such as they rarely went on with their mother, for she pandered more to the individual, taking and fetching each to birthday parties, school outings and visits to town with their friends: there was little time left over to do grand family outings and anyway she was far less able to afford them. If they could only take advantage of what each parent had to offer, and not feel that gaping, sinking feeling as their family car disappeared down the road with their mother waving manically, they should surely find life enhanced? Perhaps, in time, everything would feel more natural, once they had grown more used to their father's attention – a rarity in their old lives, but now it was overemphasised, since he had discovered he actually missed them and wanted, impossibly, to make up for what they had not shared before.

The gig that the band were booked for had been inexplicably cancelled and the evening that would lie ahead loomed large and lonely; but Connie would call up some friends and tap into whatever they were doing, with luck enough to tire her out for an uninterrupted sleep. She heaved a mound of neglected, damp washing from the machine and put on a CD of Queen, turning up the volume to lose the silence. She boogied through the kitchen with her arms full, Tramp bouncing and barking his excitement, and continued on upstairs to the drying cupboard, where she hung the load over the 'Lazy Susan', hauling at the heavily laden ropes to move the line up out of the way, where hot air was supposed to rise. Above the sounds of 'Another one Bites the Dust', she heard the distant ring of the telephone and ran downstairs, two at a time, concerned that there might be a hitch with one of the children or that she had forgotten to pack something vital.

'Connie! It's Ken: what are you up to?'

'Ken! How wonderful to hear from you – I'm up to precisely nothing, as a matter of fact!' Realising this sounded a bit lame and uninteresting she explained about the gig.

'Great! I'm glad your gig was pulled...'

'Why *thank* you!'

'I mean because I think I'm playing relatively near you tonight with Bryan Ferry. D'you want me to put a ticket or two aside for you on the door?'

'Now that sounds like an offer I can't refuse. Where are we talking exactly?'

'Birmingham.'

'*Birmingham*! That's hardly "relatively near" – I'll have to buy you an atlas sometime.' She thought for a moment longer as Ken made disappointed noises, and considered that actually, since she didn't have the children to bother over, she was free to go anywhere, which was a strange liberation indeed.

'Hold on a minute – yes! I'd love to come: I have a wonderfully whacky aunt and uncle in Worcester where I can stay – so I'll be there!' Ken was pleased with Connie's change of heart and sudden enthusiasm, little knowing that a part of it had as much to do with finding a constructive pastime until the children returned, as it did to see his concert, fun as she knew it would be.

He explained that her ticket – for she told him that there was no one she could bring at such short notice – would be found with her name on it at the box office and where to find him afterwards, when they could catch up on the intricacies of one another's lives.

She replaced the receiver with a grin! Spontaneity was something with which she was so unaccustomed – Ken wouldn't have appreciated how hopeless his call would have been at any other time. She had known Ken for many years, for they had been in a band together after they left school and had begun the passionate relationship of those suffused in a world of music, becoming for a while inseparable. However, Connie had become involved in the more academic side of music at university and Ken's continuing 'hands on' success as a lead guitarist had found him travelling the world. There was never a day when they split up; it was more that their lives drifted further afield until other relationships claimed them. They had remained staunch friends and Ken's successes in the music industry grew, while Connie's waned with the demands of bringing up a family. He would call from time to time on the off-chance, just as he had now, from exotic places, often with tickets for the variety of well-known bands for which he 'sessioned'. A further call to Uncle Gerald and Aunt Belinda had Connie packing her own bag and some dog food and skidding off on her own adventure.

Arriving at her aunt's Tudor red-bricked cottage at teatime was perfect, in that tea remained, as for her mother, a substantial meal. Aunt Belinda and Uncle Gerald sped nimbly into the yard and embraced her heartily, before leading her through the low-beamed doorway and down a dark passage into the whitewashed kitchen, resplendent in bright churchy posters and handmade pottery. A trolley, each layer groaning with a variety of bread and butter, home-made jams, sandwiches, cake and the tea things was ready prepared, to be trundled precariously (it was up a stone step) to the snug, where a fire brightened the little room with its dim mullioned windows. Aunt Belinda presided over the contents of the rickety trolley and

Uncle Gerald over the smouldering fire. Aunt Belinda was a younger, smaller and fitter version of her sister Mary, Connie's mother. She and Uncle Gerald had given up smoking and become vegetarian, growing all the necessary fruit and vegetables themselves in their large and ordered garden. For long distances they used a vintage three-wheeler Morgan, but to all neighbouring functions they rode their bicycles. This could have almost smacked of sanctimony, until it was discovered that the purpose of the bicycles was to avoid drink-driving: indeed, after one particular party, Uncle Gerald had not made it home, having taken the corner of their lane too vigorously and landed himself in the ditch! Their keenness on home-made jams and their own vegetables went beyond mere eating and focused itself in the heady realms of experimentation in vinification: they made their own wine from anything that grew in the garden, from damson to turnip, with varying degrees of success and potency, but always with a childlike enthusiasm and wonder at their abilities.

True to form, once the contents of the bounteous tea trolley had been consumed, Uncle Gerald, an ex-colonel, jumped vigorously to his feet.

'Let's get the old trolley out of the way!' he barked. 'Swede or rhubarb? At least, that's what we've got open, but come to the distillery and see the stock!'

Connie followed Uncle Gerald, while Aunt Belinda gave the trolley (which had been so carefully ministered over only minutes before) a hearty shove, landing trolley and tinkling contents against the far wall. Miraculously, not a cup was broken.

'They are sometimes,' her aunt admitted humbly as Connie admired her aim, 'it's mostly practice.' Connie was led to a large walk-in airing cupboard, much like her own. They paused for a moment outside.

'Listen!' her uncle commanded excitedly, cocking an ear to the door. 'D'you hear that wonderful sound?' He straightened himself stiffly from his crouching position, with a satisfied grin. Connie listened carefully and then became attuned to a gentle series of popping sounds: previous experience meant that she knew what it was.

'Now what *can* that be?' she asked.

'Boo *boom!*' called Uncle Gerald, throwing the door open with alacrity: all the shelves for linen were taken up by large, corked wine jars, with plastic pipes issuing from the corks. It was from these that the air was escaping, the bubbles of which were responsible for the friendly, gentle popping sound.

Each jar was neatly labelled, and displayed varying colours and densities of liquid: nettle, parsnip, strawberry, rosehip, elder – even cabbage. With practised enthusiasm Connie marvelled at the variety and the quantity.

'Wait till you've tasted the quality!' promised Uncle Gerald, with the exuberance of a schoolboy. She was led to the cellar next, to see the further process of vinification, where the bottled wines lay on their sides, now less distinctive, given their uniform covering of green glass, which hid the subtleties of their natural colours.

'This is quite a good potato,' Uncle Gerald was remarking modestly. 'By the way, we have Evensong later – and I know you have to get to your concert so we'll have to get cracking!'

'Potato sounds good to me,' answered Connie quickly.

'Shall we adjourn to the drawing room?' asked Aunt Belinda, deftly polishing at some crystal glasses, which she produced from the sideboard.

'Not on my account,' answered Connie. 'The snug is snug enough.'

'I haven't rescued the tea trolley yet, but it *will* be warmer there with the fire already lit.'

'Come on, come on, let's concentrate on the potato – never mind the tea things,' chivvied Uncle Gerald, leading the way back into the snug and kicking the fire, in front of which dozed Tramp, to set it blazing again.

In spite of it being summer, the old stone house kept itself at a fairly constant cool temperature, an ideal custodian for the wine. Uncle Gerald poured and took a long, luxurious swig, smacking his lips contentedly and pulling one ear at right angles from his head. Aunt Belinda did the same, but she held both ears out at an uncomfortable-looking distance. Both watched Connie intently, who took a sip and felt her eyes smart as the burning liquid coursed down her throat: it was extremely strong, but she was glad it didn't taste of potatoes.

'*What do you think*?' her uncle and aunt wanted to know, still pulling uncomfortably at their ears.

'It's very um… *highly proof*!' she answered with enthusiasm.

'You see?' Aunt Belinda was speaking to Uncle Gerald. She turned to Connie. 'That's what we thought – only I think it stronger than Gerald does – we measure it by how much it sings down your ears and this is our sign language: a very strong one is a "two-ear job" and a medium is a "one-ear". A low one – we hardly ever get one of those – is just a stinker and we rate it by holding our noses.'

'The code can come in useful at dinner parties,' explained Uncle Gerald.

Connie had a vision of the two of them sitting opposite one another in polite company, clutching ears or noses. She took a bolder swig – really it did have a certain something, even if it didn't resemble wine. She grabbed both ears and pulled, to the applause and merriment of her aunt and uncle.

'It has a certain *je ne c'est quoi* – but I don't know what it is!' she exclaimed.

The tautology went unnoticed by Uncle Gerald, who responded to Connie's enthusiasm by springing boyishly across the room with a refill.

Once the bottle was finished, her aunt picked up a hymn book and seated herself at the piano.

'Just need to practise the new tune to 'Oh Jesus I have Promised'. Do you know this is the fourth tune I've got!' Her aunt took herself carefully through a few verses, stopping occasionally and repeating until she got the flow just right, while singing lustily in her somewhat husky voice and inviting Connie to read the music over her shoulder and sing along. The potato had taken away any inhibitions Connie might have harboured and she joined in lustily with the somewhat jazzy version of the hymn, further embellished by Aunt Belinda's additional syncopated ornaments.

'I think that's it,' Aunt Belinda announced with satisfaction, snapping the piano lid shut. 'Of course, it's all different on the organ, but it gives me a good idea. What time is your concert, by the way? We could do with your voice in the congregation.'

'Unfortunately I was just thinking I ought to be getting ready,' replied Connie quickly, 'although, to tell the truth, I'm feeling a bit squiffy from that "two-ear job"!' Her uncle and aunt laughed.

'That's why we favour bicycles: any accidents incurred are so much slower!'

Connie ascended the steep stairs to her bedroom, where a vase of assorted flowers filled the room with their fragrance. She changed quickly into a fresh pair of faded jeans, a white tailored blouse and soft faded denim jacket. Running her fingers through her tousled shoulder-length tawny hair, she peeped into the little mirror and made a face, deciding that the sparse semblance of make-up from this morning would have to do because she had managed, as usual, to run out of time. She rushed downstairs again and received a parcel of sandwiches, wrapped in foil, from her aunt, who said that she bet Connie wouldn't bother with supper after the concert. She watched Uncle Gerald and Aunt Belinda wheel out their bicycles: each bicycle supported a large basket on the front, in which Aunt Belinda carried her music and hymn book. Connie watched them mount a little unsteadily and then, gaining forward momentum, sail out of the yard, tinkling their bicycle bells, waving and wishing Connie a good evening. Connie smiled after them, thinking of the similar exodus performed by her mother and Fish and wondered idly if the clatter and bonhomie were simply a generation thing, a family thing, or both?

Chapter Ten

Connie felt a certain energising buzz as she announced her name at the box office and received a white envelope containing her ticket for the evening's performance. Her seat was in the middle front of the upper circle of the Theatre Royal and commanded the best view of the musicians. It was a small and intimate Victorian theatre and not the kind of venue which Connie would readily have associated with a band with such a cult following.

Predictably, it was a sell-out. She twisted excitedly around in her seat, crowd-gazing and noting the wide age range and milieu.

The thrill of anticipation mounted as the support band came and went, after which there was a pause while the road crew adjusted the stage for Bryan Ferry. Connie felt the mounting excitement from the crowd and wondered, fleetingly, how it must feel to be waiting in the green room to play to these very people in this theatrical setting, where famous thespians had trodden the boards. The lights dimmed and dry ice spilled onto the stage, through which could be heard the unmistakable scratchy guitar riff heralding the beginning of 'Love is a Drug'.

As the smoke cleared, Connie was able to depict the tall lean figure that was Ken, his hair, still long and abundant, shining under the spotlights. He was standing in that familiar pose of his, with his shoulders leaning back and his pelvis thrust forward to support his guitar and the thrill of recognition swelled through her. Bryan Ferry appeared, cool and sexy in a huge white shirt, which billowed in the wind machine's blast. It was tucked into tight jeans, which were encased in long leather boots. He was standing perfectly still and apparently detached as he crooned into the mike. By the time Ken reached his solo – striding to the front of the stage to kick at his foot pedals, his body matching the sounds of his guitar so perfectly that there seemed no distinction between them – Connie was on her feet, her body swaying in synchronicity with the rhythm. Her jaw would ache from the unconscious grin that held throughout as she found herself swallowed in the complexity of levels of melody and harmony, as they coursed through every part of her being.

The encore was, predictably, 'Babylon', after which – far from soothing them into a 'going home' mood – the crowd exploded into even greater appreciation through cheers, whistles and stamping. Some had brought whirling luminous wheels and signs to wave above their heads, reading 'It's a Party!', the words in antithesis to those of the song: *'When the party's over…'*

The crowd stormed and ranted and shouted for more, as the band took their bow, Ken brandishing his guitar at the audience and getting a particular wave of applause all to himself, as he followed Bryan off stage. The house lights went up and canned music commenced, indicating that there truly was to be no more, so the crowd ceased their clamouring and turned obediently homewards, still in the claims of euphoria.

Connie hovered as the fans left in their droves and attempted to ring Ken's mobile, but either it was switched off or not in his earshot. As the cleaners entered with their vast brooms, she made her move towards the front of the stage, where a bouncer stood flexing his considerable shoulders, his shaven head protruding bull-like from his thick neck, his heavily tattooed body stretching his 'crew' T-shirt to outline every hair and sinew of his bulging chest.

'Excuse me,' Connie said shyly, 'but I'm expecting to meet up with Ken.' The bouncer looked at her blankly, knowing only the name Bryan Ferry. 'The lead guitarist!' she tried, sure that they would be well acquainted.

'*Oo?*'

'Ken – the lead guitarist – I'm a friend…'

'No fans, I'm afraid, darlin'!' replied the big man, his eyes flickering over her.

'I'm not a fan – well, at least I am,' she blundered on, wishing Ken would hurry up and rescue her.

'I'll be off duty in a minute, darlin'. I can sing good and all.' Connie decided not to attempt any further dialogue and turned abruptly away. Just then the big man called out to her. He was holding a walkie-talkie to his ear.

'Hey! Darlin'. What's your name?'

Connie was on the point of returning a suitable 'What's it to you?' when she noticed the walkie-talkie.

'Connie.' Suddenly he was all smiles.

'*Connie!* Why didn't you say so, Connie. Step this way and follow me, Connie.' She was glad that, recognising prior claim, she had ceased to be his darlin'. He led her down a murky-looking corridor to the dressing rooms.

Connie's eyes were darting every which way in the hopes of seeing Bryan close to, perhaps clad in a sarong or something equally unparalleled to his image. The bouncer knocked respectfully on a door, which Ken opened, a towel hung loosely around his neck. He was changed into a fresh, less flamboyant T-shirt and jeans and his hair was wet from the shower. He held out his arms and Connie stretched up for his salutary embrace.

'Right, leave you to it then,' called the big man as he closed the door.

Ken and Connie quickly swapped views of the gig from their different perspectives, Ken asking anxiously if she had spotted minute faults and Connie assuring him that she had heard nothing but good, picking out parts that she had enjoyed in particular. Ken told Connie she hadn't changed since she was twenty and Connie told Ken that she was seriously concerned about his failing eyesight – the banter was cut short by a knock at the door. The same roadie entered, saying that he was instructed to take Ken with the others to their hotel now. They both looked disappointed.

'We haven't started catching up,' complained Ken 'and there's so much...'

He paused, then looked up at her from beneath the thatch of wet hair: 'I don't suppose there'd be any chance of you coming to lunch tomorrow at the hotel in Birmingham? As you see, I'm somewhat grounded when we're on tour.'

Connie considered – this was spontaneity again and something to which she had rather lost the hang. She thought wildly about the timing, from leaving her uncle and aunt's to picking up the children the next day, and wondered if she could fit lunch in as well.

'I'll have to work it out,' she hedged.

'Go on: it's so good to see you. It wouldn't take you long from Worcester to here and from here to Devon.'

'Yer, right!' Connie answered in 'Ella speak'. However, she was having a break, which, after the wobbly start, she was enjoying immensely. 'I really will try to,' she finished.

'Great! I'll see you properly tomorrow then.' Ken was as confident as ever, Connie noticed enviously, as, after a hasty peck on the cheek, he grabbed his guitar from its stand and, packing it into its case, hurried off in one direction while the roadie escorted her, respectfully now that the bond was properly established, to her car, which was virtually alone in the vast car park.

The following morning Connie arrived downstairs to find her aunt and uncle already breakfasted and absorbed in doing the *Telegraph* crossword.

They broke off when they saw her, still continuing to suggest ludicrous solutions to the words that they couldn't get. Connie asked them if there was anything major planned later for, if not, she had a lunch invitation. They were pleased for her and insisted that nothing had been decided, urging her to go.

'We come with a government health warning: do not keep company with aged soaks for more than twenty-four hours, after which contagion sets in!' Connie laughed.

'Under those circumstances I feel it incumbent upon myself to go out to lunch forthwith!' They had a knack of making her feel good about anything she chose. After 'elevenses' of coffee, washed down with a smattering of 'gooseberry', Connie departed accordingly for Birmingham and found the hotel without mishap.

Ken came down to meet her and took her to his rooms, where he offered her a drink from the fridge. She asked for a 'gin and tonic without the gin' because she would be driving later and she had already sampled Uncle Gerald's gooseberry (which had been another 'two-ear job'). The rooms were of more modest proportions than Connie had expected, given the high profile of the band. She broke the ice by asking if they ought not to behave in a way appropriate to 'rock star status,' and whether they weren't meant, perhaps, to throw one or two items of furniture out of the window? Ken assured her, however, that on the contrary, nearly all the bands he worked for were quite homely on the quiet. It was true that some of them were a bit faddish, but this was mostly over their creature comforts, which tended to be such conservative things as copies of *The Times*, *Racing Gazette* and *The Field*, home-made fruitcake and particular brands of spirits or fruit juice.

One band even demanded a small library of books, ranging from Elizabeth Jane Howard to Thomas Hardy. Really, he said, 'the pros' were most concerned with making each stop on the road have some familiarity and consistency. This took the sting out of the 'nomadic impersonality', which was, perhaps, what led the more brattish bands towards vandalism.

'Life on the road is essentially lonely and most people just want to feel as though their home is travelling with them. The vandalism is hugely over-sensationalised and restricts itself mainly to the heavily druggy bands that tend not to endure very long.'

The conversation drifted from this more formal interview style to situations on stage that they had both shared in the past.

'Do you remember that stage at that Arts Centre, when Terry insisted on sitting down to play his slide guitar?'

'And his chair leg went through the stage…'

'But he kept on playing as he went down!' Connie was sitting on the bed, onto which she now fell back laughing. 'What about the time when that roadie tried to adjust the mike from under Steve's chin and got a little overzealous when it got stuck?'

'And it suddenly came free and hit him under the chin with so much force that he went down…'

'Still singing 'YMCA!' This they chanted in unison before collapsing again.

'What about that time in Germany when we got lost and parked the van on what we thought was a field?'

'And when we woke up we found that somehow we'd parked on the town football pitch with houses all around.'

'And then we couldn't find the drummer – what was his name?'

'Rumpty – because his surname was Tumm. (Can you *believe* he was called that?) We found him knocking desperately on people's doors saying, "*Zimmer fur toiletten?*" '

The idiocy was finding a momentum: Ken had thrown himself onto the bed beside Connie, where they laughed until the tears flowed. The tensions each encountered in their private lives, so far unshared, were washed away in floods of hysterical mirth.

'It's so good to see you again, Connie,' sighed Ken.

'I'm really glad I saw sense and came here!' This was her way of echoing his thoughts. Little bubbles of laughter were still punctuating their words.

'I feel so close to you. Can we have a cuddle? Oo, doesn't that sound like a cliché?'

'That's because you are close and it is a cliché!' Connie giggled, as she rolled slightly sideways into his arms. They lay there embracing and laughing at themselves for some time, enjoying the unaccustomed warmth of one another's body, shaking as one, with uncontrollable mirth. Ken drew Connie closer still.

'Ahem, Ken: I'm beginning to think this isn't a good idea.' Ken continued to fold her closely towards him, his breath tickling her chin.

'That's strange because I'm beginning to think this is a great idea!' he answered huskily, in a voice she had forgotten, his guitarist's fingers playing an irresistible pulse down her spine. It did actually feel rather heavenly. Connie broke away.

'No, Ken, we haven't had anything to do with each other – that is, not like this, for years.'

'And I'm beginning to wonder how on earth we've survived not *"having to do"*!'

'And I'll have to drive home soon.'

'And I'll be thinking of you all the way home…'

'But I'd be feeling so guilty.'

'*Guilty but nice!*' Connie was beginning to concede inwardly that he was probably right there, but she had to look at the impossibility of the situation.

'I've never had a one-night's stand and I don't want to start now.' She was aware that here she and Ken differed, for his philandering nature was not something he ever attempted to conceal.

'Who said anything about one night- or, to be pedantic, one-afternoon stands? Connie, I've always been wild about you…'

'Ken, you're doing clichés again!'

'Impressive though, isn't it?' She couldn't help laughing again. 'But actually I'm serious. You have always claimed a soft place, and not a little wistfulness, in my feelings and I always feel so much the better for seeing you,' he coaxed, running his hand gently down the length of her tangly, auburn hair, stretching out a ringlet, then letting it ping back into place. He looked at her, his dark eyes twinkling, the crow's feet tightening at the corners. He was so persuasive and such a practised tease: was he teasing though? Could it actually be that this hunk of an old friend did actually feel something special towards her? How much did it matter?

'No, no – I think we should just restrict things to cuddles. Apart from everything else, I might miss you too much.' She realised as soon as she had said this that it was a provocative thing to say – especially with the size of ego Ken had always enjoyed; but much to her surprise, he took it at face value and moved away a fraction, murmuring that perhaps she was right and that he couldn't go through all that missing her all over again.

The two friends then lay companionably in one another's arms, talking easily. Lunchtime came and went, neither wishing to mention it, for fear of losing their delicious closeness earlier than was necessary. Connie was scratching Ken's back between his shoulder blades, where he said he couldn't reach and Ken pulled her closer again, explaining that this was 'so that she could reach him properly'.

'*That* is the lousiest excuse I've heard!' said Connie, but she didn't hold back this time – it was too comforting, too delicious. Instead, she looked at him steadily and he kissed her experimentally, as she had now hoped he would, in spite of her earlier protestations. He waited, afraid that by this action he might have broken the spell and she would pull away again.

She *did* pull away and Ken cursed himself for his rashness. *Couldn't he for once have settled for the cuddle, especially since it was Connie and she truly was special to him? But probably it was better that she thought he was simply flirting, as was his style.* However, he seemed to be wrong again, for the actual reason for her pulling back this time seemed to be for another overwhelming convulsive bout of giggles. Relieved that he had not apparently wrecked things, Ken began to laugh with her and as they laughed they held one another closer and the holds became less hold-like and more like caresses.

This is Connie Sharland, teacher and mother of four being spontaneous again, was what Connie had actually been thinking, as she allowed the present moment of voluptuous pleasure and desire to invade and sweep her along on its hedonistic tide. The onus was now on her.

'Forget every pompous thing I said before…' Connie managed to gasp, abandoning herself to the situation and arching her body in delight. 'Life's too short!'

Chapter Eleven

When Connie arrived home, the telephone was ringing and she had to run to answer it, before the answer machine and it's message about 'not being available right now' cut in. It was Ken, and Connie grinned all over.

'Hope you're not feeling too guilty?' he teased.

'Actually, I haven't stopped laughing all the way home!'

'And I haven't wiped the grin from my face either!' They giggled together again conspiratorially and each felt deeply happy. They talked of nothing in particular, but laughed uproariously at everything that was said. Ken assured her that he would have a gig in the West Country soon, this time with the Pointer Sisters, when they could meet again. Connie told him she didn't want to know the date because it was bound to be too far away: 'i.e. not this evening!'

'I'll ring you again tonight after the gig,' Ken promised, and then, remembering that he must try to consider Connie's very different lifestyle, with children and school runs, added politely, 'that's if you don't mind my ringing you so late.'

Connie, careful to conceal the fact that she would probably be tucked up with a mug of Horlicks and Poppy beside her by ten, (for fear of her lifestyle sounding too contrastingly dull and conventional) answered that she would love him to ring and to hear how it went. Ken said that he was being summoned for a sound check and Connie answered that in any case the children were being dropped back at any minute.

'I'll be thinking of you all evening,' assured Ken, 'and I'll see what I can squeeze out of my guitar for you tonight.' Connie was about to retort that she wished she could hear it, but, realising that her life could be made sad through wishing, answered that it would be incomprehensible not to think of him all evening either – after this afternoon! At this they laughed again as they rang off and Connie found herself experiencing the weighty sensation of her whole body being relaxed for the first time since the tensions of the past few months. There was none of the usual altruism in her sudden *joie de vivre*; she had taken part in delicious abandon and remained in its thrall.

Almost immediately the telephone rang again; it was her mother this time.

'You sound chirpy! I was calling because I know the children are away and I've been wondering how you're coping?' A stab of guilt at the mention of the children and the fact that actually she was feeling better than she had for ages and this had no connection with them, was followed swiftly by defiance at herself: who would have gained if she had sat at home on the sofa all weekend, moping and missing everyone, while she clutched a cushion for comfort? Far better for all if she was happy and took advantage of what could be termed a break by being *spontaneous*. Her grin returned at the thought. She told Mary a good deal about the weekend with Aunt Belinda and Uncle Gerald, only missing details of the final afternoon. Her mother was full of interest over news of her sister and brother-in-law and said she hoped that they hadn't sent her any gooseberry or potato with Connie as, she felt, it was more 'gut rotting than thirst quenching'.

In spite of Mary's enthusiastic chatter, Connie felt she spotted something not quite right.

'What's been going on with you, anyway?' she asked, hoping to throw some light on things, but knowing that her mother was so much happier talking of other people rather than herself.

Her mother's laboured breathing could be heard in particularly short breaths before she answered, 'This is going to sound ridiculously self-centred…'

'You… self-centred?' Connie mocked, knowing the opposite to be the truth.

'When I finally got to tidying away the *Scrabble* after Fish left, I happened to notice our scores – do you know, she won every single game throughout her stay!'

'That's quite unusual, isn't it? But perhaps you just had useless letters – it happens sometimes and you can't do anything other than lose a go and swap them.'

'Well, maybe once or twice – I can't remember – but every single game!'

'Perhaps you weren't concentrating or you just had some off-days, like we all do.' She could tell this was really bothering her mother and was uncertain what to say or where Mary's thoughts were heading. For someone who had played a part in breaking the Enigma code, *Scrabble* was a very simple exercise and, when her father had been alive, her parents had played it daily after meals. Now that she was on her own, her mother particularly looked forward to a game and would always ask anxiously, 'You're not getting the board out just for my sake, are you?' when, in fact, they were. Fish was someone with whom Mary was equally matched and who loved the game with a similar passion: they would be positively greedy over the number of rounds they could cram in on the occasions when they were together.

'Do you think,' Mary continued, 'that I'm losing my marbles?' Connie was taken aback: her mother was the brightest person she knew – forgetful, now that she was older, but so well read and informed and so witty.

'Is that what's been bothering you? No, of course I don't. You are my walking encyclopaedia.' Mary didn't laugh.

'It's not the losing – obviously, since I didn't even notice – but you know, if I had Alzheimer's, you'd have to put me under a pillow!'

'Don't be so *One Flew Over the Cuckoo's Nest*, if you don't mind: if you had Alzheimer's, you wouldn't even remember the word!'

'I suppose there is that: so you really don't think I'm going batty?' Her mother sounded somewhat mollified by Connie's reassurances but her confidence wasn't totally restored.

'Batty? Aren't we all batty?' she tried.

'Well combatty then.' At last Mary was sounding more herself.

'Ah, *com*batty! Perhaps a little of that. And tonight you should eat some *cia*batty.'

'Ciabatta to *cheer batty* me!' They both laughed in relief.

'Do you know, you've made me feel so much better.'

'Glad to be of service – that's what you're always doing for me. Are you going to have a little snifter to celebrate?'

'Good idea again: I'll look toward you!'

'And I'll bow accordin'! Yur'z to us!'

'None like us!' rasped the response and Connie felt a further flush of pleasure at being able to administer the cheer for once. She wondered though, what *had* made her mother lose quite so many games?

As time drifted into a new season, it became the norm for Connie to receive telephone calls from Ken at two o'clock in the morning, just as he had come offstage. Although this usually woke her from deep REM slumber, she was able to be alert instantly and enjoy his tales of the gig and on the latest accommodation to which they had wound up. She found it hard to make her own life sound at all thrilling and would wonder during the day how she could tell the small incidents in a way that would amuse him when he rang. They had snatched a few more occasions for fleeting meetings, when she had refused supply work, saying that she was busy (no lie, she told herself!) and they had met at train stations for as many hours as they could steal. Each moment was precious in its very existence and painful in its passing. This fulfilled the romantic fantasies fuelled by similarities to *Brief Encounter*, not only for Connie, but also for her friends, who fed eagerly on news of the latest rendezvous for Connie and her rock star! It seemed bizarre to her that while this seemed so exciting to them, her life sounded so mundane when she talked of it to Ken.

Ken, for his part, was fascinated by the trivial, saying that he was envious of normality and felt proud to be 'going out' (for this was the term they euphemistically used) with a 'normal' person outside show business; but Connie's self-esteem did not rise, as intended with this attempt at flattery.

Once he was able to come to one of her gigs, which made the rest of the band very nervous. They invited him up on stage with them in some trepidation, where he calculatedly knocked the socks off band and audience alike, with a blistering solo in the break of Connie's song; but he contrived to make Nigel feel comfortable too, by admiring his abilities and that of the band, so that everyone appreciated and felt better for his presence. Ken loved the adulation of the small stage: 'Just like the old days,' he said.

When Connie told Pete that she was seeing Ken, he had cried and remonstrated, just as if his relationship with Connie had still been ongoing. She had gone on to say that it was clear that they couldn't see each other, even platonically, for a while because experience had proved it 'just didn't work'. In fact she had already taken that decision afresh after the James Bond ball, but he blamed it all on Ken.

'How can you see someone else when you know that I love you?' he had repeated querulously. She found his lack of logic impossible to argue against verbally, since, once he was in full flow he refused every interjection. She therefore resorted to letters and email, which provided her with a certain catharsis, since the written word at least allowed her to follow a line of reasoning without interruption. After she had written all she intended to, as kindly yet as firmly as she was capable, she would announce that she had no more to say. Following this, however, a veritable bombardment of texts and taunts ensued, to provoke her into further protestation and thus communication; but his persistent telephone calls were on the decline and Connie realised that, if she looked back, the situation had gradually become easier. She fervently hoped that this signalled a renewed interest in the outside world for Pete.

The summer was a long hot one and Connie reminded the children of their good fortune that the place where many people chose for their holidays was actually their home. 'You mean we can't afford to go on holiday ourselves,' Ella interpreted astutely.

'Well, that is true too,' admitted Connie, wishing that Ella wasn't quite so good at dampening, 'but who needs holidays by the sea when we've already got them?'

'*I* do,' said Ella lugubriously, 'and preferably away from my immature little sisters!'

'Well, *we're* all really happy and bestest where we are so that makes you the odd one out,' snubbed Sophia unwisely, as the others murmured support.

'Frankly, I'd rather be odd than even amongst *you* sad lot.' Ella had recently taken on the mantle of teenage angst with apparent determination and it was hard not to be affected by her negativism. More often than not, Connie's loving, comforting hugs would be shrugged off, while the others seemed to have to endure perpetual criticism or derisive sneers at each small joy that they attempted to express. She was seeing less of Carl too, because she said he, also, was too immature (possibly because he derived pleasure from playing with the younger ones, Connie interpreted). From her general aroma it was clear that Ella had acquired a fairly constant supply of cigarettes 'from a friend', and Connie had said everything that she could to put her off becoming addicted, but to little avail. The non-verbal agreement between them seemed to be that as long as it was done outside the house, Connie would leave her to it, hoping that this might give Ella less to rebel over and she would find out for herself that the expense was not worth the illicit pleasure. The idea of her cigarettes being provided by friends did not hold much water, for their pocket money was no more substantial than Ella's.

On the last day of the holidays, they took advantage of the hot

September day to visit again the wide sandy beaches of Westward Ho! The back of the car was filled with body-boards and a picnic, with which they struggled over the pebble ridge to find a suitably sized nest of stones in which to park themselves for the afternoon. They tailor-made the nest to their own specifications, heaving the heavy smooth stones from the middle and piling them around the ramparts of their nest, to blot out the wind. The tide was relatively far out but it had turned, so, grabbing a board each, they ran into the surf. Connie was keeping an eye on Poppy and Sophia, whose swimming was not strong. However, where they did excel (as with most North Devon children) was in their abilities on the body-boards: having spent their lives thus far surfing whenever weather and time combined to allow, their confidence and agility on the boards was resultantly impressive. Connie, too, felt exhilarated from the sense of freedom derived from the propulsion of the waves and at the sight of her children throwing themselves pluckily into the crashing breakers.

In spite of her wetsuit, Connie was the first to admit to feeling the cold and called the children back to the ridge for lunch. 'Where's Ella?' she asked, feeling the quick stab of anxiety experienced by all parents who look across the expanse of crashing waves and cannot immediately see their offspring.

'She came out a while ago saying she was cold,' answered Demelza, as she lay on her board in the sun-warmed shallow water, feeling it lap over the little ridges of sand. Relieved, Connie and the others jogged back across the shortened distance of sand, to see Tramp barking delightedly at a young retriever, who was running rings around him, the sand flying up behind.

When they returned to the nest that they had claimed, Ella was not there, but they found a note, sticking out of the picnic basket, out of which she had clearly removed one or two tasty items:

Hi everyone! Carl's just texted me, so I'm meeting up with him for a space. Have taken my share of picnic – hope that's OK. C U later, luv E, xx

Connie was pleased that Ella was going to spend some time with Carl and at the tone of the note, so, as there was nothing more hunger-inducing than surfing, they tucked into the picnic with alacrity.

Demelza had brought along the metal detector that Connie had given her for her birthday and was busy skimming it over the pebbles, listening for the high-pitched squeak denoting discovery of metal; after only a short time she had assembled a small pile of rusty metal and cans, but also an impressive number of coins.

'Ha ha – this is what I planned!' she chortled. 'And now I am off to the amusement arcade to turn my findings into riches at the machines!'

'We'll come too!' chorused Poppy and Sophia, eager to watch her put this into practice.

'Keep your mobile on then,' reminded Connie, 'and I'll call you when we're leaving: don't separate – and ask Ella to "prank call" if you find her.' (Prank calling was a useful gambit adopted by young mobile users who were low on credit: they would call their mother for a few rings only, enough for their names to appear on her screen, allowing the parent to call them back at her own expense.) Connie had bought a newspaper, so she lounged with Tramp in the nest, feeling the sun penetrate her chilled back and return it to its accustomed warmth, while she read and did the crossword, peering out occasionally to see if anyone had turned up yet and enjoying the clear view across to Lundy Island.

Connie was composing a text to Ken, telling him of the luxury she was experiencing but that she wished he were here, when she was interrupted by the ring of a mobile close by. It wasn't hers; it was Ella's and was coming from the untidy heap of clothes that she had left in the nest: she must have been clad in her bikini and bathing towel when she met up with Carl. Connie picked it up and pressed the OK button.

'Ella's phone?'

'Hi, Connie. It's Carl here: is Ella around please?' Connie was on the point of saying that she thought Ella was with him, but instinct made her cautious.

'She's somewhere on the beach.'

This gave him the opportunity to say that he knew and was trying to find her, but he merely answered, 'Oh well – I was just trying on the off-chance. No worries,' and after Connie had said that she knew Ella would be disappointed to miss him, he rang off.

Ella had clearly deliberately lied about Carl's text to stop them from wondering as to her whereabouts. As Connie's anxiety began to mount, her own mobile rang half a verse of its jaunty ring tone before stopping: this she recognised as Demelza's prank call. Connie returned it hurriedly, expecting to hear about Ella.

An excited Demelza answered, '*I got the jackpot*! Loads of ten-pence pieces – I got three pounds seventy!'

Sophia had grabbed the phone, 'And we've found forty-nine pence so far under the machines – but the man told us to bugger off so we think we'd better be going.'

'We've cleaned up,' Demelza had taken over again, 'and we've found Ella: she said we were being childish, but that's only because she's jealous because she didn't think of doing it herself and now we've got more money than her!' The knot in Connie's stomach sprang free as she breathed out in massive relief.

'Where is she?'

'She's with us.'

'OK – well, I'll start packing up and you come back with your loot.'

'Can we get some fish and chips on the way home?' This was Ella herself now.

'I should think so.'

'*Wahoo!*' came from all voices.

After they had emptied the car of boards, picnic and fish and chip cartons, they trooped into the house in their beach towels, leaving salty car seats and a sticky sandy trail. As they took their turns for showers, Connie asked Ella into her snug. This was the one room in the house which was reserved entirely for Connie's use and was where she imagined the dynasties of previous vicars had retired to write their Sunday sermons. Unlike the other rooms, it was small and contained a tiny tiled fireplace, which would have been the only source of heat in earlier years. French windows gave onto the front lawn, which was surrounded by mature shrubs and trees, planted by inhabitants long since gone. The interior housed her desk, a mixture of bookshelves and a music stand, on which balanced a wealth of music and her flute. The walls were lined with hangings, copious pictures drawn by the children and photos of them with her parents and her brother's family, while the mantelpiece supported an array of scented candles, given her by the children, who knew how she revelled in their fragrant atmosphere.

Ella entered the snug's haven. She had been relaxed and fun all the return journey and Connie was loath to spoil the mood.

'Ella, your mobile went while you were on the beach and I answered it.' Ella looked suddenly wary, before settling into her defiant mode.

'You had no right to answer *my mobile!*'

'Ella, in families we all pick up one another's phones – it's not considered to be prying, it's being helpful, just as I would expect you to do for me.' Connie was already on the defensive.

'Yer, right!' sneered Ella, but Connie persisted.

'Don't you want to know who it was from?' Ella looked shifty.

'Not particularly,' she answered, but Connie could see that she did.

'It was from Carl.'

Was that relief Connie saw on Ella's face? These days it was so much more difficult to read.

'So?'

'Well, you said that you had arranged to meet up with him.'

'Well – I did meet up with him.' Ella's eyes were shifting uncomfortably around the room, away from her mother's gaze.

'But Ella – he clearly knew nothing about your being on the beach in the first place.'

'So?'

'So you lied, Ella. Why?'

'You had no business checking up on me.' Attack was better than defence.

'It seems I did – because your note was untrue. I need to know why you feel it was OK to lie?'

'I didn't actually say it was OK – that's just your sad interpretation.'

'Ella, *why?*'

'I needed some space and I didn't want all that lot crowding me out.'

'I understand that,' said Connie, glad at last to hear something she *could* understand, 'but you could have explained that to me – and got your space without lying!'

'Whatever!'

'Lying – you have known for years – is never a good solution and I don't expect it from any of my children – particularly from you, since, as you're always pointing out, you are the oldest and I expect better.'

'Sorry then!' The apology produced, Connie immediately wanted to hug her daughter in uneasy forgiveness: she opened her arms and

Ella looked furtively at the door before coming over and turning her back so that Connie could cuddle her from behind with no facial contact. Connie had found this form of apparent disdain at bodily contact from her own flesh and blood humiliating at first, but by now she was used to it. It was better than no hug at all and in this case she was glad for Ella to be facing away and therefore unaware of the ridiculous tears that were spilling again. She wondered if part of the reason that Ella had turned away was to hide her own and Connie rather hoped that this should be so.

After the children had gone to bed, their bodies stretched and prickly from the grazing of surf and sand, Connie remained curled up luxuriously on the sofa. Her body, too, felt the allure of a shower and fresh sheets, but she was reading *The Da Vinci Code* and suffering the exhausting cliff-hangers at the finish of each chapter, which willed her tired eyes ever further down the unwinding path of the intricate plot. She had not bothered to close the shutters, for it was still warm and there were few outside sounds to muffle.

Because of this, Connie noticed absently that the porch light was on, which was odd because no one had been out in the darkness: someone must have nudged it on without realising, as they stumbled in with body-boards and the remains of the picnic. With a sigh, she at last managed to put the book down and remove her reading glasses as she moved to the vestibule, where she clicked off the porch light. She was turning to close the inner door of the hall after her, when she thought she heard an odd shuffling noise outside.

Intrigued, she stood still, waiting to hear it again, but there was nothing. She opened the letterbox and peered out through the safety of the big door. From the small slanting opening she could just make out part of the bench in the porch outside and saw that there was a dark bundle lying on it. She reasoned that it must be someone's forgotten swimming things that hadn't made the clothesline and switched the porch light back on, listening for further movement, but there was none. Emboldened by this, she decided to bring in the swimming things to put them over the Aga to dry, so she opened the great oak door, which responded with a tired creak. She stretched across the porch for the swimming bundle, but her hands, instead, curled around a crisp, crinkling wrapper, from which spilled a large

83

bunch of assorted flowers! She brought them into the house, closing the door behind her as quietly as she could and returned into the light of the hall to examine them. They were certainly an exotic, multicoloured bunch, just as she might have chosen herself. Wondering and admiring, she went to the kitchen to place the beauties in water and as she removed the wrappings a scrap of paper fell out with two words written on it in pencil: *Sleep well*!

Connie thought again about the porch light, which could only turn on from the inside and decided to check all the outer doors to make sure they were each locked. She found, to her relief (as her imagination had been running in parallel with *The Da Vinci Code*), that they were. Someone must have put the flowers there that evening but chosen not to announce themselves and it was obvious that the person had to be Pete. It was his way of showing that he was thinking of her, without breaking the bounds of their agreement that he would not contact Connie. On the one hand she couldn't deny her pleasure at being on the receiving end of nature's exquisite beauty, but on the other she felt uneasy that Pete had been lurking so close to them, perhaps even looking in on them through the open window. As she gazed at the blooms in deep conjecture, she decided on the most straightforward resolution to the situation: she would simply enjoy the flowers but not contact Pete at all in their regard, for this had presumably been his purpose and what he would have calculated that she would do. She also determined to use the shutters in every downstairs room from now on.

Chapter Twelve

September was a poor month for supply work because all the current teachers, refreshed from the long summer break, were healthy and not in need of replacements. Neither were there any in-service training courses in this month, so work for Connie was thin on the ground. For this reason she accepted 'Oh no, Teaching!'s offer of work at Cornhill School, which was desperately short of resources and in the bowels of Brigstow. Morale there was correspondingly low, where muddy paths led over scrubland through a graffiti-laden and rubbish-lined play area. The mobile classrooms were long past their sell-by dates, but government funding was insufficient to support new, more permanent structures. The funding depended on the pupil intake being high and the annual budget-spending being low; however, the more discerning parents took one look at the place before searching elsewhere for a suitable school, thus precipitating the downward spiral still further. This left the children of parents who didn't have time to choose or care and who could be correspondingly disruptive and attention-seeking.

As soon as Connie had accepted the job she felt misgivings, but she focused on the huge oil bill that she had recently received and reminded herself of 'dosh, dosh, dosh'. She dressed hurriedly, as Poppy lay in the large bed, savouring the last moments before she must peel herself out and struggle into her school uniform.

'Mummy, what's that mark under your arm?'

'I think it must be an insect bite: it's itchy and I've been rubbing it, so it probably looks worse than it is.'

'It must have been a big bug: you've had it for ages.'

'Have I?' she answered, rubbing the place unconsciously and feeling the raised lump beneath her fingers. 'It should go away soon then – and you can stop looking for red herrings and concentrate on getting up!' Connie reverted to a mental plan for the day ahead: she had been told that she was to prepare for a Key Stage One class, which should not be too difficult, she reasoned, as the children would be very young. She searched amongst her resources for suitable material for this age group, while cramming a piece of toast and marmalade into her mouth and checking that the children had brushed their teeth and hair.

When Connie arrived, the head was nowhere to be found. She searched the staff room for someone with time enough to show her to the classroom to which she had been allocated, but the staff were all queuing for the photocopier, which was on the blink and producing a dark shadow down one side of each sheet of paper. Finally she found the head, Miss Stanley, waddling slowly from the direction of the staff lavatories. Miss Stanley cut a Roald Dahl-esque figure: she was very large and wore what appeared to be a long, floral print dressing gown, complete with trailing cord and large floppy sandals, from which protruded horn-like, red-painted toenails. Her long, iron-grey hair was scraped into pink scalloped slides on either side of her head. She smiled bleakly at Connie, revealing yellowed teeth, set into a purplish complexion, her loose jowls flopping beneath her chin.

'Ah, our saviour!' she said to Connie. 'I've being trying since yesterday to get a supply and finally I had to leave it with the agency. I'm so glad they found you: do leave your details with the secretary so we can get hold of you more easily next time.'

She's obviously desperate, thought Connie grimly, realising, with some amusement, that the slight was unintentional.

'We've had a bit of a change of plan,' Miss Stanley continued, sounding suspiciously chirrupy. 'We're now giving you the Year Sixes, if you don't mind – and Jane has agreed to take the Key Stage Ones in with her parallel group. We have another member of staff absent and I can't replace him at this short notice – *I think it's stress!*' she stage-whispered impressively, from behind a large red hand. Connie's groaned inwardly, for she had brought with her material suitable only for the younger children, and she explained this fact to the head, hoping vainly for some sort of reprieve. Miss Stanley apologised but didn't waver.

'The Year Sixes are a *lively* bunch...' she went on, unruffled.

I might have guessed, sighed Connie to herself.

'And they really do need a teacher to themselves more than the little ones do. Not ideal, of course, but you'll manage all right, won't you?' This felt more like an order than a question as Connie followed Miss Stanley into the joyless classroom, where samples of work sagged from the walls. Connie's eye wandered to one where the teacher had written 'This is an excellent piece of work, Tom: keep it up', and a childish hand had scrawled 'not' after the 'is' and several exclamation marks after the last three words.

Miss Stanley found the plans for the week and ran her podgy finger down the work destined for today, which included PE. Connie wondered if things could get any worse, for the voice she would need for PE would in all probability result in its singing capacity being diminished in her gig that night.

'Now, you're quite lucky, actually. Darren's away this week, which will make things much easier – he's a bit of a live wire,' Miss Stanley explained, her head on one side, confidentiality seaming her brow, 'and Ryan should be nicely "Ritalin-ed up" before he gets to us, so you shouldn't get any trouble there. He tends to get a bit uppish towards lunchtime, so you won't forget to give him his dose then I'm sure!' She giggled conspiratorially, 'Oops and I nearly forgot...' Miss Stanley was almost skipping with gaiety. 'As Mr Chuffy's replacement, you're on playground duty: sorry!' Connie swallowed, realising that things had indeed managed to become even worse, as she thanked Miss Stanley, stating, without a shred of inner confidence at what she was saying, that she was sure everything would be fine.

It was registration and things were already not going well: the list was full of Kevins, Darrens, Ryans, Waynes, Kyles and Kylies and Connie had noticed that such names tended to bring with them a certain prejudice, for it was with these that the least controllable children appeared to emanate.

Toms and Williams, just as the books suggested, tended to be mischievous, but not ungovernable; Katherines, Emilys and Jameses could be swats; while Matthews, Jennys and Sarahs tended to sit together in a little giggly world of their own, dot their 'i's with a cute circle and suffer from apparently impaired hearing to anyone other than themselves.

Connie began to read out the names from the register, asking if they were having school dinners or packed lunches. She found some of the grunted answers difficult to distinguish between affirmative and negative, yet was loath to ask for repetition, for already she was being mocked: she had read the name Robert on the register and hadn't thought to read it as 'Bob'. This had resulted in a loud eruption of shouted laughter which hadn't died down, for each time it did, someone else would call out, 'I say, Robert!' and most of the class would collapse into more raucous mirth. The exceptions were the row of three little girls, who sat uncomfortably separated from the rest, looking miserably at their feet, too embarrassed to face Connie's discomfiture or the performance of the others. A boy, Kyle, with thickly gelled hair and a nose stud, as well as the requisite three earrings at the top of his ear, had started to ping something across the class and Connie decided that this was her moment to confront them all.

'Pick that up!' she said, in a voice she reserved as her most menacing teacher's dictate.

'No!' came the cool reply as he picked up a Lego brick, preparing to lob this too, over the class. A hush descended as all watched to see how Connie would deal with this defiance. She stood up to add height and intent to its dubious advantage.

'I told you to pick it up,' she repeated, 'or otherwise I shall go home: I'm here to teach you and not act as a minder – I'm sure Miss Stanley will be glad to stand in for me!' This was a challenge and both knew it, for Connie was aware that any sanction suggested would have to be carried through. To her relief, Kyle got up, but violently – as he did so, upsetting his chair onto its back on the floor. The others laughed as he leaned down and picked up the little brick with exaggerated gesture, slamming it heavily into Connie's hand.

'Thank you,' she said brightly, hoping that somehow the situation had righted itself to a certain volatile equilibrium, 'and now pick up your chair, please.'

Not wishing to lose face further, he angled his foot, clad in a filthy trainer complete with holes, under the chair and flipped it impetuously but accurately back onto its feet. As he did so, however, his trainer, which was apparently some sizes too big, flew off his foot and whizzed across the classroom, narrowly missing the many heads in its path, coming to rest against the waste paper bin, which resounded with a suitable thwang to an uproar of manic applause. Kyle's demeanour completely restored, he doubled up laughing and looked defiantly at Connie, who might have laughed herself in less fraught situations. As it was, she wondered despairingly what she could possibly pull out now to restore order, other than walk out as she had threatened; however, this was no longer an option while the class was in this state of anarchy! She decided on a face empty of any emotion and said quietly, 'All right. Now please fetch your trainer, put it on and sit down with the rest of the class.'

Kyle smirked infuriatingly at Connie and remained where he was, at the centre of attention and popularity, while the class continued to encourage him: 'Don't bov-ver, Kyle!' 'Tell 'er, Kyle!'

Beam me up! thought Connie desperately as, still impassive, her voice quieter still, she repeated her request for Kyle to put on his trainer, which, by this time, had been usefully picked up and returned to him by one of the three downcast Emily-types.

The class became suddenly and perfectly subdued and Kyle's face changed, as he hastily began to cram on the errant trainer. Connie let out a surprised sigh, which felt like the first lungful of air gasped when emerging from a very deep dive. The class appeared to be looking at her in a kind of awe, but on closer inspection they seemed to actually be looking through her. She glanced behind her involuntarily to see Miss Stanley, her face a hint more purple and her abundant heaving chest resembling that of a Sumo wrestler. She didn't speak for a moment and merely looked, her narrowed piggy eyes darting from one face to another, daring anyone to utter.

'Well, Kyle,' she said at length, her voice one of measured fury, 'what are you doing?' Kyle's head was bowed, a sight in which Connie couldn't help taking merciless pleasure. 'Well?'

'Nothin', Miss,' he muttered.

'*Nothing*?' hissed Miss Stanley.

She's good, Connie thought.

'Do I ring your father and tell him you've been doing nothing today?' Connie began almost to feel sorry for Kyle, for he shrank at the mention of his father.

'I accidentally dropped my trainer, Miss,' he answered, his voice almost inaudible.

'And did your *accidentally dropped trainer* cause this shocking rumpus? Did it?' She looked around at the rest of the class, who all nodded sheepishly, glad suddenly that they had not been the centre of attention that morning like Kyle, who had got them into trouble.

'Get out, Kyle, and stand outside my office.' Kyle leapt to his feet as though scalded, and blundered out of the room. 'And now the rest of you – I suppose you've been a model of behaviour for our supply teacher?' Some of the children nodded and others shook their heads in confusion at the sarcasm.

'Do you think Miss Sharland wants to give up her day for the likes of you?' Heads shook vigorously. 'No – I don't think so either! What do you think she thinks of our school when you show her such rudeness?' A hand went up from a 'Jenny' genus.

'Very not nice, Miss.'

'Very "not nice"?' she asked sarcastically, staring around again, taking in each face in her shrewd gaze. Several more heads nodded. 'Very *nasty*, I would say, wouldn't you? Extremely nasty, especially compared with all the *nice* schools that I expect she's used to.' Here Connie found herself nodding vigorously as the head turned her eyes on her for the first time, searching for confirmation.

'Right – get up and sit in your Numeracy positions. Anyone who moves to a wrong position or who *utters*, joins Kyle.' The children, completely transformed, leapt up quickly and moved to their rightful places in Von Trappian order. 'Now get out your books and continue from where you were yesterday.' The children, glad to be relieved from the head's all-seeing eagle eye, swept up their books and bent their heads diligently over their work. Miss Stanley motioned Connie to follow her out of the room.

Connie was filled with trepidation, for she dreaded a similar sort of dressing down at her obvious ineptitude at discipline; however, Miss Stanley placed a kindly paw on her arm.

'I am *so* sorry about that – they can be little tykes at the best of times, but they're worse than anything with supplies: you're not leaving now, are you?' Connie assured her that she wasn't, but said that she had to admit that it had crossed her mind. 'I don't blame you, and thank you for remaining; last week I lost my supply by morning break! The kids just think they can get away with more because you're not a permanent fixture and they think, wrongly, that there will therefore be no recriminations!'

'I must say I very much admire the respect you command from your "little tykes",' said Connie in the hopes of cheering Miss Stanley. 'In fact, I'm all envy.'

'That, I'm afraid, is more fear than respect and it's only come through years of isolating myself and not letting down my guard. It's not much of a pleasure to put on a show like that' – she indicated towards the silent classroom – 'but if I weren't capable of it those children would be swinging from the ramparts!'

Here a smile creased the soft bags that were her cheeks and Connie felt a warmth and sympathy towards the worn old spinster in her dumpy dressing gown.

'Well thank you for rescuing me – I was a complete jelly in there,' admitted Connie.

'Not at all: I think you're very brave coming here and I only hope you will come again – though I don't suppose you will?' The little blue eyes were on her again, appealing.

'I really don't know,' answered Connie truthfully. 'You see I'm not very well cut out for this sort of class and I don't think I do a very good job.'

'Well, there's a lot to be said for not being a tough old boot like me!' smiled Miss Stanley and she laughed, a deep chuckle that disarranged her chins.

With Kyle properly rebuked and the threat of further interference from Miss Stanley, whose large head was to be seen poking tortoise-like around the door at indefinite intervals during the remainder of the day, the children showed a different side; a small posse of girls sidled up during Connie's playground duty, where she stood, shrugged into her jacket, her back against the wind which sucked through the small area, making the surrounding litter dance. They shyly handed her a card that they had made, which had a picture of flowers on the front, drawn in black felt pen, while inside it said 'Sorry Miss' and was signed by many of them. Connie felt touched and rewarded and told them that it was all right. Emboldened by the obvious success of the card they began to chat to Connie. After another moment and a little jostling, a rounded, reddened child, in a pink scumbly snot-clotted cardigan, was shoved forward. She smiled at Connie archly and, producing another piece of crumpled paper, invited Connie to see what was written on it.

'This is what the boys gived me, Miss,' she said in a studiously unconcerned voice, as she watched shrewdly for Connie's reaction. Connie read the sloping unformed note, written in blunt smeary pencil: *Meet up behind Class 4, 4 larding!*

The ring of girls around her stood back importantly, digging one another in the ribs at their daring. Connie was nonplussed.

'I dunno why the boys always axes me every time!' went on the cardigan, trying vainly not to look pleased.

'So this means kissing?' guessed Connie warily, for by their faces it seemed likely.

'S'not *kissin*,' (Connie conjured nasty unbidden visions of kissing cardigans) '*S'lardin*'!'

The bell had been vigorously rung for the final stint before home time, when Connie and Tramp could make their bid for freedom, so, nodding wisely at the explanation and looking at the back of Class Four with a new curiosity, she called the class back for the remainder of the day.

Miss Stanley called in for a final time to deposit a subdued-looking Kyle.

'I think Kyle has something to say,' said Miss Stanley impressively. There was a pause after which Kyle muttered his apology, so Connie thanked him and told him it was all right, but to try to think of supplies as members of the human race in future.

'Miss Sharland, please tell me if anyone else has misbehaved again today?' continued Miss Stanley, to which Connie hastily replied that they had all behaved with perfect decorum. The children smiled their thanks and allegiance to Connie, who returned the smile while Miss Stanley kept her stance of hostile impassivity, only answering that this was how it should be at all times. She then swept around in a flurry of jowls and dressing gown and, with her back to the class, gave Connie a mischievous wink. Connie, unable to return it since she faced the class, had an impulse to rush after the bloated, disappearing figure, to give her a hug and ask her back to tea – but there was Tramp to walk, animals to be fed and the school run which formed a barrier between her world and that of Miss Stanley.

'I'll do it some time,' she promised herself, 'and I will come back!' She gratefully dismissed the class to the gaggle of waiting parents, their pushchairs heaving with identical offspring, who were ranged outside the classroom.

That evening, when the younger children were in bed, Connie turned to Ella, who was sitting at the piano learning Handel's 'Art Thou Troubled' for her Grade Six exam.

'That's going to sound gorgeous with your voice: it's as though it's written for you.' If Ella was pleased she wasn't going to show it.

'Yer, right!' However, the way she sang it again, with more confidence and inflexion, showed her true reaction to the compliment. Connie hovered, in thrall at having given life to this beautiful, soaring young voice and Ella caught the soppy expression.

'Mum! You're putting me off!'

Connie recoiled, realising that openly enjoying Ella's music was clearly off-limits and that it was best to listen from a distance, as usual. She apologised and said she was just going. 'Just one thing though…' added Connie.

'What?' asked Ella, exasperated, but still tolerant due to Connie's obvious admiration over her voice.

'Do you know what "larding" is?' Connie asked impishly. 'It was mentioned today and I didn't want to look ignorant so I pretended I knew.'

'It's *sexual foreplay!*' answered Ella with a weary sigh. 'Now can I get on?'

Chapter Thirteen

Grandma was staying again for a few days, which made everything the more chaotic, though this was equally balanced, through the bonus of also being the more fun; Connie caught herself laughing at everyday situations with the children, by seeing them through her mother's eyes instead of through her own accustomed ones. Poppy had taken part in her first netball match and had been most struck – not especially by the game – but by the journey to the match on the coach.

'We played "lick dare" and I had to lick the window for twenty seconds and Nicky had to lick Holly's hair – but Holly didn't know.' This was strange because Demelza had played a game at school that day consisting of putting one another's hair under the showers.

'It was because I put lip gloss into Bindy's hair to make it shinier and she got stressy because it wouldn't come out. So I said I would wet my hair completely in the basin to make us even-stevens. Then she did it too, to get the lip gloss out, but it didn't – not very well.'

Mary's presence and popularity gave Connie more freedom in the evenings for the unessential, so she took the opportunity to take up Nigel's suggestion of a visit to his cottage, where they could compose and perhaps record some new material for the band.

That evening, therefore, with her mother's encouragement, Connie made her way up the grassy path between clumps of mallow and hollyhock and thumped at the sun-bleached wood of Nigel's front door. There was a long pause, interrupted only by the barking of Nigel's spaniel and the carking of the pheasants coming home to roost, each of which left Tramp impassive.

She hesitated to enter – as was the normal custom in Devon – for she knew Nigel to be a territorial animal and she was anxious not to appear intrusive. She knocked again and was answered by Nigel's voice from the other side of the thatched cottage. Eventually the front latch clicked and Nigel opened the door, still barefoot, having ditched his wellies hastily at the back door.

'I've just been shutting the geese down: you should have come straight in,' he said. The front door opened directly into the main room in which a fire smouldered in Connie's honour.

'I know it's really too early for a fire, but this side of the house never properly warms up and it's better to keep the damp out of the cob walls,' Nigel explained, not wanting to sound as though he had gone to any bother especially. Connie assured him that she loved fires, so much so that all her children were well versed in making them and could make excellent girl guides. She always found herself harping on about her children when she wasn't quite at her ease, well aware that she was probably being a bore but more anxious to fill awkward silences. She had brought with her, besides her flute, a bottle of wine, which she handed to Nigel and he went through to the kitchen to find a corkscrew and glasses.

Connie gazed around the little room: the inglenook fireplace took up almost one whole wall, and had little carved stools, one on either side by the vast chimneypiece. Sagging bookshelves, held up by terracotta drainpipes, took up another wall, the books in the middle practically touching those on the shelf below. A CD player sat on a low cupboard in the corner, surrounded by an untidy stack of CDs, while some fresh-cut foxgloves sprang from a tall vase on the floor by the window. A scrubbed pine table stood before the window, which was surrounded by a cushioned window-seat and through which the dim evening sun filtered. The table was strewn with cartridges, a packet of digestives and a jar of marmalade. Propped against the far wall were Nigel's guitars: his electric guitar was still in its case but his acoustic, with its much-scratched fingerboard, sat cradled in its stand, beside it. A 'combo' amplifier and microphone stood at the ready for plugging in at Nigel's whim. Connie ensconced herself on the hessian sofa and lifted her flute from its worn leather case, the lid of which displayed a history of old stickers from Connie's student days, embracing anarchy to pacifism. A CD of REM was playing and Connie huffed into her flute to warm it before playing along with it quietly, to bring it into tune.

Nigel returned with the wine and glasses and a bowl of last year's hazelnuts, which Connie delighted over.

'Food for free,' Nigel answered laconically with a grin, as he switched off the music and fetched his guitar, throwing another log on the fire before sitting down next to Connie. She played an 'E' for him to tune his top and bottom strings and from which to base the others. After this was accomplished, he began to strum an idle sequence of apparently random chords, his toes unconsciously scrunching and uncurling to the rhythm. Connie sat quietly listening as he picked through various runs, searching for a sequence from which to glean a melody – and as one began to emerge, she started to hum with it, singing any words that came into her head: '*I'm marma-lading with Nigel o-ho! Yeah, marma-lading with Nigel!*' Nigel caught up the tune and sang in harmony with Connie. She let him take over the voice and put her flute to the groove of her chin to play an interlude of rapid runs. Nigel picked up some of the runs and played them back in imitation, by which time their minds were as much in tune as their instruments and they were able to anticipate more or less what the other was going to play before it had actually been executed. Now Connie returned to the vocal: '*I'm mar-ma-lading, mellow-making*' – Nigel, in antithesis to his usual statuesque stance, was goose-stepping around the living room and taking up the vocal line in grunting syncopation: '*I'm lemon-curding, oo-ooh, yeah, lemon-curding, uh huh, Baby!*' This last was too much and they both burst into helpless laughter.

Nigel poured another glass of wine and Connie wiped her eyes.

'I hate to be a killjoy, Nigel, but I've got to drive: I've had two glasses so I'd better not have any more.'

Nigel reflected for a moment. 'Why not stay? Then we can carry on: that's just put me in the mood for a bit of indulgence.' He spoke with genuine warmth: it was rare for him to feel hospitable and he wanted to exploit its novelty.

'I'd love to,' answered Connie, 'but the children...' Then she remembered that her mother was at home and tomorrow was a Saturday, so there would be no school run. She could be back by breakfast.

'The spare room's quite respectable,' Nigel pleaded, 'but no pressure – it's up to you if—'

'Actually, I'd really love to stay and chill with you. Since re-kindling everything with Ken I've been feeding my spontaneous side,' Connie confided. 'Just let me make a call to my mother to make sure she's happy with it.' She began to search for her mobile.

'There's no signal: use my landline,' offered Nigel, refilling the glasses.

Connie accepted the glass as she phoned Mary, who was delighted to be able to afford Connie some time for herself. She said that she was quite exhausted from several rounds of *Racing Demon*. 'Anything to get them off that wretched *Old Maid*. Fish has a lot to answer for by teaching them that!' she laughed, which culminated in a bout of prolonged coughing. Connie asked her mother if she was sure she was all right, to which she rasped back curtly that of course she was, there was nothing that a 'gasper' wouldn't put right and Connie was to stop fussing and enjoy herself. Reassured, Connie put the phone down and they began to play again.

This second bout of music was not as productive as the first, perhaps due to the amount of alcohol they had consumed between times, and, after some time had elapsed and another bottle brought, Nigel said as much.

'I know: let's record that first one,' Connie suggested.

'Good idea,' answered Nigel, jumping up to sort out the recording equipment.

'Do you remember how it went?' They sat in silence, paralysed, looking intently at each other, willing the memory to return.

'I know it had something about marmalade and there was a lot of excellent non-verbal "*uhs!*" in it coming from your corner,' answered Connie.

'I remember the marmalade intimately – I just don't remember the tune!'

Nigel tried a few runs on his guitar and Connie hummed some experimental snatches, but after an interval of attempted dredging, they had to agree that the song had vanished!

'That had real potential too!' sighed Connie.

'Mm, definitely a bestseller,' agreed Nigel. 'Isn't that always the way?' He poured more wine and rolled himself a cigarette and they moved themselves onto the woven rug in front of the fire, propping their backs against the sofa and twiddling their toes before the blaze.

'Well, it's lovely to be here anyway,' comforted Connie, 'even if we have lost a masterpiece.' Nigel echoed that he was having a wonderful time in spite of the runaway tune.

Gradually the conversation drifted from music to the personal: Connie found herself talking through the intricacies of her divorce, her difficulties with Pete and the celebrated lack of complication with Ken, while Nigel confided that he found relationships nothing like what they were cracked up to be – girls always seemed to require commitment and changes for a future, instead of simply enjoying the uncomplicated present. Nigel marvelled inwardly at the ease with which he was unburdening to Connie, safe in the knowledge that whatever he said would go no further. Connie began to talk about the children and at how they seemed to bolster her when times were difficult: she mentioned their perceptiveness and the little ways in which, with a hug, they dispensed with words and used their innate sense of comfort, through touch and warmth.

'They take things in without comment; Poppy even noticed an insect bite under my arm the other day and said I'd had it for ages – which worries me slightly actually.'

'What – the bite, or Poppy's perception?'

'The bite – actually I'm sure it's grown and it won't seem to go away.'

'Shouldn't you get it checked out then?'

'Well, it seems so petty: I mean it's only an insect bite and to go all the way to the surgery and bother James just for that...'

'It's clearly preying on your mind, though, isn't it?' Connie admitted that it did pop into her mind now and then when it itched. She smiled at the admission, but Nigel didn't. He sat himself upright.

'Connie, will you promise me you *will* have a check up – if it's just a bite, as you say, then there's nothing to worry about and doctors like James are paid to check out this sort of thing.' Nigel had changed his tone from the tipsy to the serious which discomforted Connie slightly, so she promised lightly and reverted the conversation back to Nigel:

'Now about these poor thwarted girls, Nigel...'

'Actually – I think I've come all over sleepy!' he teased, stretching to unconsciously expose his tanned six pack, which was finely covered in soft, dark baby-hair. Connie had the sense to push the subject no further, for Nigel had revealed only as much as he had felt was comfortable. She admitted that she, too, was feeling sleepy and 'ever so slightly sloshed!'

Chapter Fourteen

Nigel ushered Connie upstairs to his spare room, bringing a duvet and towel from the airing cupboard and a spare toothbrush.

'Nigel, you are the perfect host!' Connie enthused, as they hugged goodnight on the landing and Nigel withdrew to his own room. Connie climbed into the high bed, appreciating the sparseness of the simple furniture and the low beams, from which hung game hooks, slung with an old towelling dressing gown and an assortment of belts and guitar straps. She felt pleasantly drowsy, very comfortable and a lot closer to Nigel; it was strange that she had known him superficially for so long, yet to have known so very little about the world he had inhabited. Within a short time sleep took over.

She was awoken by bright lights shining through the chinks in the curtains and the revving of a motor. The dog was barking ferociously from its kennel and Nigel was shouting from his room.

'This is the third time that car's done the circuit of my lane.' The landing light went on and Nigel streaked past her door towards the stairs. She glimpsed that he was entirely naked and carrying his gun. In spite of the gravity of the situation, she couldn't resist looking after his retreating form before she herself rose, grabbing an old and cracked Barbour jacket from the beam and tripping across Tramp to the window. The security light had gone on by the barn and when she looked out for the cause, she was able to discern enough purple to realise that the car must be Pete's. With a squeal of tyres the car sped from stationary to much too fast in a matter of seconds.

Connie hastily shrugged back into her clothes and met Nigel at the bottom of the stairs: he was now clad in a sparse tea towel, which he had grabbed from the Aga. At the threat of intrusion to his privacy, Nigel's entire demeanour had changed to the primeval hunter. Connie explained that she had seen that the car was only Pete's.

'Well, let him just step the other side of the gate and I'll have lover boy!' snarled Nigel, clenching and unclenching his fists, his eyes burning with indignation. 'What does he think he's doing here?' Connie realised she had no idea how he did know and felt hugely remorseful at the aggressive intrusion on gentle Nigel.

'I'm going to leave before he comes round the circuit again,' she said hurriedly and decisively, feeling crushed and miserable at the brutal way the lovely evening had been spoiled. *If this is what happens the first time Nigel opens up to anyone, he won't want to do it again*, she thought bitterly.

'You can't leave; you must be over the limit,' answered Nigel. His mind was no longer on shooting, now that he knew it was Pete, but still on exacting revenge with his fists – he was not only aerated by Pete's cheek for turning up and disrupting his peaceful haven in this manner, but also for his dear friend Connie, who had enough to deal with, without the likes of these antics.

'The alcohol was a while ago: I expect it's all been expunged,' she said, attempting to sound reassuring, for she was determined to leave her friend to his sanctuary to prevent any further mishap from befalling. Nigel was unconvinced: animal territorial feelings were still stirring in him, and he was poised to fight to protect his property. Connie recognised and feared this more than confronting Pete herself, if need be. She made for the door, ignoring Nigel's protestations and apologising repeatedly as she went. Finding that reasoning was useless, Nigel took her hand to help guide her across the lawn to where her car was parked. Her heart was thumping in dread of Pete re-emerging in the lane behind her car as she and Nigel stood together. She leapt in, promising to ring Nigel as soon as she was home.

She knew that if her car were not outside, Pete would drive on and not return as he had no vendetta with Nigel. Putting the car into reverse, she shot back into the lane and drove off, the scattering of small stones almost rivalling those made by the powerful sports car earlier.

Nigel stood just inside his gate, still wearing the tea towel. Feeling cold for the first time, he began to shiver. His anger was spent and he felt strange, as though he had lost something: he had got really close to Connie that evening and had enjoyed the sensation of sharing hearth and home, but there had been something more. Was it a glimpse of the intimacy and trust, enflamed through a truly platonic friendship, which was perhaps after all possible between himself and another female? This might have restored some semblance of faith in the female kind; but no sooner had he glimpsed it – and felt the happiness it could engender – than it had been snatched away from beneath his feet and here he was 'alone again naturally!' Except that he now felt slightly less at ease with his self-sufficiency. He wondered if he had been missing something for a long time now, or whether he had actually just been proved right: that distance was safest? Safest yes, but now he began to ruminate over whether it was happiest. He turned and went in for a mug of tea.

Connie, meanwhile, had slowed to a more sensible speed, now that she was out of the danger of confronting Pete in Nigel's lane. The roads were empty and the trees and hedges were sharply silhouetted against the light of the moon – everything was still. Her mobile clicked back into signal and reverberated its messages with a startling barrage of staccato. They were all from Pete. He knew whom she was with. He 'just knew' where she was. He knew what she was doing. Added to this, there was a stream of invective, berating her for being with someone else when she knew that she and he, Pete, could be together still. (Had he pushed Ken's presence out of his mind totally? She really didn't want to go through the business of telling him about Ken all over again, but surely the knowledge of Ken should have vindicated Nigel?)

Connie realised that Pete had probably been parked beside her car when it was outside Nigel's house for some time. When he had seen the lights go out downstairs, followed by upstairs, he had jumped to his own conclusion. Connie was the more indignant at Pete for having ignited the calm Nigel into baying for fisticuffs! She felt flat and out of her depth; the creativity, fun and friendship of the evening besmirched and regretted: when was this tirade of Pete's going to end? Each time things seemed to be improving, something else occurred to crush her spirits again. Ken wasn't close enough in any sense to help push home the fact that she and Pete were in fact trivia from a regrettable past moment that had become eclipsed out of all proportion. She also wondered uneasily again how Pete had discovered her whereabouts.

Her lights picked out a solitary car in the lay-by ahead and, once again, the purple was unmistakable! What was more, Pete himself was to be seen squatting down beside the wheel, mobile in hand: presumably he had a puncture, deserved from erratic driving down narrow lanes, which were particularly hazardous at this time of year, due to stray clippings from the newly trimmed hedges. She wondered at herself as she sailed on past, her heart thumping, instead of checking to see if she could help. These days she felt menaced by his presence at the best of times, but particularly late at night in the dark. She was unsurprised to hear her mobile ringing and found herself answering it mechanically: she put it on 'speaker' and heard him, sounding much relieved, ask where she was. He displayed a pretence of surprise to hear that she was just returning from visiting a friend, Nigel in fact, and that there was nothing more to explain. She was now on her return home and no, Nigel was not 'her boyfriend', as suggested by his ridiculous messages.

It was clear that he was not admitting to having been there himself and that he was feigning intuition ('*just knowing*', as he put it) for his knowledge of her whereabouts. He was evidently unaware that she had seen him outside Nigel's house, or that she had only a moment ago driven right past him. Connie decided to let it go and not to challenge him in order to prevent further complication. She reassured him again and continued flatly that she was tired and needed to get home and to sleep. She rang off.

As Tramp and Connie clattered wearily into the house, heading for their second sleep, the telephone could already be heard. She ran and snatched at it, anxious not to awaken and involve her mother, let alone the children.

Without waiting to hear the other end, she boiled over at yet another potential intrusion, this time to her family.

'I've said goodnight. We all need to sleep: please leave us alone!' with which she slammed down the telephone. That had been a mistake, for she had barely reached the end of the front hall before it began ringing again: she knew she should have shown more patience.

She lifted the receiver again, ready to apologise, grovel, anything to avoid further calls and allow for a restorative sleep; however, his tack had changed and he was already talking, wheedling.

'But you'd been with him all evening and I saw the lights go out downstairs and then upstairs. You see I saw. I *know*!'

'What do you mean "you saw"?' Connie's voice had dropped to one she barely recognised as her own.

'I happened to be passing Nigel's house and I saw your car. Then I saw the lights going out downstairs and upstairs in the bedroom…' Connie was no longer tired.

'No one "happens to go past Nigel's house", except to see him. And anyone who knows Nigel would know that that had to be by appointment!'

'Well, I was just retuning from South Molton and I just thought, *I know! I'll go a different way for a change.*'

'But if that was early on, how could you have been there when he went to bed?'

'Well, when I saw your car the first time, I went for a drink or two and then I told myself you wouldn't still be there…'

'So why did you go that way again then?'

'Just to make sure you weren't!' The dialogue seemed again to resemble shades of Winnie the Pooh: 'But you were!' he went on. 'I saw the car. I saw the lights on and I watched them all go off in the bedroom.'

'*If* I'd been sleeping with Nigel, as you infer,' Connie said nastily, 'then it would be entirely my business. And Ken's – but not yours. And, as a matter of fact I was! But where your detective work is defective is that Nigel wasn't in the same room – I was in the spare room, in which, before you make any further unworthy accusations, there was only Tramp!'

A stunned silence followed this: Pete found himself a little ashamed. But then, he reasoned, how was he to know? He realised he was in a spot of bother now and had better start apologising before Connie thought of any further questions. However, Connie didn't seem interested in that – she said she just wanted her household left in peace – perhaps he had better try to do that. He had better give her some space. He had time, after all.

Chapter Fifteen

Connie decided not to mention her doctor's appointment to her mother, who didn't sound too well herself, what with her shortness of breath and her 'smoker's choke' – well deserved and well worth it! She tried to persuade Mary to stay longer with them, but Mary was adamant: 'You should always leave when you're still welcome, just as you should always stop eating while you still have room for a doughnut!' Connie spent the morning doing her mother's accounts, putting together the bills and dividends into little heaps, then preparing the cheques and the paying-in slips for her mother's signature. Mary delighted in having this done for her and had hoarded them all for Connie to sort out, bragging that she was so very lazy and that their completion definitely called for a celebration lunch. They opted for an early lunch at the local pub, just the two of them, one to one, which was a treat in itself. They ordered fresh mackerel, caught that same morning, with granary bread, followed by sticky toffee pudding. Connie chose the pudding because she had always loved a version of it, known as 'treacle stodge' in her childhood, and she knew it was expected of her and would please Mary. This was washed down with the inevitable sherry (for which Connie had also rather lost the taste, but it always tasted better in her mother's company), followed by coffee.

It was during the coffee, as they sat back, uncomfortably sated and slightly drowsy, that Mary began to talk of her latest plan, which was to visit Connie's brother, Jeremy, more often, rather than at every other Christmas.

'It's always so lovely to be a part of your lives, and Jeremy's letters keep me marvellously in touch with all his goings on, but it's not the same. I enjoy all of your company so much, but that makes me the more aware of what I'm missing with my grandsons. I want to be a part of their growing years too.'

Connie had always harboured an irrational guilt at her children having their grandmother almost exclusively to themselves, so she caught at the plan with enthusiasm, asking when she planned to go and for how long.

'It'll be only for a month and I shall be visiting my other WREN cronies while I'm out there, so I don't wear out my welcome – you know that visitors and fish become unpleasant and smelly after three days!'

'We'll just have to cope without you then, but don't you think you'd better work off some of your "smoker's choke" a bit before you go? They're so much more health conscious in Australia and they might cart you off to hospital at the first wheeze!' Her mother took a long and deliberate draw on her cigarette and looked at her daughter mischievously.

'Over my dead body!' she rasped, after which, seeing that Connie didn't see this as quite as amusing as she did, she went on, 'But I shall live to be a hundred, like all our healthy old relations. Poppy will have to push me about in my Bath chair and the rest of you will be busy keeping me in my supplies of sherry and gaspers!'

'And when you do pop those immortal clogs, I suppose I shall have to ensure that there's a grand supply of sherry and gaspers in your coffin to keep you down there.'

'Oh, indeed you will – or I shall be coming back to haunt the local off-licences and will prove a huge embarrassment!'

Going '*I looks towards you*!' Connie lifted her glass towards Mary, wondering at what other incumbents of the pub were making of the macabre turn the conversation had taken. (Mary was hard of hearing, but resisted the help of a hearing aid, which she owned but rarely put in, so her voice easily penetrated over all others in the vicinity.)

'*I bows accordin*',' responded her mother, inclining her head. '*Yur'z to us*!'

'*None like us*, thank God,' answered Connie, clinking her mother's glass and aware that all other conversation had completely stopped and that their own smiles were mirrored by the inhabitants of one barstool to the next.

She waited for her mother's usual spirited light-flashing, horn-beeping departure before making the appointment with James on the same afternoon, so as to save on days off. She arrived at the medical centre and took a furtive look around, hoping there would be no one familiar, who might ask her the reason she was there. To her relief, the waiting room seemed empty of anyone she recognised. With mounting assurance Connie went up to the desk to register and be given her disk, but as she gave her name and details, she heard the familiar voice of Rowan, a friend and midwife, booming out something to do with pelvic floors. She kept her head lowered, hoping not to be spotted, but already Rowan was delightedly calling her name.

'Connie! Haven't seen you for ages! What are you doing here? Not pregnant are you?' (What sort of questions were these, coming from an averagely intelligent member of the human race?)

'May we nip that one in the bud right now!' hedged Connie.

'Pity! That could have been fun. Anyway, what a lovely surprise! I'm doing a clinic for first-timers – it's all very sweet: they're so earnest! But what ails you? Have you got a small daughter with rampant verrucas lurking around the corner, or is it you?'

'It's me,' Connie admitted, 'but I'd rather you didn't shout about it. *I've got a lump,*' she added, as quietly as she could and still be audible.

'Oh,' Rowan sounded instantly professional and lowered her own voice to match Connie's. 'I take it it's on the breast?' Connie nodded, feeling that all eyes were directing themselves upon her for the second time that day.

'You know, Connie, ninety per cent of everything that's examined turn out to be insect bites or simply benign deposits. We all get them – but panic when they're on the breast!' Rowan warmed to her pronouncement. 'Quite right to get it checked out though – you may feel a complete prat, but it's worth the peace of mind.' Connie thanked Rowan for the advice, wishing that she would stop talking about it as though it were a big deal.

'Yes, I'm sure it's nothing: I just promised someone that I'd have it checked, you know, anything for an easy life! I think I'm next anyway,' Connie went on, hoping that Rowan would take the hint and leave her.

'Promised, eh? This sounds intriguing. I've got to run anyway, but look, I'm halfway through – this is just a break – let's meet up for coffee after my class and your appointment with James. You'll have a laugh – and watch he doesn't tickle anywhere sensitive with his nose hair – it's getting distractingly long!'

Rowan's mischievous sense of humour was beginning to thaw Connie's prickliness and the sides of her mouth twitched.

'Well, I will if I can, but I have to fetch Sophia to take her to the orthodontist later in the afternoon so there mightn't be time.'

'Don't worry, Connie – there'll be plenty of time – you'll be fine!' called Rowan astutely, seeing the anxiety that Connie was trying to hide and she dashed off down the corridor, her arms full of dummy newborns.

A loud bleep announced Connie's number and she rose from her seat and walked through the swing doors towards the room marked 'Dr Haggart', at which she knocked.

'Hello, Connie! What a lovely surprise.' (Connie was becoming fed up with being a 'lovely surprise'.) 'I don't think we've seen you since New Year on Bideford Bridge – God, wasn't it wet!' Connie agreed and James went on to discuss the party that they had gone on to (dressed as carrots) for what seemed an eternity.

'But you didn't come here to talk about my carrot costume, fetching as I must say it was. What can I do for you?' Connie felt herself blush ridiculously, while inwardly reprimanding herself at the absurdity of her embarrassment: after all, James had not actually delivered her babies, but he had performed all the antenatal examinations, so why should she be feeling so fey now? Perhaps because she had been brought up with her parents' attitudes, which had seen them through the War, never to fuss and to make the least of the most. Yet here she was seeing a doctor over an insect!

'I don't want to waste your time or anything, but I've found a lump under my arm, at the edge of my breast and it won't go away – I think it may have grown. I'm sure it's an insect bite but I'm under orders to have you investigate…' She said all this in a rush, smiling apologetically. James had instantly switched his demeanour to the professional.

'Let's have a look at it: pop into the cubicle and slip off your top half.' He ushered her into a narrow room with space only for a couch, a trolley and a chair. She removed her top and bra and sat nervously on the edge of the couch. James came in and she showed him the lump, which was an angry red.

'It's that colour because I itched it,' smiled Connie awkwardly. James paid no attention and pushed it, pressed it and poked at it, asking her if it felt tender.

She answered heartily that naturally it did, wouldn't anyone's? All the while he was looking minutely at her body and not at her, for which Connie was grateful. She noticed that Rowan had indeed been right about the nose hair and almost giggled to see a rogue strand protruding some distance from his nostril, like a beetle's antenna. Finally he finished and, still not looking at her, told her to get dressed again, allow the nurse to take some blood and do a quick urine sample for analysis before returning to his consulting room.

As she got dressed, Connie could hear James on the phone through the thin wall which divided her cubicle from his office, but she couldn't quite catch what he was saying and whether it was about her. When she rejoined James in his office, he began to question her minutely.

'When did you first notice it?'

'I'm not sure: a good few weeks ago.' He had turned to his computer.

'Hm, my computer doesn't deal with "a good few"; could you be a bit more specific?' Connie thought for a minute, for she had become aware of it gradually and she truly had no idea.

'Well maybe five weeks – or more,' Connie tried again.

'Five plus – and you didn't think to come in before at all?'

'Well, I kept expecting it to disappear, you know – and then I've had my mother staying…'

'Not a good excuse, Connie – but how is Mary, OK, I hope?'

'Fine.'

He was jabbing at his computer with his index finger as the exchange continued: 'Did it change at all during your last period – get larger, or more tender?'

'I'm afraid I didn't notice if it did.'

'And when was your last period?' Connie didn't know the answer to this either and flinched inwardly at the inadequacy of her answers.

'I think it may have been at the end of last week – or the week before. Really, once one's finished I don't think any more about it until the next one.' James didn't smile but continued to tap awkwardly at his computer. Connie felt tempted to say that she could at least perhaps help him on the typing front, but refrained, since it was clearly taking up all his concentration.

'And according to this,' he glanced again at the screen, 'you are not on the pill.' Connie shook her head, mildly pleased at having a question to which she knew the answer, even though it appeared, in any case, to be rhetorical.

After a little more computer work James swivelled his chair around to face Connie. He took off his work glasses, making him look far more the person she knew socially. He looked considerately at her for a moment, smiling kindly.

'Mmm, I think you had better go for more tests, Connie. There's probably nothing sinister there and it's probably a simple cyst or what's called a fibroadenoma – but without a proper investigation I can't be certain and obviously we need to err on the side of caution.'

'So it isn't an insect bite?' asked Connie stupidly, deliberately slow to catch on and give time for misunderstanding.

'I think we can rule that out for certain – but, as I said, there's probably nothing sinister for you to worry about and the tests that you'll have will be simply precautionary.'

'What will happen?'

'Well, we'll send off your bloods and urine sample to North Devon Hospital…' (at the word 'hospital', Connie felt alarm bells reverberate across her chest) 'and I've just arranged for you to pop over now for a mammogram down at X-ray – they're ready for you and it shouldn't take five minutes – that's the beauty of our cottage hospital, there's far less fuss and queue!' (So that was what the phone call had been about.) 'Then I'm recommending you to a specialist, who's far more knowledgeable in this field than me. He'll look at the results of everything and let you know the outcome. It's possible he may do a "fine needle aspirate", which means they'll draw out some of the fluid from the lump for analysis.' At the mention of a needle, however fine, Connie shrank momentarily: in spite of being a blood donor, she was hardly a fan of needles – especially not there! James had picked up on her reaction – really he was very good – and assured her that the place would be anaesthetised so it wouldn't hurt, while she remained somewhat fazed by the unexpected.

'It'll be a piece of cake – nothing like having babies!' The initial paralysis left her, and she was able to ask when these tests would take place.

'We have something called the "two week rule", which means that that's the maximum time you'll need to wait for your appointment – and please think of the tests as just a precaution to eliminate the possibility of anything sinister.'

That was the second time he had used the word 'sinister'.

'By "sinister" you do mean Cancer with a big "C?"'

James was a professional: he looked her mildly between the eyes. 'Well, yes. But, as I said, this is simply a precaution: the majority of people find their cysts to be benign and you'd be amazed how many we see. Just forget about things if you can until the appointment with the specialist. They'll contact you with the date and time and, as I said, it won't be longer than a fortnight.' He moved back his chair, indicating that the appointment was over and, giving her hand a little squeeze and an apologetic smile, he opened the door for her.

'You know the quick way out at the back for the hospital and X-ray Department, don't you?' Connie nodded and smiled away her inner agitation. 'Bye, Connie: see you around.' James waved after Connie's retreating figure, perturbed not to have been able to have given his friend the news she deserved – but, after all, this was Connie, who was totally unfazable! James was right about the mammogram proving quick, but he hadn't mentioned the discomfort of pushing the tender place squarely between the hard, cold screens while the radiographer retreated behind the partition to perform the X-rays.

'I think I feel a certain empathy with apples entering the cider press!' Connie muttered through gritted teeth, as the radiographer shuffled back in her sensible shoes to rearrange Connie's breasts and the screens to a different angle for further X-rays, returning again to adjust and reposition Connie's hair this time. The radiographer indulged Connie with a smile.

'I'm afraid it's not very comfy, is it?' she responded rhetorically, saving Connie from further speech, 'but at least it's over nice and quickly.'

Maybe to you! thought Connie, deciding that further talk might delay the process still more.

By the time Connie was finally able to make for the exit doors of the medical centre she felt bruised, both physically and mentally; however, as she drew level with them, Rowan called out to her again. 'Hey, Connie – what about our coffee?'

Connie had completely forgotten and automatically looked at her watch. She was surprised to see that there was still ample time before she was due to fetch Sophia. The trouble was she really didn't wish to discuss the news she had just received with anyone, especially since she had barely found time to digest it herself. However, it appeared she had little sway in the matter, for Rowan, never one to hang back and with enough positivism for both of them, had linked her arm in Connie's.

'You don't mind if we go somewhere other than the medical centre café?' she whispered, so that the ladies on the desk shouldn't hear. It sounded more like a statement than a question – and one that Connie was emphatically in agreement. Rowan steered her to a shady café around the corner, talking non-stop, where she ordered a café latte for herself and tea for Connie.

Rowan scraped the rubber-tipped chair legs across the linoleum café floor with a rasping sound, and gazed directly at Connie.

'I'm getting the vibe that your appointment wasn't entirely plain sailing?'

Another statement posed as a question, and one which Connie could not avoid answering.

'Not good, actually,' answered Connie, 'but I'm a bit reluctant to talk about it.' Rowan put a comforting hand on Connie's.

'You're not going to let a little thing like an appointment with a specialist worry you? Not when you're coping so amazingly with four kids and a divorce with a known skinflint?' Rowan's lack of tact was legendary, but Connie knew that a compliment of sorts was intended.

'Strictly outward appearances – those are what I'm good at,' answered Connie, 'and I've got my mum – she helps more than she knows.'

'Well, all your problems are what I'd call major front-burners compared with most!'

'Major *Who*?' Connie couldn't resist batting back, finding herself rallying with the effort.

'Well, "*if you can keep your head when all about you*", etcetera – then a little thing like a mammogram—'

'I've had that – a needle aspirate, actually.'

'Oh, and a fine needle aspirate – (you won't feel a thing – it's done under local anaesthetic) – well, it's nothing. Loads of people have them and it's pointless worrying – unless the test which you haven't yet had turns out positive!' Connie began to see the logic with which Rowan was clumsily and sweetly trying to reassure her, and suddenly felt desperately glad that there had been this chance rendezvous with her friend after all.

'Well, can we keep the whole thing to ourselves – I don't want any of the family knowing. Especially since it's such a routine thing.'

'Mum's the word – oops! I suppose you hear that one a lot! Anyway, how was James's nose hair?'

'Tickling his vitals!' As they exploded with laughter Connie felt a pang at the way Rowan's irresistible sense of humour brought out the worst in her, for James had been so kind. However, she wasn't off the hook herself, for Rowan was still probing for further sensation.

'You have obviously not kept this totally to yourself in any case: who was the certain someone that made you promise a visit to James? I don't see you confiding that sort of thing with Ken – you don't see him enough.' Connie felt irritated at Rowan's perception, but shrugged it off.

'Only Nigel.'

'What? Not the gorgeous hunky-dory guitar-playing Nigel?'

'The very same...' – Rowan's eyebrows were arching in anticipation of glorious scandal – 'and no! Before you suggest anything – we are truly and proverbially "just good friends"!'

'How disappointing! But what were the circumstances?' (*Would she never give up*? wondered Connie.) 'I mean you couldn't have just come out with, "And by the way, I've got this lump – on my breast actually!" ' She mimicked Connie perfectly.

'No – I went to his cottage to write some stuff and – we made quite a night of it actually.'

'Huh!' Rowan pouted. 'How did you get an invite to the delectable Nigel's? Thought he was a virtual recluse! Why doesn't he ask *me* to his cottage?'

'He probably asked me because he knows me well enough to know that he's safe and that I wouldn't pounce!'

'Ah, but *did* you?'

'Well, I did see him with no clothes on!' Connie couldn't resist answering.

'What? You jammy thing – I bet he was well hung?'

'There certainly didn't seem to be anything wrong with him – but I only happened to spot him fleetingly on the way to the bathroom,' she confessed, smiling annoyingly at the thought of Nigel's inadequate tea-towel loincloth.

'*Happened to spot him!*' crowed Rowan. 'Connie, I am utterly and totally jealous of you!'

Connie was now laughing and receiving envy for her good fortune: she felt entirely restored and ready not to think of her appointment with the specialist until her next visit. Still chuckling at Rowan's reaction to her chance view of Nigel, she swept out of the car park to fetch Sophia.

Chapter Sixteen

Ken was playing for the Pointer Sisters this time, at West Point, near Exeter, and had managed to procure four tickets for Connie and three of her friends. His hotel was near the gig, so he and Connie would have time to go there after it, allowing her to return in the small hours. They were both particularly excited because he had been touring Japan recently and the children had been on their summer holidays before that, so it hadn't been possible to steal any time during the day to see each other. Their phone calls had continued, of course, at odd hours of the day and night, and text messages about how much they missed one another ping-ponged between them, providing each with an inner glow, which helped to bolster them against more trying times. Ken purported to have the idyllic life, playing music, being adored and never so much as having to do his own laundry; but overriding all this was a need to be needed and to be missed and Connie was fitting into this niche rather comfortably.

West Point was a huge hangar of a place and was used for motor trade fairs and exhibitions, as well as concerts for big bands, in a festival setting with standing room only. Connie first invited Rowan to the gig, knowing that she would be less interested in the band itself but more in the general ambience: she wanted to meet the members of the band and wondered if there was a 'fit black bass player' to whom Connie could introduce her.

Connie explained that she rarely even saw the rest of the band, since they very often went their own ways after the gig and as Ken was simply a session player, he wouldn't know the other band members especially well: Rowan's spirits remained unchanged, however, as she winked at Connie saying, 'Where there's a will, there's a way!' Next, she invited Max and Clara, to which Max agreed enthusiastically but Clara said she felt too heavy and cumbersome in the late stages of her pregnancy to envisage an evening of jostling and standing – much as she would normally have loved to come. 'Next time,' she said resignedly, 'when I have returned to my sylph-like state.' For the third ticket, Connie turned to her own band.

Nigel didn't like big jostling crowds (much to the chagrin of

Rowan!) and she didn't want to ask Andy, in case his ego suggested that she might have some ulterior motive and that perhaps she was harbouring regrets at having turned down his proffered attentions. Cake was the obvious choice and was thrilled, not only at getting a 'freebie' to watch a big band but also for reasons antithetical to Nigel, for he loved a festival, a demonstration, a crowd: the more strangers who were in one voice, the better.

Connie insisted in going in two cars, which gave her freedom of movement after the gig to go home in her own time after she had spent glorious time with Ken. Connie was amused to discover butterflies in her stomach, in much the same way as she supposed Ella to have, when she anticipated a meeting with Carl. These mounted as the day wore on and as she prepared the children an early supper. She reminded the younger ones that Ella was in charge and that she herself was only at the end of her mobile, should any of them fall ill. She also took the precaution of having a private word with Demelza not to wind any of her sisters up.

'But I never do – it's just that sometimes they can't take a joke!'

'If they can't take a joke, don't make one – just keep it for me later,' instructed Connie and Demelza, mollified that at least her mother found her jokes funny, agreed to desist for the evening.

Connie hugged all the children goodbye, thanked Ella for being so grown up as to babysit, adding that it was a lovely feeling to know your babysitter this well and that she could be totally trusted.

Ella answered laconically that this was no problem, but she was subdued despite the flattery, which had typified much of her recent behaviour. She smiled wanly, looking far beyond her just fifteen years, while Connie's eyes gleamed bright with excitement and anticipation. It seemed almost as though a role reversal had taken place between the mother and daughter.

During the drive to Exeter Connie had time to reflect on her strange relationship with Ken. Certainly they got on well, but she was unsure if they knew each other better, simply because it had been for such a long time: they had hardly played an important role in one another's lives during all those years between the first bloom and the second. Their companionship seemed to be bound in the elixir of youth, which was the circumstance surrounding their first acquaintance, when they were in their late teens and early twenties, the memories of which, childishly, vainly, they nurtured when they were together. This was fine, as far as it went, but was there anything on which to base their present lives? Ken clearly tried to show an interest in the children he had never met and Connie was certainly intrigued with his existence as a nomadic musician. Perhaps the glory and chemistry lay, therefore, in the sheer difference between them – and in the security provided by the fact that there was no possible threat of a compromise to reach? Her mind thrummed on in this vein as the venue at West Point drew ever nearer.

Rowan found Connie, through the use of their mobiles, at the bar: the fans had to follow a one-way system, so as to avoid collisions with drinks, which could, in turn, cause possible ill feeling. This was most unlikely, however, as the prospective audience consisted largely of seasoned festival goers, their tankards dangling from their belts in readiness for a cool pint, and Diana Ross lookalikes (both female and male) for whom the dressing-up held equal significance with the gig itself. They flaunted and flirted in their elaborate wigs and tastefully scanty clothing. Part of Connie began to long for Ella's presence, knowing how much she would enjoy the sensationalism, while the other part was ridiculously full of girlish anticipation at the thought of seeing Ken in this setting.

'Have you *heard anything*?' Rowan was asking the inevitable question, after taking an exaggerated look around to make sure they were queuing at a safe distance from Cake and Max. Connie found herself mildly irritated, for she was far too caught up in the present to wish to concern herself with any problems outstanding.

'As a matter of fact I have and I'm going for the tests next week,' she replied, 'but do you know I really don't care about it now? It just feels like a time-waster for the NHS and me.' She hoped this would quell any further discussion, but Rowan returned that this attitude was a very good thing and that she had always admired Connie's level-headedness. Perversely, this suggestion of her being sensible made her feel uneasy again.

'I gather that breastfeeders of far too many children run less risk of developing breast cancer,' she defended, as though Rowan had suggested that they did, 'and, of course, I breastfed all mine for ages just for a peaceful life.'

'I remember: you always seemed to have a little pair of feet sticking out of your misshapen jumpers!'

'Thanks!'

'Oh, but it was so sweet!' Rowan tried again, attempting vainly to cheer and support her friend. 'And then, of course, there's your diet.'

'Or lack of it!'

'I mean all those vegetables from your garden – frightfully organic – couldn't be healthier!'

'Ah, but think of Linda McCartney!'

'She's simply an exception – think of Kylie Minogue!'

Thanks to Rowan's well-meant assurances, Connie had returned to the thoughts that had actually been nagging her subconscious for the past few days and which she had only today succeeded in dislodging. She bought a round of drinks, and Cake – always adept at receiving, due to his apprenticeship with the begging bowl – suggested that they all took two drinks, one for each hand, to save themselves queuing a second time. It seemed a sensible idea and when all eight drinks were lined up at the bar, Cake kindly offered assistance, magically managing to carry four at once between his powerful drummer's paws, while Rowan and Connie managed with the remaining two apiece.

A voice boomed through the intercom announcing that the support band was about to begin and they fought their way through the mass of bodies, which had accumulated in the main arena, to an agreed spot where Max was valiantly attempting to hold a space for them. This was near the front by a conspicuous pillar that Ken had spotted during the sound check. He had explained to Connie that if she were in this particular place, he would be able to focus on it, warmed in the knowledge of where she was positioned, and direct his energies towards her, in spite of the lights being too strong for him to actually see her!

The support band began and the crowd started to sway gently, like ripples over a streambed, infused and enthused. As it became closer to the time for the Pointer Sisters' appearance, the crowd around the pillar became more dense and they could feel the heat from the surrounding bodies, which pressed ever forwards. Cake was in his element, his two pints clasped protectively to his chest, his elbows turned outwards to prevent anyone from taking his body space. He was bouncing lightly from his ankles, as if connected to the pedals of his high-hat symbol and base drum, while his head moved keenly forward and backward to the rhythm. Rowan had, somewhat unwisely, placed her drinks between her feet. She stood with her feet therefore rooted, while her knees and shoulders twitched self-consciously sexily, to the bass beat. Max, in contrast, stood stock still, an intent look on his face, his eyes slightly narrowed in his attempts to see as much as he could without his accustomed glasses. A very slight inflection of his head, redolent of that of the nodding dogs to be seen in the backs of cars, was his only perceptible movement.

At last the support band, good as they were, had left the stage and Connie could feel the knots tying themselves tighter in her stomach. When she had watched Ken at the Bryan Ferry gig, simple recognition had been a thrill, but this time, knowing that Ken was with her and that they would be together later, she felt positively enflamed. Rowan looked significantly at her and bit at her finger dramatically, which Connie answered with a widening of her eyes and a glance at the stage as the familiar introduction could be heard playing 'I'm so Excited!' (*'and I just can't hide it'*). The lyric matched her mood as she strained and craned around the gyrating crowd to see the one she was really here for: the stage was necessarily large to accommodate all three sisters and their backing band. Ken was standing in profile, his lanky legs well apart to support his guitar, which was slung so low it was almost at arms' stretch. Connie was singing along with the lyric: *'Tonight's the night we're going to make it happen, tonight we'll cast all other things aside'*. Ken was joining the numerous harmonies in the refrain: *'I want to love you, feel you, wrap my legs around you'*. As she watched him crooning this (Connie had thought that the music itself and the nearness and knowledge of Ken could leap no higher within her) she realised he was singing the words apparently directly at her – and then he grinned and winked! Connie squealed and pogoed up and down.

'*Did you see that*?' she shouted to Rowan.

Rowan, who had been keeping a keen eye on Ken herself, hardly able to believe the luck of her friend, the free ticket, the connection, replied by pretending to put her fingers down her throat: '*Pass me a sick bucket!*' she bellowed.

The band continued to whip the crowd from one frenzy to the next, each of the Pointer Sisters taking turns to come to the front of the stage and dance deliciously, provocatively, to a tumultuous reception. Connie was hoarse from singing along at the top of her lungs and fuelled with an inner anticipation, engendered partly by the music and its lyrics. She danced from the hips, which saved her feet from trampling on those of others and ensured their small space in the crush, which pushed its way ever further forward, while heavy-shouldered bouncers, their T-shirts rendered transparent through sweat and being stretched to their limits, formed a human cordon below the stage to stop the 'moshers' from reaching it. For the encore, by which time the crowd were stamping, whistling and shouting at fever pitch, the tempo was brought down with 'I want a Man with a Slow Hand', ('*I want a lover with an easy touch*'). Again, Ken seemed to be directing himself exclusively at Connie and she giggled and shuddered as he left the stage, waving with his guitar in her specific direction.

'Just as well we did stand by that pillar,' said Rowan, 'or he'd have been doing all that sickening carry-on to someone else!'

'Bah! I never saw anyone so green!' answered Cake in support of Connie.

The crowd was leaving, suddenly spent, in their droves, trampling the crackling carpet of polystyrene cups in their path. The cleaners were already tackling the mammoth task of clearance before the exhibition the next day, pushing their vast brooms, which spanned a metre across. The four friends loitered a little and were told to move on.

'I want to stay and be introduced to Ken,' insisted Rowan. 'I'm hoping he might introduce me to one of those big burly bouncers.'

'Hands off, he's mine!' said Cake, who was known to be a little ambidextrous when it came to choosing gender.

'Come on – I have to get back to Clara and we should leave Connie to get on with her romantic liaison with that scruffy bloody guitarist!' Max winked at Connie conspiratorially and she smiled back at him gratefully, for she was hoping to get Ken alone for as many moments as possible and didn't want to waste time on the niceties of introductions.

Rowan saw Connie's look and spoke reluctantly.

'OK, we take the hint – but how about just one little look and I promise I won't cramp your style?'

'No – we're going, and you don't want to lose your lift,' said Cake firmly, taking Rowan by the shoulders and propelling her firmly towards the exit.

'Don't I?' smiled Rowan, but she put her arm around Cake and blew Connie a reluctant kiss: 'Ah well – enjoy!'

A doorman had come over to usher them out.

'I'm with one of the band,' said Connie, rendered suddenly shy at seeing her friends leaving.

'I bet that's what they all say,' laughed Max. 'Goodbye, Connie: have fun and try to do anything we haven't!'

Chapter Seventeen

Connie waved her friends goodbye hurriedly, because she had seen Ken, coming from beside the stage area. When he saw her he held out his arms and she ran to him, nestling into the soft denim of his jacket, smelling the freshness of what must have been a very hasty shower. He held her tightly as they hugged and kissed and delighted at one another's presence, their conversation disjointed.

'You're all warm and steamy – it was – brilliant!'

'*Am* I? *Was* it? High praise coming from *you*. You smell wonderful – all perfume and perspiration! You *did* stand by that pillar?'

'Yes, and you were looking right at me!'

'That's what I intended... I could sort of feel you there... everything I squeezed out of my guitar tonight was 'specially for you...'

Connie loved the idea of this, but wondered briefly to how many others these glib, smooth, familiar words had been uttered? Ken was carrying his guitar in one hand while his other was around Connie.

'I've told the others I'm not going back to the hotel in the bus, so I can come back with you straight away.' He said this between murmurs of how wonderful she was looking, always looked, never changed. Again, Connie felt inside that this sounded a little slick, but she couldn't help revelling in it, her self-confidence soaring: it was an unaccustomed and glorious feeling.

'Right – what are we waiting for?' she answered and led him in the direction of her car. The long file of cars awaiting the exits was still in evidence, so they climbed into the car, stowing the guitar carefully in the back and waited, unable to keep their hands still from stroking and caressing.

'I've been looking forward to this so much for so-oh long,' Ken was saying when Connie's mobile began to ring.

'I'm sorry, I'm afraid I'll have to answer this – it's from the children,' Connie said glancing at the word 'Home' on the front of it.

'Of course you must – go ahead!' said Ken, his arms loosening a fraction as she answered it.

All she could hear at first was very loud bawling and then Demelza's indignant voice: 'Be quiet! I'm telling Mummy! Mummy, Ella kicked me really hard and she swore and she's spilt water all over Poppy's prep on purpose!'

'And what did you do to provoke her?'

'Nothing. I was just watching a programme and she took the controls and changed it over so I mentioned her spots – which is only truth and not a joke. Then she kicked me, the water went over and she never even said "*sorry*" and then she—'

Poppy had swallowed her bellowing for a moment and had grabbed the phone: 'And then she said the "poo" word!'

'The what?' Connie had to think for a moment.

'The *poo* word – *you* know!'

'Does it begin with an "S"?' Connie asked carefully.

'Yes – well, a sort of "Sh" actually.'

Connie attempted to sound very stern. 'I think I'd better talk to Ella, please.' There was another scuffle, because Ella had evidently walked out of the room. A furious dialogue followed in the background, with Demelza insisting that Ella had to come to the phone because Mummy said so, while Ella, after mimicking 'Mummy thed!' answered that she was the boss so she didn't have to do anything. There was more pressure from the younger ones for Ella to answer the phone and after a dignified interval she picked it up, speaking icily.

'Hello – and now I suppose you are going to have a go at me as well!' This rather took the wind out of Connie's sails.

'Actually, yes, Ella – I am – I left you in charge.'

'Yes – you left me in charge and I told Demelza to go to bed and she refused – I had every right over the TV controls since I had sent her to bed. Then she defied me – she's such a little *baby*!'

'Kicking is never the right thing to do, no matter how much you are provoked.'

Ken's eyebrows lifted in surprise, not only at the content, but also at the as yet unheard severity in sweet Connie's voice.

'She's exaggerating as usual – I hardly touched her! But of course you're not going to listen to *me* when dear little Demelza says anything different,' answered Ella, cleverly shifting the accusation.

'So you're admitting that you *did* kick her. I'm glad it wasn't as hard as it seemed, but any time you hurt someone physically you put yourself in the wrong, no matter what they may have done to you.' Demelza could be heard screeching in the background that it was a really hard kick and that Ella was lying.

'*And* you swore!' Poppy and Sophia were shouting at Ella. Ella was apparently now clutching the receiver above the heads of the others who, judging from the sound of their baying, were all trying to wrest it from her.

'Can you hear what I'm having to put up with? They're all such babies!' The squabble began to abate as Ella continued, but this time to Demelza. 'You can have the flipping phone – all you have to do is ask me nicely, you *baby*!'

Demelza responded, 'All right – *please* may I have the phone, your *Majesty*!' There was a pause while Ella evidently passed it to her, but Demelza could be heard to say, deliberately loudly, 'There's no need to throw it at me!

'When you get back,' said Demelza, calm now, 'you will see my bruises, which are coming out already – and then you'll know how hard I was kicked, won't you?'

'I will,' answered Connie, 'but until then, do you think you could all just go to bed and when you wake up I will be there! I'm sorry this happened, Demelza. Ella should never have hurt you – although it does sound as though you provoked her, after I'd specifically said not to. And now, could you put me through to each of the others?' Connie spoke to them in turn, soothing, comforting, reassuring. She told Demelza and Ella to apologise to one another, which they played lip service to, with an exaggerated 'Sorr-*eee*', after which she told each to go to bed and not refer to the incident on their way.

Finally Connie was able to put the mobile down and Ken nuzzled her to him.

'Wow! That was a diplomatic masterpiece,' he breathed, in genuine awe.

Connie nestled up to him, urging herself to feel the excitement engendered by his physical presence as she had earlier, but her mind was elsewhere, cartwheeling through the trauma of the family drama which had taken place *when she had not been there*. Had she been there, all the same things might have happened, but not to the same intensity – and not resulting in the same sense of inadequacy that she now felt over her absence when she had been needed and, worse, at the fact that she had been spending it out having frivolous fun!

Ken was gently stroking her hair and brushing her neck with soft kisses and Connie tried to lose herself in the comfort of this, but the impassioned scene of her children distraught, crying and hurting one another raced across her mind's eye, veiled in red, as if skewered by the pause button. Demelza's confident voice reverberated in her head: 'When you get back you'll see my bruises...' *When you get back*.

'Well – all's well now: shall we venture back to the hotel, raid the fridge and see what we can lug out of the window?' cajoled Ken. 'That is for starters!'

He looked at her doe-eyed and mischievous, willing her to snap back into being the uncomplicated fun-loving Connie that he knew and understood.

Connie turned the keys in the ignition and began to bump out over the rough ground towards the car park exit. Ken took on the role of raconteur, talking animatedly about the band, about the people he had met recently that they both knew, about the latest modifications to his guitar. Connie made all the non-verbal sounds cognisant of one enjoying the repartee, but she said little. Ken was finally running down on topics; he took her left hand between gear changes and stroked it.

'I've been so looking forward to this,' he finished, his words sounding somewhat hollow now and in need of an echoing reassurance from Connie.

They had reached the hotel and were about to get out, but Connie hesitated.

'I'm so sorry, Ken,' Connie said dully. 'I can't do this – I was really looking forward to it too, but now – I just need to get home.'

Ken looked at her miserably – this was the feeling he had interpreted at the pit of his stomach and had been trying so hard to smooth away. 'But I thought it was all sorted...?'

'I think it is, but – I'm not sure you'll understand – it's just that I need to be there, to see for myself that they're all right.'

'But they'll all be asleep by the sound of things?' Ken pleaded.

'I'm sure they will – I hope they will.'

'Then isn't this a little bit irrational? I mean, couldn't you come in for a minute or two and maybe I could help take your mind off things?' His hand continued to stroke the knotted column of her back.

'It isn't irrational – it's *maternal*!' Connie answered peevishly. 'I said you wouldn't understand.'

'OK, OK... it's just a little hard for me to understand, not being used to this sort of thing – and I'm sorry if I was sounding self-centred. It's just a bit disappointing – that's all.'

'Oh, Ken – it's for me to be sorry – but I'm afraid I simply won't be good company until I've seen them all tucked up and cosy in their beds. I know it sounds idiotic when by now they must be in bed because they'd ring again if there was any more trouble.'

Ken could see that her departure was inevitable and that he would come out in a far better light in his own estimation, as well as that of Connie's, if he accepted it.

'Right, well, I'll just get my guitar out of the back and you'd better whiz along home.'

'Oh dear – this is a side of me you haven't had to see and I feel *so* bad for messing up this lovely evening!'

'Not your fault,' said Ken gallantly. 'Anyway, another time, hm?' Connie realised that there was more to this apparently casual question than it seemed. She neither assured nor denied.

'Another time,' she repeated. 'Oh, Ken, I really am so very sorry for dragging you into all this.'

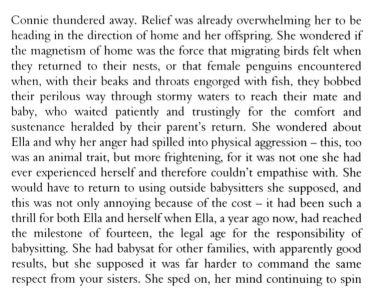

Connie thundered away. Relief was already overwhelming her to be heading in the direction of home and her offspring. She wondered if the magnetism of home was the force that migrating birds felt when they returned to their nests, or that female penguins encountered when, with their beaks and throats engorged with fish, they bobbed their perilous way through stormy waters to reach their mate and baby, who waited patiently and trustingly for the comfort and sustenance heralded by their parent's return. She wondered about Ella and why her anger had spilled into physical aggression – this, too was an animal trait, but more frightening, for it was not one she had ever experienced herself and therefore couldn't empathise with. She would have to return to using outside babysitters she supposed, and this was not only annoying because of the cost – it had been such a thrill for both Ella and herself when Ella, a year ago now, had reached the milestone of fourteen, the legal age for the responsibility of babysitting. She had babysat for other families, with apparently good results, but she supposed it was far harder to command the same respect from your sisters. She sped on, her mind continuing to spin during the frozen gulf of shortening distance between her physical presence and her nest.

Ken stood in the hotel car park, waving at the rapidly disappearing car. It was ill-suited for this sort of place, he thought, with its vastness, its mud-spattered sides and manure-caked wheel guards. Ill-suited – as perhaps was Connie. He returned slowly to his room and it ceased to be the haven, represented by his personal belongings, from the antiseptic environment of the hotel, that he had hitherto seen his own hotel spaces to be; for now it seemed suddenly barren and un-centred. He thought of the contrast to which Connie would be returning: a house humming with the vibrancy of life, and he realised a completely foreign feeling of envy. Envy at her surrounding chaos, her lack of time and space, the consequent disorganisation and freedom from personal introspection – in which he found himself so frequently dogged.

Ken considered the slinky, nubile backing vocalist who had asked him earlier, in an unmistakably meaningful way, if he were coming to an after-gig party, which he had turned down easily through preference for his new and old love, Connie. He decided that perhaps he would go after all – that would bounce him out of this unfamiliar melancholy. He sat down on the bed, disturbing a piece of paper on the pillow as he did so. It was a frivolous note he had written earlier in anticipation of Connie's amusement: *Hello and welcome!* it began. He sighed and put his head in his hands: Connie! This time he had really thought that perhaps he had found a helpmate and lover all in one, who actually understood and enjoyed both the confines and the possibilities of his lifestyle. What he had never thought to take into account, however, was the need in this instance to consider or understand hers! He had hoped that he would, in time, get to know and enjoy her children – he always got on all right with kids, recognising that he would never allow for the commitment of having any of his own. Beyond all this, he had let his defences down unpardonably and allowed himself to become unusually attached. He had come to hope for what he now realised to be the dream of an incurable romantic: that their two lifestyles could merge, somehow seamlessly, into one happy family! How had he let this happen, when he knew from experience that his lifestyle and commitment were not compatible partners? He stretched for his acoustic guitar and his fingers spilled through a series of minor cadences. His voice was constricted from the tightening in his throat and as he played the haunting melody, which was revealing itself, one word presented itself repeatedly in the lyric: 'Connie!' All thoughts of that backing vocalist and the party had vaporised as he let the balm of the music assuage him as nothing else could.

Some hours later he glanced up, his fingers sore from playing, to see dawn glinting through the curtains.

I should call Connie now, to make sure everyone's all right, he thought. Then it came to him that the reason for his call was more for him to feel all right. He pictured her 'all tucked up and cosy', as she had put it, surrounded by her little ones. Unlike him, she had a relentless timetable to be up in time for and she would need all the sleep she could steal most nights, he considered. He decided that, in view of this, it would be better to leave ringing her, perhaps for a while: Maybe she'll ring me? he thought, to buffer the realisation that this somehow felt very unlikely. He picked up his guitar again; that song he'd been playing – it was really rather enchanting! He played it again, thinking that perhaps something good had come out of all this heart-wrenching after all – such was music.

Maybe I should call it 'Connie's Legacy', he mused.

Chapter Eighteen

As Connie began the bumbling negotiation of the pothole-ridden drive, she felt a sense of calm: her home, her family, represented from the distance in warm yellow, was glowing ever stronger through the murky trees. She clambered out of the car and fumbled at the lock, the light from the moon, obscured somewhat by the dense weight of wisteria, dappling the porch. The key finally turned, allowing the door to thud open and the rush of the familiar churchy smell of dampened wood and floor polish mingled with the lingering toasty odour of cooking.

Connie took the stairs at a run and entered her own bedroom, where Poppy and Sophia lay, mouths gaping, lips full as ripe strawberries, their hair tousled and mingled across the pillows. Connie manoeuvred them deftly across the bed to allow a modest space for herself, wedging a large teddy behind Sophia's back to stop her sleepful weight from returning to its former position. Loud snores issued from the furthest side of the bed and Connie paused briefly to stroke the warm, soft head of Tramp, who snuffled and thumped a weary tail. (Tonight he had allowed himself upstairs before Connie's arrival, sensing the younger children's need.)

She moved now to Demelza's room, negotiating the tumble of books, posters, sports kit and photos of friends, in her foray to the bedside. She stroked the sleek dark hair and tucked Demelza's secret evening read, entitled *Full Frontal Snogging*, more securely beneath the pillow, whispering the familiar nightly pattern of assurances and love as she did so. It was time to check on Ella now before Connie herself turned in, after what had been a wonderful evening – until the moment it had been so suddenly curtailed. She made her way to Ella's room where the light was still on – but when she looked in, it was empty. Connie tried the lavatory and bathroom before searching the downstairs rooms, but, with mounting dreaded certainty, she found that they, too, were without a sign of Ella. Grabbing her discarded jacket, Connie scrambled for the front door.

She hadn't stopped to search for a torch but the moonlight was enough to make her way up the drive, heedless of the toe-stubbing potholes that impeded her speed. She realised that she was without a definite plan and that her remaining children had been necessarily abandoned by a babysitting figure. A cloud slid from the moon's honey pot, making the way instantly clearer and as it did so she saw the shape of a car at the bend in the drive and knew, with sudden intuition that it was – a purple sports car!

With a sickening lurch of the stomach, Connie heard Ella's voice, all chirpy on the midnight air. She screamed Ella's name but it came out as little more than a croak as she ran, stumbling, towards the car: it thrummed into life, but she was there in moments and it needed to turn around before it could leave. She wrenched at the door before there was time to reverse.

'What have you been doing with my daughter?' she rasped.

'Ah! So the wanderer has returned! Was the evening not up to standard? (I was *only* returning her from the pub!)'

'Mummy, I'm really sorry! I thought I'd be home before you got back. I'd had that mega row with Demelza (which was totally *her* fault, by the way) and I just needed a drink, so when Pete phoned my mobile—'

'*Pete!*'

Connie's brain felt numb and turgid in her efforts to grapple with what she was learning: she wanted to be concise and lucid, but her maternal exasperation was letting her down. 'She's just fifteen – she shouldn't be drinking there anyway!'

'Oh, it's OK, everyone thinks I look old enough when I'm with Pete.' Ella couldn't resist bragging.

'Here, Ella, you'd better take another couple of cigs with you – you'll need them since your mum's in such a stress!'

'So you *took* her there too?' muttered Connie, as her brain filtered one fact at a time.

'I'm really sorry, Mum. He just always wants to know what you're doing and I really like getting out. It's more fun with a grown-up sometimes – I never drink too much and weed's less harmful for you than cigarettes!' As Ella blundered further in her agitation, Pete lost his assurance and, seeing the harrowed look on Connie's face, began to look quite nervous.

'Oh, it's drugs now as well! I really can't believe—'

'Just *weed*!' Ella corrected. 'It's only a class C!'

'So this is how you "just knew" where I was on all those occasions when you claimed psychic understanding?' A number of apparently coincidental sightings of the purple sports car flew to Connie's mind, in particular the absurd flight from Nigel's.

'You've been using my child to carry out your perverted, stalking games, filling her up with, now let me see, not merely flattery and cigarettes, or alcohol on licensed premises, but drugs too; when I've been thinking she was tucked up in bed! And you purport to be *fond* of me? There's nobody I know who could do such a completely self-centred... s... s...' She was floundering for something vile enough.

'I never touched her!' he blubbed.

'Oh, so that makes it all all right then! Am I supposed to *thank* you for that? In fact, the idea must have occurred to you, or you wouldn't even have *said* that! Pete, may I remind you that you're thirty-four and she's just fifteen!'

'I wouldn't have let him anyway!' put in Ella. 'Number one, I don't fancy him and number two, I've got Carl!'

'No, it truly is true. I never ever thought of that until now.'

Connie saw he meant this.

'I only wanted to be close to you,' Pete sobbed. 'I just wanted to know what you were doing and if you had anyone!'

'And, of course, I'd share all that with my fifteen-year-old! I may be a little immature but my selfishness doesn't extend quite that far!'

Ella was crying now, both at seeing her mother more distraught than she had ever been and at the realisation that she had been the cause. Connie put her arm round her.

'I'm totally furious with you, Ella,' she said, 'for allowing yourself to be so easily manipulated by this – as you named him – "Psycho!" You're old enough to realise how completely you've let yourself down while I was trusting you to look after your sisters. But I can see you realise that now! But Pete!' Her voice was gravel now. 'Listen to me – we've all had *enough*!'

Pete had been muttering: 'Psycho? Psycho? Why Psycho?' His apology was genuine and, for him, succinct. 'I *am* sorry, Connie, really I am.'

'If you are, then would you do something for me?' He nodded. Connie didn't recognise the lioness's growl that was issuing from deep within her: 'Never *ever* go anywhere near me or *any* of my family again!'

Pete, white-faced in the moonlight, nodded and Connie turned on her heel, taking Ella's arm in her own.

They heard, rather than saw, the powerful car reverse crazily back and forth across the short corner of the driveway. The lights disappeared with the roar of the engine, intensifying the darkness that they were now plunged into, as a cloud slid across the moon. They could taste the arid dust which the scorching tyres had disturbed into a flurry before silence and stillness resumed their claims.

'Mum, you were so-oh cool!' confided Ella in awe. At this Connie felt another bolt of anger butting at her chest.

'Ella, I was not cool – I was terrified for you, furious with you both, not cool! I'm a harmless, hippy-type, dedicated to love, peace and whoopee: I never expected to feel like this in my life! And you don't even like him! What made you...?'

'I'm *sorry*, I suppose I just didn't *think*! I was just bored – and talking to him and doing all that stuff was exciting! It was him I was with that day on the beach when I said I was seeing Carl. And those flowers you got? He gave them to me to leave for you, so he could say it wasn't him, because, technically, it wasn't. (I'd only just got in the side door before you found them too!) He's the one who gives me fags as well and now I'm really quite addicted, I think, because this evening I've had about five and a spliff.' The words were spilling out of Ella's mouth, tripping over themselves in their eagerness to be free from the dark bonds which had harboured her secret for so long: 'I hate him again now. He's mad about you though, you know.'

'You're right about the mad bit!' Connie answered, piecing together the many fragments, which seemed so obvious now, but which she had failed completely to connect with her daughter. Failed her daughter, in fact.

'And he's always thinking you've got another man – even though I told him you hadn't... you haven't, have you?'

'Not really,' answered Connie, wondering about Ken for the first time since they had parted so abruptly this same evening. Not after tonight, anyway, she thought as, tucking Ella's arm under her own, they stumbled down the gloom of the drive to curl up on the sofa until dawn, too wired for sleep, drinking mugs of cocoa – talking, explaining, each blaming themselves and both of them blaming Pete.

In a solitary hotel room in Exeter the song, *Connie's Legacy*, was by now almost complete in its composition.

Chapter Nineteen

Connie's head was still whirling as she bumbled through the routine of the school run on Monday morning: she felt distanced and betrayed by Ella one minute, wondering when she would be able to trust her again, and closer than she had been for a long time the next, due to the distances they had covered from their soul-searching talks through the night. Ella had spent most of Sunday in her bedroom, from which pulsed the sounds of Slipknot, the most raucous of her heavy metal music. She only emerged when Carl came round, with whom she could talk and easily ignore her surroundings.

When they went for a walk, Connie discovered an unknown urge to follow them, her stomach churning needlessly until they returned, hand in hand, smiling. A residual guilt lurked in her subconscious for ever having allowed herself to be taken in by Pete's charm and *joie de vivre* in the first place, for if she hadn't accepted the attentions of this younger man and had behaved with a modicum more decorum, Ella's predicament would never have arisen! She wanted badly to ring her own mother and tell all, so that somehow the brunt of the situation wouldn't feel so firmly lodged with her alone. She needed to hear Mary excuse her and say that although she had been thoughtless, wouldn't we all behave differently in harsh situations with hindsight?

However, she felt it would be kinder to leave more space between now and talking it over, when she could be more distanced from the event. Therefore she resolved to leave the unburdening until the evening, when she might speak more objectively and less emotionally.

It was the day for her check-up and she realised that she hadn't given it a thought over the last two days. Now she thought of the appointment as mere routine: she would arrive, be clucked over, which might be quite pleasant, and everyone would assure her that nine out of ten of these tests proved to be benign and hers had been one of them!

As she rolled into the heavily congested car park at North Devon Hospital and attempted to negotiate with the machine at the ticket barrier, her mobile rang. She wrenched her ticket from the jaws of the machine as the queue mounted behind her, and shunted off the path, lunging for the mobile but as she picked it up, it stopped! Looking at the receiver she saw it had, in fact, been her mother. Here she was, in the hospital car park, going for tests she hadn't mentioned to her mother, besides which there was the situation with Ella, also yet to be discussed! Connie considered leaving calling back until after she had at least dealt with the appointment, but it was most unusual for Mary to call her mobile, since she treated them with mistrust and felt that nothing was so urgent that it couldn't wait. Connie's dilemma was taken from her as the mobile rang its silly, jaunty ring tone (selected for her by Sophia) once more. She found herself automatically answering it, deciding that there was still no need to mention everything right now, for the evening and a glass in the hand was always a better time for discussion.

'Hello, Mother! Two calls in two minutes – proud to be of service!' Connie awaited her mother's incredulity at how she could possibly know who was calling. She was already sifting through some suitably ridiculous responses to set them off laughing where no one else would find amusement, while also keeping an eye on the time for her appointment. The voice at the other end of the phone, however, was not that of her mother but her mother's home help, Jane.

'Is that Connie?' Jane's normally warm Cornish burr was clipped and somehow formal. An icicle stabbed at Connie's solar plexus.

'Jane! Tell me: is something wrong?' she asked, willing Jane to return an affable negative, but knowing within that this was not going to be.

'It's Mother! I'm sorry to tell you 'er's died in the airing cup-board!'

Connie felt the colour drain from her face and the life from her voice. 'What? When? How?' she began, in a bemused rush.

Jane explained in doleful, funereal tones that she'd let herself in as usual and found the television still on, which was odd. Then she had called out and, getting no answer, had trawled through the house. Eventually she had found the door to the walk-in airing cupboard open ('which 'er never doos, as you know!') and had found Mary curled up on the floor, still clutching the washing basket.

'I said, "Whatever have you been and gone and done now?" 'Er fag was all ashed out on the floor – a mercy 'er didn't manage to cremate the place there and then – the "lazy Susan" rail had come out of its hoist and 'er was all over damp washing!' Jane continued dramatically, indulging, slightly, at the importance of being first on the scene.

'Yur! I've got to move now – they're bringing Mother down the stairs! Don't mind me: I'm really upset, Lover, 'er was like a mother to me and all! I can't take it in!' Jane's hiccupping sobs were beginning to render her inarticulate.

'Jane, you've been marvellous for her – and thank you for finding her. She'll be glad of that...'

Jane began to talk again disjointedly, for she was clearly suffering from shock, but Connie interrupted her, being unable to take in any more and fearing she couldn't hold it together for much longer.

'Look, Jane, I'm coming down to the house...' Suddenly she realised that Mary wouldn't even be in it, for already she had been claimed by the state and it had assumed the right to take her out of her own front door, without so much as a by-your-leave. Her mother didn't belong to herself any more.

Another thought struck Connie: 'That is – Oh God, Jane, I'm sorry – but where is she?'

"Er'z on 'er way to Truro 'ospital, Lover!'

'You don't need to stay there at the house all on your own. I'll come down directly I've called my brother and some of the family. Thank you for everything you've done! Um, I know Mother always knew she could count on you.' Connie switched off the mobile, realising that she had just spoken of her mother in the past tense, which would always be so from now onwards!

Connie put her arms around Tramp's warm, rumpled body and shook, tears spilling into the curly tufts of fur, then sat up abruptly for there was so much to be done and all of it rested with her: just now there was a son who thought his mother was still living! She sped home, far too fast, for the tears kept tumbling from her eyes. She stopped crying directly she had found her brother, Jeremy's, phone number and called him gently, giving him the bare facts as she knew them. He said he would check flights from Australia and come directly, as she knew he would, and there was immediate relief in knowing he would be there to share the grief, the understanding, the responsibility. Only after she had put the phone down did she realise that it had to be the middle of the night in Australia. Next, to set the family and friends network rolling, she rang Aunt Belinda and Fish.

She marvelled at the way she found an ability to speak to these key people in a factual, compassionate way, matching their own calm strength, almost as though the loss was the more theirs than hers; but the moment she had replaced the receiver the shaking and tears would resume the stronger for having been checked.

The most important calls done, Connie jumped back into the car to speed down to Cornwall. She now began to consider the children and how they would cope with the loss of their grandmother – and Ella. The drama of the weekend was eclipsed now as she mused at the 'special relationship' Ella and Grandma shared – and how Ella had never given way to teenage angst before the myopic gaze of her fond but steely grandmother! How was Ella going to cope with this?

The Cornish lanes became ever deeper and the banks correspondingly higher and bedecked with wild flowers, which obscured all views of sea and countryside, through the history of vehicles that had created them. So numb was Connie that she barely noticed when she had reached Pol Kerris and found herself stopping the car. She let Tramp out at the drive of her mother's house, realising she would need to use a key at the door, for the first time.

She found it in its obvious location in a patum paperium jar, under a frond of campanula by the porch.

The door clicked open and Connie was to feel the loneliness steeling over her as she wandered aimlessly from room to room, smelling the mixture of damp Cornishness and cigarettes. Jane had left without tidying up and Connie found herself mechanically washing up the evidence of a rather meagre supper of faggots, carrots and potatoes, followed by a portion of apple crumble, the rest of which was in the larder, divided out to last a week before a replacement was to be made. She had obviously had supper then, had taken her tray through to the kitchen and was perhaps just popping some clothes from the washing machine into the airing cupboard when…

Connie had known her mother hadn't been in the best of health for an age, remembering the sawing sound of her breath down the phone, but she had always been told that everyone in their family lived to be a hundred 'and you'll be fed up with pushing me around in my Bath chair!'

She visited the conservatory, where the sun-bleached table supported a brimming ashtray and the *Telegraph* newspaper, open at the crossword, which had been completed in her mother's neat hand, the pen and a coffee cup lying beside it. She closed the open skylight and wandered back to the hall. She felt compelled now to go to the airing cupboard on the first floor, appreciating the steepness of the stairs and imagining the weight of the often-carried laundry basket. Someone, presumably Jane, had re-hoisted the 'lazy Susan' with all the washing, which was still damp from the washing machine.

The familiar, slightly worn M&S olive-green jersey was there, beside her favourite viyella paisley blouse, along with sundry other garments for the elderly ('I'm into Damart undies! Makes such a difference!'). Seeing Mary's still-damp clothes looking so natural drying there, Connie could barely believe the scene that must have been depicted so recently. She knew that she and Jeremy would have the painful task of taking all the good clothes and bed linen to the WRVS (of which Mary was organiser for the Restormel district), for she remembered her mother insisting on washing all her father's clothes after he had died, for this purpose.

Connie returned now to the drawing room and there, next to Mary's chair, was a sticky empty sherry glass, another nearly full ashtray and most of a packet of cigarettes. She could hear her mother joking in her head: 'There was no way I was going to pop my clogs without first finishing my sherry!'

Connie picked up the bottle – a very little left in it – and up-ended it herself. *That's my girl! Here's to us! None like us!* echoed through Connie's throbbing brain. She raised the last dregs of the sherry bottle towards the skies.

'I looks towards you, Mother!' she called, and then gave the answering phrase, which was her mother's line: 'I bows accordin'!' Then she scooped up the cigarette packet and lighter and closed the front door, for she knew now what she had to do.

Travelling to Truro now, she called the children's schools, explaining what had happened to the respective secretaries, who grappled with saying the right thing. Connie asked if the children could stay on after school and to tell them she was held up at Grandma's. This would not be too much out of the ordinary for them and they would accept it without questioning further.

Once she had seen her mother she hoped she might feel more composed, for each time she had to tell another person that Mary was dead, the words twisted themselves on her tongue and she felt that catch arising in her voice and, what was becoming familiar, the knot, pulling ever tighter inside her.

She explained herself at the hospital and was sent into the bowels of the building, following signs for the mortuary. Once there, she was told she must wait, for her mother 'wasn't ready for her yet!' Connie almost laughed! Mary was dead and she was still keeping her waiting! What could they mean? She expostulated, explaining that she had to get back for her children (mentioning children often moved mountains of bureaucratic tape!) so could the hospital staff hurry? She was informed next that they 'liked to make their bodies look nice, with a spot of make-up, a brush to the hair'. At this, Connie exploded: complete strangers were dictating that her mother didn't quite look presentable to her own daughter and that her daughter should wait until they had got her mother looking the way *they* thought she should!

'I'm sorry, you don't know, but my mother would not thank you for putting make-up on her: she has never worn it! Please don't do that to her!'

'But we haven't got all her personal effects off, like her watch, her wedding ring!' they demurred.

'She wanted to be buried with her wedding ring on – please don't *think* about removing it!' replied Connie, becoming further distressed, 'and I'll take her watch off myself!' Finally, but with an obvious reluctance, it was agreed for Connie to be allowed to visit her mother and she was asked if she would like company. Connie vehemently refused this too, longing by now to drop her facade and be with the person who knew her the best and the longest.

A nurse took her to a little cubicle and hovered at the door, saying she would be close by, should Connie need her. Connie pushed the door open gently to see a small trolley-bed, on which her mother lay. An armchair was positioned at her mother's side, on which was placed a large box of tissues. Mary was covered in a white sheet, with just her face showing on the pillow. An outsider had pushed her white silky hair off her temples, and Connie hastily pushed it back across her forehead and in front of her ears.('There's no need to show too much face! I don't want anyone to die of shock!' Mary's voice spoke, disrespectfully, in her head.)

'So I've got to believe it now! I'm so sorry, so very sorry I wasn't there…' Connie heard herself mutter, for until this moment she had half-expected this whole episode to be one of her mother's more macabre practical jokes – how she wished it had been! At first she wept uncontrollably, grateful for the inclusion of the tissues. She kissed the forehead and wiped one of the unseeing eyes, which almost seemed to be in sympathy. Then began a stream of words from Connie, confidences, recriminations.

'You *can't* do this to me now – you know how much I need you. We *all* do!' she reproached. 'And what's Fish going to do? Who will she play *Scrabble* with?' and then a string of apologies again in a mechanical mantra for not being there, for finding her like this, looking so… Connie folded back the sheet and took Mary's left hand, reassuring herself that her father's wedding ring remained – the fingers were too swollen to remove it anyway. She peeled back the sleeves of the hospital gown that her mother was wearing and removed her father's large, flat gold watch, that Mary had insisted on wearing since his death, in spite of its absurd size on her tiny wrist. She kissed the hand and folded it gently back. She then rummaged in her handbag for a moment, bringing out the cigarettes and lighter and laid them at her mother's side.

'I wouldn't let you lie here without these, much as you know *I* don't like them!' Connie whispered. 'A promise is a promise! You didn't leave enough sherry in the bottle though, so I'll have to get you some next time I come – Jeremy will be with me then.' The thought of how her mother had hoped to see Jeremy shortly, filled her with confusion: how much point was there now she was like this? Then she reasoned that everything was going to be how Mary would have wanted her death to be. All her best people would come to see her off and she had left them with no fuss, and fuss was something she had always hated: she had even managed to cheat them all out of saying goodbye! Connie looked back on her last hasty visit, only a week ago.

'Of course, if only I'd *known* I wouldn't have fussed around getting all that financial claptrap sorted! And we could have gone to somewhere far better than the local pub!' At this Connie managed a rueful smile. 'But how could we ever have said goodbye? Oh Mummy!' she had reverted to the name of her childhood: 'I've never had such laughs with anyone!' She was calmer now and reluctantly accepting the inevitable. 'Good job the children haven't seen me like this: it's you that has to put up with it, as usual! Talking of children, I'll have to fly – you always say I'm in too much of a hurry! I'll be back though and I'll bring you the sherry – and flowers. Loads of flowers – from the garden – you won't know yourself!' Kissing the thin pale skin of her mother's forehead, Connie backed out of the room.

Connie asked the nurse on no account to remove the cigarettes and lighter – she didn't seem as surprised as Connie had expected, so perhaps the bereaved were slipping afterworld memorabilia beside the deceased as a matter of course? Next, she was confronted by a plastic bag containing all the clothes her mother had been wearing when she died, including shoes and holey tights ('Thoroughly unholy!' her mother would have said.) Connie took in the familiar worn herringbone tweed of her mother's skirt and the navy cashmere jumper (which was going at the elbows) and wondered desperately whether it would be less upsetting to ask this stranger nurse, who had presumably been intimate enough with her mother to change her from these remembered clothes to the stark hospital gown, to now dispose of them, or to take the clothes home and wash them with reverence before, well, throwing them away, she supposed! She muttered to the nurse that she would be grateful if the hospital would dispose of the clothes, after which she had a disturbing vision of them being thrown into an incinerator! As she thought to change her mind, she was further disturbed at the notion of the children seeing their grandmother's clothes in the back of the car, all compartmentalised in their plastic, hospital carrier, and she realised this could prove the more harrowing to their sensitivities than her own.

Connie let the nurse gather up the bag as she signed for the watch and a haze of other forms.

'There's just one more formality,' the nurse said gently.

What now? thought Connie.

'We need you to sign the consent for the post mortem.'

'What on earth do you need a post mortem for?' asked Connie, the strain and frustration showing in the shrillness of her voice.

'We need to establish the cause of death,' the nurse answered apologetically.

'But she's nearly eighty! She smoked like a chimney! Her doctor saw her regularly and – I deeply regret – she was alone when she died, so – oh, I do hope you are not thinking of foul play!' *Wycliffe* had been a favourite of Mary's and it might have tickled her to think of herself immersed in a posthumous 'whodunnit' of her own!

'It's a formality that has to be undertaken,' the nurse repeated sympathetically. 'No one will be suspecting foul play, I assure you! Wouldn't you prefer to know yourself?' Connie was too overwrought to be able to consider any such thing and realising that it was useless to argue she grabbed the papers, signing illegibly under next of kin, then, reminding them again about leaving off the make-up, she fled from the antiseptic environment where she had left her mother.

On her homeward journey, having seen her mother, Connie had composed herself enough to face the children. She felt as though she had just had one final chat, from which she had drawn the usual resilience and calm. She decided to tell them all at one time, fearing that repetition might wear her down from managing the job properly. She had intended to wait until they had returned to the house, but, on her second pick-up, at Poppy's school, they all got out to try to find Poppy, and Sophia asked how Grandma was.

'It's not very good,' answered Connie, making the understatement of her lifetime, 'but let's all get into the car and I'll tell you.'

'She's not dead, is she?' asked Ella quickly.

'Don't be such a drama queen!' retorted Demelza, but she trailed off when she saw Connie's face working. Now they were all looking at Connie.

'I'm terribly sorry to tell you that Grandma died this morning,' she announced miserably, and as she clung to them she added over their quiet tears and stricken faces that it had been very sudden, with no pain (how she hoped that this was the case!) and that Uncle Jeremy was coming.

The children huddled together quietly for most of that evening, as Connie yo-yoed to and from the telephone, for the news had filtered through the sagging network of friends and family from the many factions of her mother's life, both in war and in peace, all of whom joined one another in stoical sadness and sympathy. Ella was completely silent and white: she seemed to understand the strain that Connie was undergoing on so many levels, and to have time to consider her through her own grief. She heated several cans of tomato soup for all, with much Marmite toast, and quietly fetched the family for supper. No one felt much like eating, but they did, in recognition and appreciation of Ella's efforts.

'You need to eat!' she told her mother, when Connie had started to say she would have her soup later and, through the warmth of Ella's kindness, Connie did eat and was grateful to her, accepting and giving the hugs of empathy they all craved.

Chapter Twenty

The night was fitful: Poppy slept in Ella's arms in Ella's room, amongst the pin-ups of Kerang stars, minimally attired. The room was redolent with the pungency of aromatherapy oils, which, in their turn, masked the faint, acidity of deodorant. Demelza and Sophia shared with Connie, who badly wanted to get up, make tea and read poetry, in the hopes of inducing sleep; however, she was too fearful of disturbing the others, who were sprawled across her like puppies, waking occasionally, sighing and stretching out for Connie's sympathetic arms.

Uncle Jeremy had offered to get a train from Heathrow, but the family wouldn't hear of it. The children announced that they weren't up to going to school that day, being too tired and sad, and Connie felt the same about the school run. Therefore after breakfast, the whole family chugged off up the M5 to meet Jeremy's plane at midday: it felt better for Connie to escape the telephone for a space and to have something positive to do. The huge excitement at the prospect of Uncle Jeremy was muted by the circumstances and Connie found herself almost resentful when she considered the impact Jeremy's visit would have engendered, had their mother been there to share it. She comforted herself with the thought that their mother would have so much appreciated his presence at her send-off also.

The plane was on time and Jeremy was one of the first of the dazed and shuffling passengers to emerge from the arrivals gate, pushing their unwieldy trolleys. He strode past the others and stretched over the cordon to the eager flurry of arms awaiting his. He seemed remarkably wideawake, which he put down to some 'knock-out sleeping tabs' which he had managed to procure for the flight. To Connie, he looked every bit the same sibling hero: the low autumn sun glinting into his spectacles, his unruly hair the more tousled from his flight and the irrepressible banana-split grin that he and Connie shared.

The children were momentarily bashful, now that the so much talked of Uncle Jeremy had materialised and Connie found herself overwhelmed by the relief of sharing: the bereavement was their equal burden and the emergent empathy that this knowledge produced, bolstered her energy and resolve.

Wasn't it Piglet who had said that it always felt better with two, Pooh! – and so it was. How many times had Mary repeated that she wished she could do something to help during Connie's separation from her husband, and how many times had Connie answered that her mother was helping, just by being there? Connie felt her soul lurch at the question which had kept her awake all the previous night: how would she cope in times of crisis without her mother's earthy levelness and humour down the telephone? However, here was Jeremy, who would know, who would understand; and she could cling to this right now and adopt her Scarlet O'Hara mode of thinking about the future tomorrow!

Connie told Jeremy that she had already given their mother the cigarettes and lighter and he simply said, 'Good on you!' appreciatively, which made her feel as though she had been awarded the form prize! She went on to explain that it hadn't been quite possible to put in a bottle of sherry because she had finished it herself and Jeremy said that they would have to sort that one out. Here was her sibling, with whom explanations were unnecessary; for their upbringing, knowledge and intuition had not dimmed over time. When, some time later, they had returned home and she was receiving a particularly poignant tribute from one of their mother's friends from the WRENS, a glass of gin and tonic was fitted into her hand, just when needed, mixed just how she liked it and, because it was Jeremy, she didn't need even to turn her head, for he knew she was grateful and *she* knew that *he* knew!

The week tumbled on for Connie and Jeremy with plans for the funeral and visits to Cornwall, where they went through the house and Mary's possessions, agonising over keeping, choosing and discarding numerous items, treasured by association of place and time. They visited the family solicitors for a formal reading of the will – in which certain items, such as clocks and pictures, were mentioned in their mother's 'wishes', for various people who were key to her past. There were jolly messages, jokes and instructions enclosed, showing that their mother had clearly enjoyed the task.

She had written a little message for both Jeremy and Connie, addressed to Superson and Superdaughter, but Jeremy was mysterious when Connie quizzed him over the contents of his.

'Just a legacy, Sis. I can't tell you about it now!'
Connie's read:

Darling Superdaughter,
Keep your chin up and remember that you do a wonderful job as a
mother and a daughter. I hope that I will have left you with the
wherewithal to cope with your divorce and dreaded school fee situation,
so you won't need to negotiate much further with that unmentionable
blagueur! (I have instructed your brother as to my legacy to the
aforementioned Unmentionable, which I hope he will deliver.) Should
you embark on another relationship, I hope you will be more
circumspect in giving a wide berth to any who could become interested
in developing their skills in the tyrant area! Darling, the sky may be a
little grey today, but what FUN we've had! The sun will shine again
soon for you all and you can think of Daddy and me looking down
from our cloud and playing with the light switch!
    'I looks towards you!'
    All my love,
    Mother
    xxxxxxxxxxxx

'*I bows accordin'*,' muttered Connie automatically in answer to the
family toast, as she folded the note, her eyes misted but shrouding a
rueful smile.

So she must have written this lot since the divorce began and it seems she
knew she wasn't going to last, even though she continued to talk of living to a
hundred! Connie thought back uneasily to her last meeting with her
mother, the shortness of breath, the rasping cough, each of which
had been there for so long and had always been put down to
smoking: 'A vice with which I intend to leave this world!' Mary had
always retorted, in answer to suggestions that she should give up.
Perhaps, though, these ailments had increased imperceptibly over
time and had Connie been less wrapped up in her immediate family
she might have been able to bamboozle her mother into discussing it
with the doctor. However, Connie smiled grimly again, she should
know how badly her mother, one who had made decisions for herself
and others pretty well since World War II began, took to any form of
'bossiness', as she would think of it! Anyway, this little note, written
in Mary's scratchy, blue, fountain pen in her familiar slanting script,
would help Connie in times of low ebb, for she would be able to read

it and think of her parents on their cloud where she could be a child again.

'Jeremy! Please show me what's in your letter – mine refers to a legacy for Stuart – what is it? Come on, I'll show you mine if you show me yours!'

'I'm not showing but, all right I will tell you what the legacy is if I must!'

'Oh go on!' Connie realised the letter must include things about herself: perhaps asking Jeremy to look out for her when she had her family wobbles, which he wouldn't want to disclose. She felt a pang of guilt for having persisted, mixed with warmth towards his quiet kindness. 'Just tell me the legacy bit,' she corrected.

'She says her legacy to Stuart is a punch on the nose!' Jeremy laughed.

Connie giggled. 'Oh, Jeremy! Are you going to do it?'

'What do you think?' Jeremy puffed out his stubbly cheeks and made punchy gestures in the air, and Connie knew that he had no more intention of delivering it than his mother had in suggesting it!

The will was relatively straightforward, with various items bequeathed to close relatives and carte blanche for Connie, the executrix, to give away anything appropriate to those who had not been named, yet might appreciate a keepsake of sorts. The rest of the estate was to be divided equally between Connie and Jeremy; and through the attention they were receiving from the bank dignitaries, it seemed they clearly thought it was worth 'more than a sniff', as their mother had indicated. The school fees for all the children, including those of her grandsons, had already been taken care of by a trust fund, to paid into from her estate which saved Connie from any further sleepless nights on that score. Although her mother had promised to help, Connie hadn't thought she would have had the time or the inclination to start this particular ball rolling.

On one journey to Cornwall, Jeremy and Connie had resolved to combine the removal of yet more effects from Mary's house, with providing their mother with the promised bottle of sherry. By this time her body had been moved to a chapel of rest near St Austell. On the way, Connie had decided that she wanted to know not only the result of the post mortem, but also if there was a possibility that her mother had suffered for long in the airing cupboard with no one to help or call an ambulance. She was aware that she would continue to ponder over it indefinitely if she couldn't simply know, rather than speculate, the worst. Jeremy differed, saying he really didn't want to know, in case it was bad news. Connie left Jeremy in a lay-by while she climbed out of the car, heart pounding, to make the call. The coroner, who seemed thoroughly understanding, explained that Connie's mother had suffered from oedema, which explained the laboured breathing and the swollen fingers. This had resulted in a massive ischemic heart attack, which, the coroner explained, had been brought on by furred-up arteries, caused by smoking. She kindly assured Connie that death would have been instant and there would have been nothing anyone could have done to prevent it, beyond stopping Mary from smoking a long time ago; something that could only have been her mother's own choice to make.

Connie thanked the coroner profusely for her candour and ran to the car.

'I don't want to know!' said Jeremy firmly, his fingers stuffed in his ears.

'Oh, but you will if it's good news! Please let me tell you – you'll be so relieved!' Jeremy assented, relieved as much to see Connie's radiance as the obvious result that his mother hadn't suffered long. Now perhaps his sister could stop blaming herself over not being clairvoyant!

'She said it was instant! Nothing other than giving up nicotine could have prevented it.'

'Well, none of us would have dared to attempt to enforce that!' answered Jeremy heartily. 'And now let us get back to this chapel,' he continued, for they had already visited it earlier to give the staff some clothes for their mother's burial.

Choosing something for someone to be buried in had not been easy: Connie had preferred the idea of comfortable warm corduroys and a woolly jumper, while Jeremy had felt that this was what Connie would prefer for herself and might not be their mother's choice. He said that warmth didn't come into it, so why not one of their mother's favourite dresses? Connie was forced to see the wisdom of this and she selected a pinkish summer dress in an Aztec pattern, which Mary had always favoured; however, Connie wouldn't be moved from her choice of fluffy bedroom slippers, rather than shoes, which somehow seemed more homely.

On arrival at the chapel of rest, Jeremy fetched their bunch of flowers, the sherry and a prayer book that Mary had always carried, from the debris of belongings on the back seat, and handed them to Connie.

'Hey! You come too!' Connie rounded.

'No! No – I'm not going in there. It's right to put them with her but it was *your* pact.'

'But you agreed. Can't you come with me?'

'I *do* agree, but – sorry, I can't!' Connie realised that while she saw her mother at least once a fortnight, for her brother, seeing her annually at best, visits were necessarily far more precious. To see her now, in a state of death, was more than even steadfast Jeremy could entertain. She took a deep breath and, hiding the sherry under the mantle of her coat, while holding the prayer book piously in front of her, she knocked at the heavily studded door: it was answered immediately, without pomp, and she was conducted to the room where her mother lay, for their final encounter.

With a pious inclination of his head, the usher tactfully withdrew, leaving Connie alone with Mary, who was now lying in the coffin that was to be her house for evermore. It was made of light oak, lined with Barbie-pink satin. The hospital had kept to the request for no make-up, but they had brushed the hair off her mother's face again, making her look like a stranger. Connie felt better able to cope this time as she swept the hair deftly back to its familiar disarray over her mother's forehead, and marvelled at herself as she whispered, 'I've got the sherry, like I promised: now you and Father can have a real party! And here's your prayer book! I knew you'd want it. The flowers are all picked from the garden, which is looking great; the roses are from Ella, the Cornish lilies from Demelza and Sophia – and Poppy and I picked the pink clover from the paddock.' She slid the worn little leather volume, a dedication written by her grandmother, into her mother's folded hands and arranged the flowers, like a garden, all around the inside of the coffin. She placed the sherry at her side, next to the cigarettes, amongst the ample folds of the pink and beige Aztec dress.

The job now done to her satisfaction, she looked at her mother lying peacefully amongst her garden of flowers and felt reluctant to leave; however, she knew she couldn't be late, thereby causing the children any further anxiety.

'Thank you! Thank you for *everything*!' she said. 'I really wish you hadn't gone and done this, but Jeremy and I will manage – and you wouldn't believe how helpful Ella's been! I'm not sure how I'm going to manage this one without your help...' she faltered, 'but goodbye, Mummy!' She kissed her mother gently on the forehead and hurried out to where Jeremy was waiting.

This time, however, she had the strange sensation that her mother had no longer been there and that she had been speaking to herself!

'Job's done...' she sniffed, 'and nobody spotted the bottle!'

'Good work, Con!' answered Jeremy grimly, as he revved the car out of the car park in the direction of the school run.

Much later that evening, when all were resting their aching, exhausted limbs, Connie crouched on Tramp's worn sheepskin beside her bed and buried her face in the soft fluff on top of his ancient head. 'Oh, Tramp! Don't you die on us – we need you too much, you hulking old puppy dog!' He snorted down his grey whiskers and whirled the remains of his flag of a tail, theatrically, in what she took to be a tributary denial.

Chapter Twenty-One

It was on the morning of the funeral that a call came from the hospital. Jeremy took it and assumed it was further bureaucracy to do with their mother; however, the voice the other end was insistent that they speak to Connie herself, for it was personal.

Somewhat disgruntled, Jeremy handed the receiver to Connie, who took it gingerly and proceeded to speak in an undertone. She began to apologise for something and then to consult her diary, finally agreeing, without much grace, that tomorrow would do if it had to.

'What was all that about?' queried Jeremy. They seem a might pushy – you'd think they'd be a *bit* more sensitive!'

Connie lowered her voice. 'Actually, they were just being professional,' she began. 'It was an appointment that I never kept. I was on the way to the hospital when Mother... and I really haven't had the time or inclination to give it another thought since.'

'Nothing serious then, I take it?' fished Jeremy, as he fetched another vase for the copious bunches of sweet-smelling flowers that had been dropped off regularly at the porch.

'I hope not – I'm sure not,' mused Connie. 'All right, I'll tell you, but don't mention it to the children, will you; they've got enough to think about.' She looked around quickly as she spoke.

'Mention what?' Jeremy began to sound anxious.

'I found a lump on my breast,' answered Connie casually, 'so I had it looked at – you know, just to make sure that it wasn't – and now I have to have more tests and so on, which is why they wouldn't discuss it over the phone.' She paused, seeing Jeremy's expression of concern.

'Now, don't go all Australian on me and start fussing!'

'Fussing!' Jeremy was quite rattled, but realised that he shouldn't upset Connie by showing this. 'Well, you're right! This is not the day to be thinking about it, but I'm coming with you tomorrow!'

'OK, thanks – I'd like that.'

Connie had great concern over Ella, who had become so calm and kind to her sisters in this last week that she seemed to have almost taken on a new mantle. Connie wondered when and at what moment it might remove itself to reveal a shaken teenage child, shattered at the loss of the one person for whom she had *always* shone. That morning Connie had overheard Ella telling her sisters in a fierce hiss: 'Whatever Mummy says or asks today, however stupid it is, you go along with it: this is going to be even stressier for her than it is for us!'

'But Mummy's never stressy!' Poppy had put in loyally but unwisely.

'Shut up and don't even try to understand!' Ella had snapped back.

'Well, who's stressy now?' Demelza had commented. Connie, impressed by Ella's lack of retort was also touched, but she pretended not to have heard.

The family had decided not to wear dark clothes, for the funeral was to be a celebration of a long and happy life: to this end, they were wearing bright autumnal colours. However, there had been much dissent from Poppy over wearing a dress: she had chosen a pair of golden corduroy dungarees, but when Connie had remonstrated that on this particular occasion a dress was needed (even though the dungarees were indeed lovely), a fierce look from Ella sent Poppy trotting out of the kitchen to change. At the door, however, she turned: 'But I know Grandma liked these...' she faltered, but another swift glance at Ella's stony face sent her upstairs without further argument. Connie sighed, and wondered, as she usually did, whether she had got it wrong, but when Poppy re-entered in a flowery viyella dress from Next, which, with its deep sash, complemented her unusually well-brushed ringlets, she was delighted to see her youngest transformed from tomboy to little girl – and Poppy seemed mollified by the admiration she received.

It was twenty to two when the hearse appeared and slid noiselessly to a graceful halt outside the house. The children walked out demurely with Uncle Gerald and Aunt Belinda in what was, for once, an awed silence, while Connie and Jeremy issued final instructions to the team of caterers who were preparing tea and drinks for the wake. Aunt Belinda, Uncle Gerald and Jeremy filed in beside the coffin, which was decked with a multitude of heavily scented flowers, while Connie drove with the children in their own car, which had been especially cleaned for the occasion. She had in her lap the music, which she knew by heart, for the song she had chosen to sing for her mother at the funeral. Nigel had agreed to accompany her and would be waiting with his acoustic guitar at the church: everyone had been so kind in their offers to do anything to help, but this had been the only one she had taken up. Jeremy had the address that he and Connie had prepared, safely ensconced in the top pocket of his suit.

A pale autumn sun shone through the orange leaves of the churchyard from a brilliant sky, and Connie looked up at one white puffy cumulus cloud, which she had somehow known would be there. She took a deep breath and clambered out behind the hearse, where the pallbearers (all nephews of the deceased, who knew one another best from weddings and funerals) were getting their instructions from the undertaker to take the coffin to the lychgate.

The little village church was so full that benches were being moved in from the village hall down the side aisle and in front of the belfry. The bell was muffled and tolling slowly as the cross-section of people shuffled to their places. A row of elderly ladies in petrol-coloured WRVS uniform, stood respectfully neat, their broad, shiny, sensible brogues twinkling like chestnuts, while another small row of retired naval personnel, including Fish, stood in tweedy suits, sporting clanking rows of medals. Jane and her boyfriend were conspicuous in their black. They already shared a limp-wet hanky with which Jane was attempting to suppress noisy gulping sobs. She was as yet unaware of the modest sum that Connie and Jeremy had decided to bestow on her, on their mother's behalf, from the estate.

The coffin was shouldered down the slippery cobbled path to the church entrance and the congregation stood. Jeremy and Connie had been arranged by the funeral director behind one another, male before female, as etiquette demanded, to follow the flower-bedecked coffin, but they had broken ranks and walked arm in arm, as though at a wedding, Poppy holding Connie's free hand and the other three children taking up the rear. They kept their eyes lowered to escape the looks of sympathy and sidled into their pew at the front.

The parson had known their mother well and welcomed everyone with warmth and a little gentle humour before the first hymn, 'Through All the Changing Scenes of Life, in Sorrow and in Joy'. After this, Fish rose from her seat and walked with stiff dignity down the aisle: her osteoporosis seemed to have lowered her height even further since a short time ago, for it looked as though it might have been more suitable for her to speak from beneath the lectern. Instead she stood at the front, next to the coffin, her wild, white dandelion hair shining brightly in a shaft of light from the stained-glass windows. In a composed and homely voice she read a poem of her own choosing, by Joyce Grenfell, which ended:

> Weep if you must – parting is Hell!
> But life goes on, so sing as well!

Fish then bowed to the alter, giving a long and fond look at the coffin and limped, unhurried, back to her seat. Jeremy's voice was a little unsteady, in contrast, when he began his address, but he grew more relaxed as he tracked through his mother's life, drawing on a few unsavoury anecdotes to conjure up the infectious humour, as well as the distinction of the person they had all gathered to appreciate. Aunt Belinda had chosen to read verses from Proverbs about there being a time and a season for everything under heaven. She said that she knew, as a sister, that for Mary it was 'time' and as she said this, she managed a generous, but slightly trembling, smile.

After the next hymn, 'All Things Bright and Beautiful', it was Connie's turn to sing her song. Nigel had already given her a significant look from his place in the side aisle opposite Connie, to make sure she was prepared. It was an Annie Lennox song, the lyrics, of which Jeremy had adapted slightly to be more pertinent to their mother. As the final verse of the hymn began, Connie tried to sing out to warm her voice, to let out the last of her emotional wavers and to breathe more evenly. It was then that she noticed Poppy beside her, singing the hymn she knew best, her eyes shining full but without tears, while down one skinny brown leg and beneath the pretty floral dress, golden, corduroy dungarees made their wriggling descent! Poppy stopped singing when she became aware of what was happening, but by this time the other leg had begun to slide out of concealment! She snatched at the descending trousers and attempted to defy gravity and stuff them back above her hemline, taking a wary glance at her mother, in the desperate hope that she hadn't noticed: Connie, however, was convulsed by a mixture of mirth and misery. The fact was that there was one person in this church who would find this display as funny as she – but that person was in the coffin.

The hymn had stopped and the congregation had sat down, all expectantly waiting for Connie and her song. Nigel had shuffled out of his aisle and was looking at her in alarm, as the tears of laughter and sadness made their mingled descent down her face, making her body shake. The silence began to be punctuated by coughs and the rustle of people shifting positions, but Connie remained where she was, her head bowed, waiting miserably for the paroxysms to subside.

The sound of footsteps echoed hollowly through the hush of the church and Connie looked through screwed-up eyes to see Ella, completely composed, standing beside Nigel. She was holding the lyrics that Connie had laid beside her, and with an imperceptible nod to Connie she turned to Nigel, who began to play the introductory bars. Ella lifted her pointed chin and sang with a simple clarity, not once faltering, her eyes fixed on a bell rope at the back of the church. Connie had stopped shaking, but the tears continued to course down her cheeks, as she held Poppy's hand tightly, patting it reassuringly.

She was moved now by another sheer emotion, which was simply that of love and pride as Ella's notes soared, dipped and resonated their way to the song's conclusion. When it was over Connie reached across to where Ella sat, wedged between Demelza and Sophia, and squeezed her hand. 'Thank you!' she whispered. She felt Ella's hand trembling, heard her breath panting and saw the brave tears, the first she had shed. Connie realised that although Ella had seemed so cool, she was now, naturally, quite overcome. Sophia and Demelza had their arms linked about her as they knelt in prayer for their grandmother, who was here beside them but who, at the same time, was not here for them any more.

The congregation left the church and followed the coffin out into the blinding low western sun of the graveyard. The grave, exposing damp clods of red Devon clay, stood beneath a giant oak tree: the children had picked posies of pink clover and given them to Connie and Jeremy to scatter on the coffin, which was being expertly lowered into its resting place by the solemn, fresh-faced nephews, after which there was a short blessing. Connie thought briefly of the same red clovers that she had arranged inside the coffin. Sophia handed Jeremy a crumpled piece of A4, containing her poem to Grandma. It began with the dedication: *Never mind, Grandma, you will be able to see Grandpa now, but please hurry back soon*, and Jeremy let it flutter into the grave unread. He and Connie then stood in silence together, arm in arm, locked in their own thoughts for some time, before they moved quietly away to help with the wake at the house ('the bun fight!' as their mother had always named such events), and to face a new chapter – of life without parents.

'Yur'z to us!' The words of their special toast rang hollowly around Connie's throbbing head: '*None like us!*' None like us. None like us at all.

As soon as she found a moment between dispensing the sandwiches and cake, Ella tugged at Connie's sleeve and pulled her into the kitchen.

'Mum, was I all right in the church?' she fished.

'Ella, you were fantabuloso – you sounded amazing – and without any rehearsal! Much better than me – you were my saviour and I was so proud!' enthused Connie, fondly, watching the pink glow ascend Ella's neck and cheeks.

'So I did do the right thing? I mean, you looked so incredibly sort of crumpled, that it seemed…'

'Darling Ella – you saved me from total undignified disaster on the most massive scale! Thanks a million from me – and from Grandma too!' Grateful, happy tears welled into Ella's beautiful toffee-coloured eyes.

'Oh Mum, I miss her so much already: what's it going to be like in a month? Two months?'

'Actually time will make it easier as we adjust. Grandma never let on when she was sad, but I think that over this we must sometimes try *not* to be brave and just accept that we need her, but be glad, too, that we had her. We'll talk about her and we can laugh and we can cry too.' Ella hugged her mother until her tears had ceased and Connie found herself holding back her own and being brave just in the way she had advocated they should not.

A moment later, Poppy, golden dungarees no longer in evidence, sidled up. 'Mummy, I'm sorry I kept my dungarees on: I thought they'd stay up in my knickers and then Grandma would be the only one able to see them – and she did like them!'

'Yes, she did, and you know what? I think it was a good thing you had them on because otherwise Ella wouldn't have sung the song!'

Poppy looked relieved but persisted still: 'But what happened to you, Mummy? Did I upset you very badly?'

'Poppy, you made me laugh for two! You made Grandma laugh inside me and that's why I shook so much!'

'Oo! Is she going to stay inside you?' asked Poppy, examining Connie's midriff carefully.

'I hope she will – there's a little bit of her inside all of us – and every time we think of what she might say, that's her coming out!'

Poppy's eyes rounded in wonder and delight as Demelza, who

had been listening, asked innocently, 'Does that mean we're all going to grow white hair and say "crawse" instead of "cross"?'

Poppy took a sharp intake of breath at the irreverence of this remark, but Connie laughed, happily this time, and they realised that sound had been missing for some time as it spread and infected each of them.

'We'll manage – and it must be snifter time!' Connie consoled herself, unconsciously adopting her mother's well-worn phrase, as she bustled out of the kitchen to rejoin the ranks of sympathisers.

Chapter Twenty-Two

After the school run, Jeremy and Connie drove to the North Devon Hospital for the long-overdue appointment with the specialist, concerning the lump on Connie's breast. Jeremy did his best to sound positive and jolly, but this to Connie, who knew him so well, belied his true feeling of nervousness.

Connie was calm, for she had a certain faith in things not being able to get any worse and in not being kicked when you were down. 'He that is down need fear no fall,' she told herself consolingly. She was so laden with missing her mother and trying to cope without their frequent phone calls (for no one else would be sufficiently interested in the little anecdotes that she would save for her mother's ears only) that the possibility of the lump being malignant had not been given serious consideration since the eternal weeks of her mother's passing. They arrived at the hospital in good time and Connie was careful to avoid the spot where she had precariously parked to answer the call from Jane. The memory and the associated numb misery, however, would be imprisoned for her in that particular space, forever.

A bright, confident-looking nurse, who looked little older than Ella, issued Connie into a cubicle and plied her with issues of *Hello* while she waited for the specialist to speak to her. Connie leafed through pictures of the Royal family, smiling at a shot of a crimson-faced Prince Harry apparently brawling with paparazzi outside a nightclub. At last the specialist bustled in from a side door and shook her hand. Connie apologised for not having kept her previous appointment, explaining the situation, for which she received professional sympathy and understanding. The specialist had a large pile of notes in front of her and was studying these intently – Connie began to wish she would get on with it.

'Well? Am I doomed?' she smiled. She was disconcerted that the specialist barely bothered to twitch a response.

'Hmm. This is a little difficult.'

Connie's heart sank: no! It wasn't possible that it could be positive – that would be too much! There really wasn't the window for further complication within the family.

'I'm sorry to say...'

Connie barely heard any more: her body and soul were rebelling. This was too unfair!

'...that the results of your mammogram and those tests carried out by your medical centre have proved so far to be inconclusive: you clearly have some kind of cyst on the upper-outer quadrant of your left breast, but the results do not indicate if it's malignant or benign. I'm sorry – this does sometimes happen – but we'll have to run some further tests, which I will arrange for you to have here today, to determine exactly what we're dealing with.' Connie caught at the straw.

'So, if the tests are inconclusive, there's still a chance that it is simply just a cyst?'

'Yes, certainly, it could still be a fibroadenoma, which can look almost identical, but we'll have to take a fine needle aspirate to remove some cells from the lump and we'll also need an ultrasound.' Connie was reeling between relief that there was still a chance that she was cancer-free and feeling aghast at the possibilities that were spilling before her, should cancer, after all, be confirmed.

She was asked to slip on a hospital gown while the specialist went out to arrange for the tests. Meanwhile Jeremy came in, his eyes illuminated large and concerned behind his glasses. He attempted as much encouragement as he could, by making light and cracking jokes.

'Actually I'm quite relieved: I thought that the very fact that they wouldn't give you the results over the phone meant that there must be something wrong!' he explained cheerily.

'But there is something wrong: it's inconclusive.'

'But that means there's a strong chance that it's nothing, which is much better than I thought...' Jeremy continued to blunder miserably around with his attempts at encouraging interpretations.

'There's also another "strong chance" that I may have cancer! What would I do? Mother's not there to look after the children and you've got to get back.'

'I could prolong my stay!'

'But not for months of chemotherapy or whatever – you have your wife, your work, your children to get back to!' Jeremy realised that she was right and felt his loyalties splitting in two.

'Hey, let's not jump the gun here!' he said. 'So far nobody says you have *anything*.'

'I know, but I need to prepare myself: I could be walking around this moment with cancer and maybe I have to think that one all through…'

'Well, if that's what you want, but why don't we take this one step at a time and deal with each eventuality *if* and when it happens.' Jeremy's level-headedness was doing her good, although he didn't know it and it was draining his reserves.

'Constance Sharland!'

Connie sprang from her seat, nervous energy spilling through her, as she followed a nurse through to a suite of rooms where she was first given an ultrasound test. Connie lay on a couch, while her lump was wiped with oil, after which a cold probe was run across and around it, and a television screen recorded the findings. Connie was at least no stranger to scans, but previously they had always served to delight and excite when they recorded first sighting of her babies in the womb. Further examinations to her breast ensued and some cells were removed from the lump with a very fine needle, as James had warned on her visit to the medical centre, what seemed so many moons ago. She should 'barely feel a thing', she was told, if only she would relax; but relaxing while a needle was inserted into her breast, of all places, was quite out of Connie's power, so she pulled faces, held her breath and ground her teeth, determined not to let out a sound! No one was seeing her face, however, and Connie considered that if medics did look at some of the faces pulled as a result of their torturous exploits in the name of healing, they would barely be capable of continuing in their vocation. As the needle was removed and Connie let out her breath, there was a pause and then an apology.

'I'm so sorry – we seem to have misfired – I'm afraid we'll have to do this one again. The fluid hasn't drawn into the test-tube.'

Misfired? *No!*

'Oof!' exclaimed Connie, through gritted teeth. 'Does this often happen?'

'Not very often – you're just unlucky!' answered the nurse who was assisting, in a clumsy attempt at reassurance, as she got ready a fresh needle.

Connie began to feel like something on a conveyer belt, for her breast began to get the same sort of scrutiny as a picture in a gallery and she felt as though it was no longer a part of her. Finally she was told that the tests were complete and that she could get dressed.

'But when do I get my results?' asked Connie.

'We'll make you another appointment in a couple of days: we should definitely know by then and – I know it's difficult – but please *don't* worry, it is often nothing at all.'

Connie found Jeremy sitting on the edge of his chair in the waiting room examining, but unable to read, the *North Devon Journal*. They left the hospital for the nearest pub, where they downed a couple of gins and had a lunch of pasty and salad. Connie phoned Nigel, as she had promised long ago the first time, and he asked if she would like to cancel the gig that night.

Connie said the gig would be the perfect distraction, which, beside being the truth, she was aware needed very much to take place, since the band had missed two gigs since Mary had died – and she knew that certain of the band members would be depending on the dosh.

Jeremy was keen to watch Connie's gig, but she asked him to babysit instead, knowing that this time Ella *would* cope well with her sisters but that it might be too soon to depend too much on her, for she didn't want to succumb to the temptation of leaning on her. If she did have to have any therapy, she realised that leaning would be precisely what she would need to do and while they still had Jeremy it seemed pre-emptive.

She was also uncharacteristically glad to be alone with her own company for the journey to the gig, for she could stop being stoical and wallow in a few moments of unadulterated panic! How would she cope with the school run over the period of a mastectomy? She would have to depend on taxis and the help of friends. She hated feeling beholden, but she would have to view it that if it were the other way round, she would, of course, want to help others all she could. Then a most unworthy thought went through her: Why me? What have I done to deserve this shed-load? She knew she would make awful jokes, if she had to have a mastectomy, and saw herself carving a chicken.

'Now who would like some breast? Me, I think!' and so on.

The gig was a thumping success and Connie was on top form: her voice was cutting through well and she managed to put over the songs with complete absorption and conviction. She lost herself so utterly in her flute solos, that she felt quite detached from the mechanics of producing the sounds. It was as though the flute were actually playing itself and she was the lucky custodian for its performance. After the gig they went for the customary 'egg-burger without the burger' at the hot-dog wagon and Connie became loud and vivacious, the adrenaline still pumping. Nigel was the only one who knew about the test and he looked on encouragingly as she fooled about with the subsequent ice cream cornet, inverting it on her nose like Pinocchio while crooning 'Just One Cornetto!' By the time they had dropped her off at home, she was completely exhausted: she heaved the unwieldy oak door onto the waiting Tramp.

'Right, puppy dog!' she whispered. 'We've now got one day down and one more to go! Let's hope tomorrow will be as speedy!'

Tramp snorted his agreement before giving in to the pleasure of the instant head-heavy slumber he had been waiting for!

Chapter Twenty-Three

Purgatory!

Darling Connie,
*I heard recently about your mum and was so very sorry, firstly that you
didn't think to tell me in time for me to have sent some flowers at least
by way of condolence. But actually, you probably DID think and
decided not to tell me, due to my dastardly behaviour of recent.*

*I know you were really close to your mum and I was always
looking forward to the point where you would introduce me. I suppose
you wouldn't have done anyway now, as things turned out, so her
dying hasn't stopped me from ever knowing her, which is really sad to
me. I truly hope things haven't been too awful and that you are getting
enough help moving her things and such like, but I'm sure, what with
your brother and all those friends, you won't be short of volunteers. I
would offer, but I know you don't want to see me again and so would
have turned me down.*

*This brings me to a further point, which is that I am off to Sri
Lanka on one of my jaunts to pick up gems at amazing prices – except
this time I think I'll stay out there. At least for the foreseeable future. I
am so ashamed of my recent behaviour and I feel burnt-out here. Never
forget that the reason for it all was my love for you, which you spurned,
so, like it or not, you are at least partially to blame! If you had taken
me back, none of that stuff with Ella need have happened – it was only
because I was so very lonely without you and I needed to know how
you were and what you were doing. I STILL do, which is why I'm
planning to distance myself. So you may thank me for that if you wish!*

*Please be aware that, whatever you may think of me – and I DO
feel bad – I'm doing a noble thing here. It's not as though I particularly
WANT to go to Sri Lanka and you only have to say the word and, of
course, I won't think of going. Somehow, though, I fear you'll prefer
me out of the way which, given what's gone down, I do understand.*

*So remember I'm not all bad, and remember our good times, which
I regularly do, and one day maybe we can become friends again. The
sooner the better in fact. Now, rather than later, if at all poss.*

Also remember that all this mess is because I love you and I wish you would understand that,

Pete

Dear Pete,

Thanks for your kind (she wanted to put 'well intentioned') *letter.*

Yes, it has all been pretty ghastly losing Mother. Although, as you say, you never met her, she did know of your existence and was glad that I had a 'somebody', as she put it. The fact that you didn't meet, means no one can say you didn't get on, which is sort of good, I think. Anyway, I miss her loads and it was good of you to write. I think it brave of you and – dare I say it, SENSIBLE to choose to go away for a while. With a space, I think you'll wake up to the reality that I'm not the person for whom you have made a pedestal.

But what I am is a parent, which has to come first and foremost of everything – and it is not something I should have to apologise for. The wide-ranging ramifications are too hard for someone not directly related to my family to take on. That is why your 'stuff' with Ella hurt me more than you would have understood. I know I love to act daft sometimes and I'd probably do that more if I were free from family ties, but I always have to think before I'm daft when I'm around my children! And I'm sorry but I couldn't be happier with them, even though relationships are important to me and I do feel lonely without one. In fact, I must admit there are times when the children make me want to stick my head in the oven – but, oddly perhaps, even then, they still come at the top of my pop chart!

You need someone who can give you so much more time and consideration than I and I hope that one day soon you will meet that right person for you and, in time, you may even have children yourself – don't think I'm being patronising, but I think that only then will you understand my feelings.

I do wish you well but I do also endorse your plans for leaving – 'there are plenty more fish in the sea', as the Streets so eloquently put it – and I hope you find happiness ASAP. This has been a bad time and it will be mended the sooner on new exciting shores.

Who knows? We may be friends again, when we're old and grey, but right now, I need to mend. Forgive me if this is not what you were hoping to hear.

All the best and good journeying!
Connie

Connie reread her letter and wondered at its harshness, but there was truly nothing else she dared say, in case Pete interpreted any tiny nuance into an excuse that really (she might not know it yet) she wanted him to stay!

She was not proud of the relief she had begun to feel at the prospect of his being oceans away, especially in the small hours, when her fears were magnified and the normally comforting homely sounds of pheasants carking or wisteria branches tapping the window, made her hold her breath for the dreaded strains of the purple sports car, its door slamming and his footsteps on the gravel. She selected another letter from the sheaf of black-bordered cards, with which Poppy was adorning the house. This was from her favourite cousin, Boo, with whom she had been at school and through no end of scrapes in her early years: this might keep her gainfully occupied from demon flashes of positive test results for a little longer.

Dear Connie-cuzzy, it began,
Poor, poor you! You must miss Mary so much! I remember at school being just a little jealous of the relationship you had with her: you seemed to be able to tell your mother ANYTHING and she invariably thought it funny, which gave us the sense of proportion that whatever trouble we were in, it couldn't have been SO bad! She was also one of the few adults I found myself able to talk to as a teenager, because she seemed genuinely interested, non-judgmental and on the same wavelength! That is surely something to aspire to. Mind you, you must be a chip off the old block because we were all really impressed with your Ella at the funeral – she sang like a veritable angel (just like you, dear!) and seemed very self-possessed, which, I think showed great maturity and promise! You and Mary must have done a great job – lucky you! (If you only knew, thought Connie, still swelling at the compliment!) *My two teenagers are both hideous – you should HEAR the way they speak – nay, BELLOW – at me! I'm sure WE weren't that ghastly! Or were we? Don't let's dwell on that!*

Anyway, this is my thoroughly clumsy and indulgent way of saying I don't know what to say because you were both so close and you probably need her even more at present, what with the revolting, curmudgeonly Stuart and everything! (Didn't I TELL you not to go marrying him?)

Dear Jeremy will be busy being a brick, I know, but after he inevitably leaves for Aus., couldn't you get away for a weekend and you and I could hook up, get sozzled and behave badly? I could get rid of my ghastlies with their father and couldn't you send your sweeties – (I know you ADORE yours!) to THEIR father? Say yes – you need a break and I know Mary would be the first to agree.

Loads of love and hugs and hopefully C U soon!

Boo

xxxxxxxxxxxxx

Connie smiled wanly at Boo's infallible mixture of kindness and irreverence but, as she began to reflect, she found the idea of behaving badly with Boo and without the children rather appealing! She smiled the more broadly at the realisation that the following letter that she would write was to be somewhat antithetical to the smugness displayed in the one to Pete, that had directly preceded it.

Dear Boo-boo,

Thanks for your lovely letter: it is indeed awful to lose Mother and to realise that one has orphan status. Who was it that said that no one truly becomes a grown-up until both their parents are dead? Well, it seems to be true a bit, for I feel I may have lost some of my 'inner child'. It's like the buck stops here and there's nobody sort of senior to pass it on to – if that makes any sense. You are right, of course, that lovely Jeremy, identically bereaved, is holding the plot together tremendously for both of us; but he's put his flight off once already and now he must travel back in two days' time. Thus I find it incumbent upon me to take up your jolly good offer to come and stay soon, sans famille, to rediscover my child within and all things badly behaved! I'll ask Stuart if he can have the children soon, once things have died down a bit more: it may divert them from noticing the hole Uncle Jeremy will leave too keenly!

Thanks again and hope Abyssinia,

Love, Connie-cuz

Connie picked out another letter, the opening of which she had deferred for some days and rebuked herself as her heart responded with a familiar lurch at the sight of the spidery handwriting. Why, when they were so very 'finished' in all senses, did this annoying reaction refuse to leave her? Was there some truth in Dylan's 'thin line between love and hate'? After time and tide, her feelings were certainly lacking warmth or respect, but she didn't feel she had the capacity to hate; love then? Surely not – and for the same reason. She slit the familiar vellum of the long, cream envelope jaggedly open and hastily flipped open the contents.

Dear Connie,

I don't know what to say except to offer my heartfelt condolences! It would be hypercritical of me to feign a closeness with your mother, but she did have my deepest respect and I realise that her sad death will be a dire blow to you because you WERE both so close. She was indeed a fine and intelligent person. The children will miss her too. I won't come to the funeral, obviously, but please know that I will be thinking of you and the children and willing you through. I expect you will be singing and it will be uplifting to everyone – difficult for you, of course, but I know your resources.

I have been waiting for an appropriate moment for some time to tell you something that's happened to me that's important – and since I am already writing to you I hope you won't mind my mentioning it right now (although it makes the aforementioned sorrow none the less sincere, and if there's anything I can do to help in any way you have only to say). I've been going out with Sue (from Accounts) for some months now and it seems (fingers crossed, etc.) to be going well. In short, we wanted you (after my parents) to be the first to know that we are expecting our baby in December! This has, of course, happened rather quickly but although it is not something I had budgeted for (!) I think the news is great and it will help to fill the void that I experience in missing bringing up OUR own children. Maybe I'll do it better this time and perhaps the fact that it seems to be a boy (Sue is one of those who prefers to be prepared in advance, which I must say I admire) will make for a healthy alternative. Anyway, I will tell the children only when YOU feel it to be right.

I realise it will be hard for you to be happy for us just now and I repeat that I'm sorry to mention it at the same moment as the sad thoughts I expressed earlier, but I needed to let you know as – although I haven't admitted it to her – Sue is just beginning to SHOW and questions will soon be asked!

All the best to you and the children,
Stuart
PS: Do we still have the Moses basket?

Connie's stomach churned and turned ever-greater cartwheels as she read this, scanning quickly at first, greedy to absorb it all, before reading it again, more slowly and carefully. She knew Stuart better than to blame his insensitivity – indeed, she was touched at his efforts in expressing his sympathy over someone with whom, although inevitably close, he had found no rapport. However, Connie was experiencing an irrational creeping, seething loathing. Presumably it was directed towards that red-headed (loads younger of course!) 'Sue in Accounts'. And the mention of his 'budget'! Had this been dropped in deliberately, to warn her that her maintenance would have to be trimmed accordingly because they were expecting another 'and you know yourself, having babies isn't cheap'!

Connie leapt up, still holding the letter, and strode to the kitchen cupboard where she deftly drew out, from amongst the assortment of jams and marmalades, the digestive biscuit tin, its cylinder shape fitting the contents snugly. She returned to the snug with the tin and munched through the biscuits methodically as she read and reread the letter in an attempt to absorb and understand how its contents affected her.

Gradually the initial impact of resentment began to subside and Connie began to question herself: wasn't she, Connie, happy with her four bouncing, healthy exuberant girls? Of course she was. Did she want more children? She didn't. Would she have wanted to have had a boy? Certainly not – she wouldn't have known what to do with one. Was she jealous of Sue in Accounts then? Here she pondered, but no – Sue was really nothing to her either way and if she succeeded in keeping Stuart happy where she had failed, then good luck to her! The red hair was probably dyed and that amount of make-up didn't constitute a look over which Connie was envious; in fact, she found herself wondering, slightly anxiously, if it hid any insecurity, for Stuart would find that soon enough! Connie could have done with Sue's comparative youth, enabling more time, but then there was little she would wish away! Her own children, then? How might this affect them? Suddenly, unbidden, a picture of Sophia, her gentle smile suffused with the kind of maternal pride she showed towards her teddies when she thought no one could see, cradling the baby – her *half-brother* – stole across Connie's subconscious. A half-brother to her children but of no relation to herself, Sophia's mother! This, then, was from where the wrenching twisting feeling had come.

Connie had found it out. She had diagnosed the pain and what she had revealed about herself was not pretty! She scanned mentally through each of her children in turn, imagining how they would react to their baby brother and finding herself envisaging, as she did so, their delight with the news and adoration for the baby.

Connie could allow herself to feel totally excluded – or perhaps there was another way. She turned her consternation inward and considered further: how could she, Constance Sharland, mother of four delicious babies, possibly think of resenting those same precious people the beatification they would no doubt feel at the emergence of another (albeit half) sibling of their own? She continued to munch slowly and absently through one digestive after another, musing all the while. A soft breeze stirred the bowl of the lime tree outside the French windows and the squirrels danced from branch to branch.

With huge relief, Connie felt the contortion in her face relax, as she slumped more comfortably into the folds of the battered armchair, an empty digestive box at her feet and crumbs speckling the soft, faded denim of her jeans. If the children were happy then, simply and naturally, so was she!

There was a moment when she automatically reached for the phone – her mother would want to know about this latest bombshell – and also at the way she had handled it! Her face fell again as her hand dropped back by her side and she immediately realised *why* she had managed this alone. The fact remained, though, that she had and now she knew she should be able to cope with future wobbles! In a moment she would tell Jeremy about it calmly and he would, hopefully, be impressed; but before the mood deserted her there was a letter that needed an answer.

Dear Stuart,
Thank you for your kind thoughts. It's awful but we're coping. Wonderful news re. you, Sue from Accounts and the babe to be! The children will of course be thrilled, but may I suggest you introduce them to Sue before you tell them about the baby? (Since they don't know her they won't know if she's changed shape.)
I wish you both (I mean three!) a healthy and happy future together.
All the best, Superdad!
Connie
PS: The pram and Moses basket are still in the cellar, which might save you a bob or two!

Chapter Twenty-Four

Sophia was particularly slow to get down for breakfast and when remonstrated against, she retorted that she didn't think she was quite well enough to go to school.

'Bet there's a test!' Demelza stage-whispered.

'There is not!' answered Sophia, anxiously glancing at Connie, who, in her turn, was appealing with her eyes to Jeremy; for the last thing they could do with was a sick child at home on the day of Connie's test.

'In what way do you not feel well, Sophia?' asked Connie, ignoring Demelza.

'Well, it's no special place, it's kind of all over!'

'She feels doomed!' chortled Demelza, her hand against her heart in a mock faint. Connie felt the smooth forehead, which, to her relief, felt normal.

'You don't look unwell, Sophia – how about if I write a note to say you're off games because we think you may be coming down with something…?'

'We-ell,' muttered Sophia, looking uncertain, although off games was worth something, for she lacked what her teacher fondly called 'the killer instinct' for ball games and loathed them accordingly.

'A good breakfast and a good off games note should soon put you right,' urged Jeremy and Connie looked at him gratefully as Sophia meekly stretched for the Shreddies: life without Jeremy was going to be difficult, for they had all warmed to his enthusiastic but gentle good nature. Connie wrote the note at speed, assuring Sophia that if the ill feeling persisted she could be off school tomorrow – though that, she thought wearily, was going to be Jeremy's last day.

They all piled into the mud-spattered four-by-four, Jeremy driving and Poppy in Connie's lap: it was reassuring to feel Poppy's soft, warm weight, to feel the peachy cheek against hers and to smell the 'little girl' smell of soap powder and porridge.

I wonder how long it will be before I can cuddle if I have a lumpectomy or worse – a mastectomy? she found herself musing.

Jeremy was executing the school run magnificently, teasing Ella about her penchant for piercings and tattoos, asking Sophia which colours she had not yet selected for her brace (this was changed at six-week intervals, with an impressive choice of all colours of the rainbow) and encouraging Poppy to recite her seven-times table without Demelza's promptings. At last they were able to go directly to the hospital, Jeremy keeping up his badinage throughout, partly for the benefit of Connie and partly in an attempt to stop himself from thinking too much. He had prepared for the shock of losing his mother many times during his pondering, wondering hours at his own home, which didn't mean he didn't miss her dreadfully; but the notion of his sister being unwell was something totally other and he felt wretchedly inadequate.

They waited in the Oncology Department amongst a sea of other apparently normal-looking people, each wondering at which stages these other people had reached, and how they had reacted to the news that 'the big C' was a possibility, a probability, or a cert. Connie attempted to hang on to the naïve hope that life couldn't do this to her because she was far too busy and necessary at present. She wanted to do a deal with God: 'If you'll let me off now, I'll have it later. Just not now – not when the children are missing their grandma so much: the timing would just be too unfair!' She wheedled in her head for a while, but then felt instantly ashamed as she looked around her at those who must have equal or greater importance in being needed than she – one woman had a child in a pushchair, another was grappling with a Zimmer frame – statistics were that the majority of people in this room would turn out to have malignant cancers of some sort.

They watched one person after another being called in for their fates to be decided: a look at their expressions as they left the consulting rooms told the diagnoses plainly and Connie was distressed to see the woman with the pushchair come out with her eyes brimful of tears. When Connie's name was finally called she had lost all faith in her own invincibility, for she had now come to the conclusion that there could be no one for whom it could be considered a right time for a positive diagnosis. Each person was therefore equally undeserving.

She sat down quietly and attempted to compose herself as a nurse handed a thin, grey-headed, weary-looking specialist her notes, which he was reading without expression. An X-ray of what must have been her breast, with the lump showing darkly, was highlighted on the wall and the specialist glanced up at it occasionally, presumably for reference. After what seemed an eternity, he looked at her for the first time over the rims of his spectacles which were positioned halfway down his nose.

'Well…' he said.

For God's sake spit it out! thought Connie.

'Yes?' answered Connie, her smile brittle and over-bright.

'A fibroadenoma!'

If the moment had been less tense Connie might have responded with 'Bless you!' and proffered a handkerchief, but instead she remained in dumb, compliant patient-mode: 'I beg your pardon?' He was smiling kindly now – was it because he felt sorry for her?

'A fibroadenoma… it's a sort of collection of fibrous glandular tissue which knots together to form the lump you're experiencing. It's almost identical in composition to a cancerous lump, which is why they can't always be identified without further tests – as in your case – but it's perfectly harmless. We can remove it, of course, but I'm happy to say you're in no danger!' The specialist had warmed to his explanation, for he had been the bearer of bad news to several that morning and it was always such a pleasure to be able to reassure. 'So go home to your husband and family,' he expanded, 'and tell them the glad news!'

Connie felt her thanks to be pitifully inadequate, so she repeated them several times over. She stumbled out, trying to compose her features for the sake of those with different news to hers, but Jeremy had read her face and his own beamed no such scruples!

Once the swing doors had swung to behind them Jeremy made a fist and leapt into the air, with a '*Yes!*' Connie was skipping down the slidey linoleum corridor.

'Oh God, I can't *believe* how relieved I am – how *lucky* I am!'

'You should be so lucky – lucky, lucky, lucky! But you'll have to keep on supply teaching!' chanted Jeremy.

'Oh! Perhaps I should have a little cancer then, after all! But right now I think I could do a round at St John's and still come out smiling!'

At the foyer, a lady could be seen selling daffodil badges for Cancer Research and Connie began to scrabble in her handbag. She pulled out all the notes she had, which came to sixty-five pounds, and began to roll them up and push them into the delighted lady's tin.

'Conscience money,' she said to Jeremy. 'There, but for the grace of God, go I!'

Nodding, Jeremy too began to manically turn out his pockets and produced another forty pounds. 'Have a wonderful day!' he said to the astonished lady.

'Yes,' laughed Connie, 'please have lots and lots!' They walked out, arm in arm, into the sunshine, smiling.

'Do you think there's a cash point around here?' asked Jeremy.

The rest of the day vacillated for Connie between a beatific haze at being spared the complications of cancer, and of emptiness at seeing Jeremy pack. The children were subdued at the thought of his parting for such a very long time, after they had begun to depend on his high spirits geeing them all along and his gentle understanding. He had small packages which he found a private moment to give to each individually: to Ella, he gave matching earrings and a belly-button stud, which, reading from one ear and across the navel to the other, read WI – CK – ED! Ella pounced on them, exclaiming, 'Wicked!' and laughing easily at her own stereo-typicality, which was something she would have been incapable of doing some weeks ago.

'Ella – you know your grandma would be really proud of you, the way you're supporting your mum: you've grown up so much and she really appreciates a 'nearly grown-up' around the place. You will keep it going, won't you?' Ella was blushing a very girly pink as she smiled shyly and said that she had every intention of 'keeping it up', for this, indeed, was the new her! She then gave Jeremy a big hug and snuffled something about missing him into his hairy bush sweater.

Jeremy gave Demelza a horror make-up kit, complete with blood capsules, one of which she immediately bit, 'Just to see what it tasted like!' She then let out a few blood-curdling growls, but the words being uttered belayed her true feelings. 'Don't dare leave us, Uncle Jeremy, or I shall have to eat you *bodily*!' she drooled, mock blood spilling down her chin. After a couple of lunges at Jeremy she sped away to don more of the horror make-up with which to frighten the rest of her family.

Jeremy discovered Sophia up a tree, reading *Jane Eyre*. 'I know why you're here because Demelza told me: if I *don't* have my present, will you have to stay?' she called down.

'Oh, Sophia! Don't make this any harder – I hate to leave you too,' Jeremy said, with feeling, 'but think of your aunt and cousins back in Aus, wondering if I'll ever get back – I need them too!'

'So when you're here you miss them and when you're there you miss us!' sighed Sophia.

'Well, yes, I guess that's exactly how it is. But you know I'll be thinking of my best nieces and telling them all about you – and maybe, before too long, you can all come and stay with us in the bush. There wouldn't be room for all of you in the house, you know, so some of you would need to sleep in a tent!'

'Ooh! Could that be Demelza and me? We love camping,' smiled Sophia happily.

'I think that could be arranged…'

'But,' Sophia's face had fallen again, 'I don't know if Mummy could afford it?'

'I think you'll find that Grandma's taken care of that sort of thing,' Jeremy answered. 'Everything may be just a little easier from now on.'

'Well, I can't wait then!' said Sophia easily. 'So now you may give me your present, if you like!' Jeremy produced a heavy-looking package from behind him, which Sophia ripped open: it was *Pollyanna*.

'*Yes!*' cried Sophia excitedly. 'I've seen the film and I've always wanted to read the real book!'

'Well our grandma – your great-grandma – used to read it to your mum and me and you rather remind me of Pollyanna and her "glad" game!'

'Do I? Well, I shall read it forthwith and then give you my comments!' So saying, Sophia propped *Jane Eyre* against the tree and peeled back the crisp new flyleaf of *Pollyanna*!

Poppy was helping Connie to catch the strawberry hen, Bustle, who had escaped through the netting again and was stalking slowly back towards the open door of the hen run; however, instead of going in, she hesitated. Poppy clucked behind her, at which Bustle changed her mind and scuttered on past the door! At this point the cockerel stepped out of the open door, followed by Bashful, Bustle's companion, whereupon Connie slammed the door to all, after which all the remaining inhabitants of the chicken run began to cluck and carp! Next they reopened the door, by which Connie stood sentry in an attempt to stop any others from escaping, while Jeremy and Poppy rounded up the three absconders to hoosh them back home. Once all this was accomplished and Connie had announced the need for gin-but-go-easy-on-the-tonics, Jeremy produced their presents: Poppy's was a beautifully inlaid oaken box, with a secret spring. Inside were all Jeremy's old school medals for sprinting and long jump. Poppy's mouth formed a perfect 'O' when she saw the medals.

'Wow! Are they real antiques? Did you actually win these? And the box is cool as cool! Thanks, oh thank you, Uncle Jeremy!' She flung her short arms around his neck and he whizzed her in a circle.

Finally, Jeremy picked up Connie's somewhat bulky present, complaining that she was a real problem to find a present for. Connie stretched out for it but Jeremy held it above his head. Connie chased him, attempting a rugby tackle while Poppy tried to pin his arms. He broke free and then threw it for Connie, calling, 'Don't drop it, little sister! It's glass you know!' Connie shrieked as she fell backwards, holding the tatty parcel aloft triumphantly. Covered in mud, she began to rip at the slippery Sellotape.

'It's not glass at all – I can feel!' she complained, exasperated by the confining wrapping. 'All that falling over for nothing!' But at that moment out fell a large, smiling, cuddly Koala bear, wearing a pair of racy boxer shorts!

'Oh, Jeremy, he's gorgeous! I love him!' laughed Connie, cuddling the bear.

'His name is Bruce and he's under strict instructions to guide you and the kids to his homeland before long...' said Jeremy and then, more anxiously, 'I'm sorry: I couldn't think what to get – you *do* like him, don't you?'

'Like him? I think Bruce is wonderful and he and I will get along famously! Couldn't want for anything – cuddlier!' she giggled.

'There's a refreshing change!' remarked Jeremy archly.

Chapter Twenty-Five

The goodbyes were accomplished as cheerily as possible, with the promise that they would all be visiting soon. Jeremy took his final school run in the morning, for Stuart had readily agreed to pick the children up from school to spend a quiet weekend with him, while Connie returned Jeremy to Heathrow and went on for the promised visit to their cousin, Boo. Tramp took up the back, surrounded by an assortment of suitcases, severely bubble-wrapped packages containing pictures, and smaller items of furniture – not to mention several bottles of wine, a prerequisite for seeing anything of Boo.

Jeremy and Connie chatted easily as they cruised up the M5 and M4, but as they neared Heathrow an awkward silence descended, each feeling the awe of the moment and finding nothing worthy enough to say.

'Look,' began Jeremy as they swung into the vast impersonal multi-story car park, 'you don't need to spend a fortune on parking. Just drop me off and I promise not to make a fuss!'

'Oh no! I'm seeing you properly onto that plane! We couldn't have you carrying all that stuff by yourself!' Connie excused herself lamely. The truth was, she needed to see Jeremy off 'properly': he had been such a boon to them all in so many ways and she wanted to do something demonstrative to illustrate it. Also, there actually were so many of their mother's possessions (some of which were to be put in the hold as extra baggage, while a container was booked for the rest at a later date) that extra hands would be genuinely useful. Jeremy gave in gratefully as they commandeered trolleys, which they attempted to control down the invasion of lifts and conveyers. After a gruelling check-in and much scrutiny of baggage and form filling, they ditched the trolleys and made their way towards the departure lounge. Each was busy with their own thoughts while attempting to make light, knowing the other was feeling the absence of their mother acutely. For here she should have been with her stiff upper lip, cracking bawdy jokes and allowing no chance for sentimentality; she was so much better at this sort of thing, due to the years of their being shipped off to boarding school. In the midst of her misery at her own inadequacy, Connie heard the sound of quick footsteps and her name being called. She whipped around.

'So you *came*! And you had me thinking you didn't care!' Pete was beaming, Jeremy looked confused and Connie was gaping!

'Pete, this is Jeremy, my brother,' Connie said weakly. 'Jeremy, you remember my telling you about *Pete*?' She gave Jeremy a significant look of desperation.

'Not all bad, I hope. Good to see you: I've heard a lot about you. But Connie!' he turned to her delightedly. 'How did you know the time of my plane? I'll cancel: I'm sure they can recall my luggage – talk about the *eleventh hour*! But all the more of an adventure for that.'

'Yeah – just about all bad, as I remember!' Jeremy was snarling.

'Oh, I'm so sorry at how it looks, Pete,' Connie answered despairingly, 'but I'm just seeing Jeremy off to Australia. I'm afraid I didn't know you were here – in fact, I thought you had probably already gone to Sri Lanka!' There was a lengthy pause while Pete absorbed this latest emotional boomerang.

'Ah,' he said at last, in his Eeyore-ish manner, 'easy mistake, I suppose – um. Well, I'm going via Singapore,' he tapped the side of his nose warily, 'I heard of a bit of a deal – no, it's all above board!' he added, as Connie's eyebrows rose. 'But I must say I feel rather dashed seeing you and…'

'Bit of a shock for us all,' said Connie sympathetically.

'So it turns out I'm seeing you onto this plane because I go via Singapore too!' Jeremy muttered darkly.

Connie had begun to feel very sorry for Pete, for this was one awkward situation which he had not engineered, and yet he was suffering. Her voice softened.

'In fact, it turns out I'm seeing you both onto the plane! And maybe it's made an opportunity to part without the ill feeling we may have been feeling!'

Pete looked somewhat restored at this logic. His face lit up.

'I bet it was actually all meant to happen – I'll look it up in the *Ai Ching*! Maybe we can view this as a healing, karmic experience!' he enthused, much mollified.

'I'll go along with that – on condition that my niece stays out of your cosmic sphere!' Connie looked gratefully at Jeremy for putting into words what she was thinking.

'Oh, absolutely! That is all a part of a past of which I wish to be expunged!'

'Sponge away then!' smiled Jeremy less grimly, and, although there was still a certain awkwardness, the atmosphere warmed a little.

'Good luck, Pete – I am actually glad we ran into you.' Connie was surprised to find this to be true.

'Me too! And I'll take good care of Jeremy to Singapore!'

'You and me both!' Jeremy grinned.

'Oo – I'm feeling all loved up!' sighed Pete. 'But that'll be partly due to popping my last 'E' so that I could board the plane ecstatic and totally clean.'

He wiped a tear dramatically from his shining cheek and searched Connie's face for approval. Jeremy snorted disbelief while Connie smiled encouragement.

'Goodbye, Pete, it sounds as though you've taken all the best decisions – and now, do you mind if I have a moment with my brother?'

'Not at all! All the best Connie,' said Pete a little shakily, but he smiled bravely before kissing Connie's cheek. 'Bygones and all that?'

'All that.'

Pete lifted his shoulder bag back onto his shoulder and shambled off.

'Wow, Connie! *What were you doing with him?* I'm really glad I can watch him going!' volunteered Jeremy, his consternation overruling any consideration of tact.

'My self-esteem was particularly low: I was flattered, I was lonely, he made me laugh – you know, nothing much!'

'Hmm – well, you're not going to let that sort of thing happen again, are you? I mean there are loads of much nicer fish…' *Wasn't the fish bit what she had told Pete, too? It was clearly a catchy phrase in these situations.* Jeremy was looking piercingly at her from behind his spectacles and there was a flash of their mother's level gaze, reserved for the rare moments when she was in earnest. Connie smiled wryly.

'No, I'll be more careful in future. And actually I'm starting to quite like being single – except I do get empty when the children are away!' she corrected candidly.

'Oh, Sis – Bruce will look after you!'

'So he will! And Tramp!'

'Connie – you know Tramp won't last for ever!'

'Shut up! "I'll think about that tomorrow for tomorrow is another day",' she quoted. 'And now,' she smiled bravely, 'you have a plane to catch, your long-suffering family to catch up with, and I have a cousin Boo, who was mentioning something about a party!' She hugged Jeremy and his fleece tickled her nose.

'Be safe, Jeremy – and thanks – I couldn't have coped without Mother without you!' Jeremy gave her a squeeze and his voice had now lost all authority.

'Neither could I, Connie, neither could I – you have no idea. Goodbye, little sister!' He turned abruptly and didn't look back. Their family had its own routine over this sort of thing and each knew what to do – Connie turned away too and began walking as briskly as possible in any direction, without a wave or backward glance.

Marching determinedly out of the airport, Connie began to realise that she had no recollection on which deck they had parked, for Jeremy had been driving and her mind had been dealing only on the immediate present.

Feeling the emptiness she had so recently described to Jeremy, she floundered up and down lifts and around countless shady-looking pillars behind which her car could be lurking. She thought of poor Tramp in the back of it and of the mounting parking fee and was on the verge of a minor panic, when a voice hailed her.

'Excuse me – this is probably a stupid question, but you haven't seen a vivid-green BMW on your travels? Sorry to ask, but I noticed you two floors ago and you look as though you're looking for something too!' Connie looked up briefly, relieved that there was someone else in the world in as daft a position as herself.

'I'm really sorry, but I'm afraid I haven't noticed...' she began, while thinking that, of course, she had hardly been looking. Then it occurred to her to try his rather ridiculous tactic herself. 'But I wonder if *you've* noticed a rather dingy, dirt-coloured old Discovery, with an even older dog in the back?' The large man, in a distinctively well-cut dark cashmere coat, sporting a floppy black felt hat, looked at her excitedly.

'I should think I have! He began barking as I went past – a sort of brownish hairy-looking chap? Quite a veteran.'

'Oh yes!' called Connie happily. 'I wish he'd had the brains to bark at me! Where, please?'

'Definitely in a corner and I *think* it was the floor below this one. If not, the one below that...' he wavered, 'sort of in *that* position.' He indicated where it would be had it been the floor they were on. Connie thanked him and wished him good luck in his own search while she hurried to the lift.

Sure enough, the car was exactly where the man had described on the floor below, with Tramp sleeping soundly again, only waking to thump his tail as she unlocked the door.

'Clever boy! You helped me find you!' Connie enthused, as she wondered briefly if the other person responsible had found his own car. She sped for the exit, keen to pay-off her still-mounting parking costs, but as she did so her mobile was beginning to ring: she answered it as she negotiated her payment. It was Ken. He was apologising sweetly for not having been in contact for the past few weeks and Connie explained about her mother and her brother, while thinking to herself about the other things she had left out, such as Ella, Pete, the cancer scare...

Connie returned to the car, feeling less stressed and switched the mobile to 'hands free' mode.

'Ken...' He was busy being sympathetic about her mother, about whom she didn't want to think just now – or of Jeremy, if it came to that. 'I think we both know why we haven't been in contact and I've been wondering how I'd talk to you when we did get time for each other again.' Ken sounded relieved.

'Me too, actually – I could have called from New York but... I know your kids have to come first and I did understand when you had to rush off after that gig; but you didn't really give me time to say so – and then I felt it might be best to cool things, or at least see if you rang me!' Connie warmed, as usual, to his candour.

'I know I didn't treat you very fairly, but the thing was I couldn't have had a good time with you, knowing there was a problem which was possibly unresolved at home...' She broke off, as she considered how things might have run on had she not gone straight home and discovered Ella's outing with Pete. 'Sometimes you get an instinct for things and at others you get it all hopelessly wrong – but I just always need to be sure either way.'

'I know – well, I can imagine. The thing is though, Connie, I was getting quite fond of you and when you left like that it left me realising that I would need to accept that kind of thing at any time – that it could never really definitely be just you and me… Oh dear! How self-centred a confession is that?'

'But, Ken, you've got it exactly right – which is why we weren't destined to become involved again. When we were together before, we were *both* entirely autonomous, but now it's only one of us, so things are completely different. I think we were simply revelling in the past – but we did know really that things had moved on and couldn't be…' She had left Heathrow behind and was following the signs south-eastwards, towards Kent.

'Well, I have to confess that I had started to think that a musician could have a settled home life and that a mother could have one too – with that musician,' he began.

'Purely in the abstract sense!' said Connie, keen to keep the conversation light.

'Well not entirely abstract—' continued Ken, sounding rather too serious for Connie's liking.

She interrupted: 'You know what? I think you're right to a point – that it could work for a while – like it did – but then the musician always being in other parts of the world, in an antithetical lifestyle to the mother (who had all those children to put first) would begin to create its own friction – and then they mightn't be the friends and soulmates they always intended to be!'

'It was always great fun, from my point of view, but then I never actually saw you at home with all your broods!'

'We were never ever certain enough for that – but *I* had a great time too, having you in a little world away from my broods!'

'A touch of the fantasy then?'

'Perhaps – but the very *wonderfullest*! Oh, Ken, I've missed you too! I want you to be my friend forever and I've been so afraid that we'd feel too awkward to see each other again and I'd lose you!'

'Let's agree to be friends forever then, and not to have any awkwardness.'

'Ken, I would like that more than anything! And will you still come and see me and invite me to your gigs when you're nearby, like always?'

'I promise! Where are you going this evening, by the way?'

They both burst into laughter at this and Connie explained about Boo, while Ken said that if there was a party on that was near London (where he was to be stationed for the next three nights), he *might* be able to fit it in and would Connie please furnish him with all the necessary details.

When he finally rang off, Connie had left London and the zenith of her feeling of emptiness behind her, to be brooded upon another day, when the pain of parting was a little duller. The restraint between her and Ken was gone too, and the original easy harmony restored.

Chapter Twenty-Six

As Connie and Tramp pushed their way in through Boo's little cottage door, a scurry of cats marked their arrival, to which Tramp gave gameful chase.

'Yahoo-oo!' called Boo over the barking, hissing hubbub as she trundled in from the garden. 'Is that you?'

'Certainly is Cuzzywuz!' called Connie, as Boo bounded towards her, beaming her greeting. Boo was the same height as Connie, but probably almost twice as wide. However, far from this being any sort of visual disadvantage, her ampleness was a thing of voluptuous beauty, which exuded a 'Ma Larkin' sense of sexuality, rendering her irresistible to a number of people: her skin was of a pink and white English rose hue, with barely a line to be seen, in spite of her being well into her forties. There were just a few fine creases, however, around her shining eyes and deep red, generous mouth, to give away her irrepressible good humour. She was naturally dark, but today, she was sporting a veritable wealth of blond streaks and splodges, matching her leopard skin mini-skirt. After a couple of glasses of wine she would launch, if encouraged, into a torrent of intriguing stories concerning infatuated, highly unsuitable and undesirable men, with whom she had accidentally entangled herself, and the incumbent extrication process that had been necessarily adopted. Many of these unfortunates had found themselves much smitten, to Boo's surprise and genuine distress, for she never apparently took any signs seriously. To Connie she was a wonderful tonic, confidante (for she could listen too) and comrade as well as cousin, and they each shone in one another's company.

Boo was quick to fill the glasses with a rich, oaky Merlot, while deftly lighting the fire with her cigarette, by tossing it onto a well-soaked fire lighter.

She fell back into the ample sofa with a giggle and a flurry of large white legs and petticoat. (Who else, besides my mother, would bother with a petticoat at home, thought Connie.)

'I bet you're laughing at my hair!' interpreted Boo. 'Do you think it's a bit too OTT? I fear it is rather wild – I did it myself!'

'Well, knock me down with a feather – I never would have guessed,' answered Connie cheekily, 'and yes! It's outrageous!'

'Goodie! That's what I was hoping,' chortled Boo, enjoying Connie's frankness, as Connie had intended. 'And now! Tell me about the men in your life and I will tell you about mine,' she said, curling her legs under her, the skirt strained to bursting.

'Well, actually,' answered Connie, realising she was about to sound rather lame, 'there's no one – friends but not relationships, if you know what I mean.'

'Ah yes – I know: sort of "pausing between courses", as it were!'

'In fact, I've had rather a bad time lately…'

'Tell me about it!' interrupted Boo, flinging another log on the fire and refilling glasses, all reached from her station on the sofa.

'To the extent,' Connie continued, 'that I am really quite enjoying the luxury of being single. Unless, that is…' she said, slurping delightedly, with the hint of a glint in her own eye, 'unless Colin Firth were to burst through the door at the party, like he did for Bridget Jones!'

'Only if he was wearing his reindeer jumper though,' added Boo.

'Oh, then – and only then!' agreed Connie, the strain of the last few weeks receding to dullness as she swilled and chilled with her lifelong companion.

'But not if I see him first!' pronounced Boo.

'Ah well – I concede that if you see him first there'll probably be no chance even to see the reindeer!' Connie teased as she manoeuvred herself onto the floor for a safer, warmer position, nearer the fire and second wine bottle, on which they had already embarked. Boo then launched into a lurid story of a Danish cameraman she had met in Mexico (she was in the film industry) who had such a penchant for her tummy that she had wound up with it covered in love bites, resulting in her not being able to wear her bikini for a week and being unable to find a replacement swimming costume generous enough to accommodate her. Connie countered by describing one of her adventures with Pete when, after smoking a hubbly-bubbly pipe, he had insisted that he could walk across the estuary at low tide from Instow to Appledore, clad in a pair of flippers and little else, and he'd had to be rescued by the lifeboat.

After much further banter, Boo pulled herself up to a more upright posture and wagged a finger at Connie.

'We must remember, Connie!'

'Mm?'

'We must remember we have *a party* to catch,' she swung herself up from the sofa and tottered towards the stairs, 'and I don't know about you, but I'm *hungry*! Do you want the bathroom first while I prepare us a little something to munch on the way?'

'OK – yes, I think food is something I shall need in some quantity if I am to get *anywhere*!' Connie rose from her place on the floor and stamped the numbness out of her legs, after which she mounted the steep stairs. As she took a hasty shower and grovelled in her bag for her party clothes she shouted down, 'Boo! You remember Ken?'

'What, *the* Ken?'

'Well, you know – session guitarist Ken?'

'Yes, *the* Ken. Ah! What about him?'

'Well, he rang today and sounded at a bit of a loose end, so I told him about the party and gave him your address. I hope that's OK – I mean, I doubt if he'll turn up or anything.'

'Well done! Let's hope he does – we can leave him a note on the door or something.'

'Yes, I think that would be better – I don't want to ring him in case it sounds like I want him to come… you know…'

'Ah, but you *do*!' answered Boo with a chuckle, as she crossed the crowded room with a plate of tempting-looking sandwiches, to fetch the writing pad on which to write the address of the party for Ken, ignoring Connie's protestations and explanations.

When they were both finally ready and had gobbled some of the sandwiches 'because it never does to arrive and make too obvious an attack on the food,' Boo had cautioned (her firsthand experience with this sort of faux pas being clear), Connie fetched Tramp's lead.

'You're never planning on taking him, are you?' asked Boo. 'I mean, I know you're attached at the hip, but I'm sure just for the evening…'

'Oh, it's not that I mind leaving him behind, but I know he's chased your cats out of their home and they'll be wanting to return – he won't hurt them, but he's capable of causing a heck of a rumpus – it rather depends on what your neighbours may have done to deserve it.'

'And, in fact, the cats are capable of doing damage if barked at,' considered Boo. 'I do see what you mean.'

'Then I'll take him along – he'll just go to sleep under a table or something – he's very experienced in these matters.'

'Well, perhaps it would be simpler,' mused Boo. They were now more sober and better prepared for the bracing walk down the village street. Boo's heels were impossibly high and pointed.

'I know they're not designed to do anything more than support the horizontal pose – they're not called "do-what-you-will-to-me" shoes for nothing!' Somehow, however, they complemented the deep, blue, velvet dress particularly tastefully. Connie, in contrast, wore her black silk trousers that she wore for gigs, tucked into long boots and a white cotton, open-necked shirt, revealing her mother's short gold 'snake' necklace, as they had always called it. They perched the note for Ken visibly under the doorknocker before teetering down the uneven pavement. Now the alcohol had worn off, Connie was less confident, realising that she was about to enter a room with a host of people whom she had never met – and she was without a partner as such.

She wished she could be more like Boo, whose brazenness and infectious *joie de vivre* highlighted what she felt to be her own inadequacies. However, she could remain with Boo and enjoy the party from the security of her generous shadow.

'Colin Firth, here I come!' said Connie bravely, taking Boo's arm, as much for Boo's sake as her own, for Boo was struggling dangerously in her fashionable, pointy-toed excuse for shoes, while Tramp trotted cheerily alongside.

A sudden wave of voices and music assailed them as they entered the semi-open door, each conspicuously clutching a bottle. A hearty host welcomed them enthusiastically, planting a smacking kiss on Boo's cheek and exclaiming that she smelt yummy! They took their coats off in a bedroom upstairs and then made their launch on the party. Boo introduced Connie to several jovial people, with whom she enjoyed affable pleasantries, mostly concerning Tramp (how old was he and what breed?). 'Ah! A mongrel! My uncle had one once – lived to be over a hundred in doggie years – marvellous companion!' and so forth. Always at home at being a conversation piece, Tramp stood squarely beside Connie, stomping his flipper-like front paws alternately, his tail an indicator to his enjoyment at the attention he was receiving. Gradually Connie was beginning to shed her mantle of awkwardness as the wine kicked in again and she discovered the food table, into which Boo was tucking with alacrity and under which Tramp retreated for some peace.

'It seems a great village to live in,' enthused Connie, 'they're all so friendly and easy-going!'

'Yes – I do feel as though I've fallen on my feet, tentatively speaking!' Boo answered absently, as her practised eye roamed the convivial crowd. 'Excuse me a sec, though,' she said, bolting the last piece of smoked salmon canapé. 'I just want to talk with that guy over there – I did a shoot with him for a holiday commercial and he was really intuitive. Are you all right here?' Connie could tell that Boo wanted to have one of her highly technological talks, where anyone outside the film industry needed an interpreter for every second word; so she assured Boo that she was fine and continued with her difficult deliberation between the choice of a delicious-looking humus dip or the mushroom pâté.

As she refilled her plate with both dip and pâté, she became aware of a voice coming, as it seemed, from beneath her, and she looked down to see a pair of neatly polished brogues jutting out from below the tablecloth! The voice was getting no verbal response that she could hear, but it was taking both sides of the conversation.

'Are you having a good time? You are? Well, so am I! And may I say, you are looking particularly ravishing this evening! Oh, excuse me! I hadn't noticed you were a boy – no offence, mate, but you're exceedingly handsome, just the same!' Connie became intrigued as the voice, to which the brogues must belong, continued to discuss the world from beneath the table and other shoes, which could be observed more minutely from thence.

'What did you think of those? Yes, *infinitely* chew-worthy, I'd say too!' as Boo's 'do-what-you-will-to-me's' receded from view.

'Now these unremarkable black boots belong on someone quite remarkable!' enthused the voice. Connie found herself taking a quick sideways check at her feet, which were indeed encased in unremarkable black boots, and she couldn't help giggling.

'Why, I do believe they must be mine!' she exclaimed.

'She appears to have remarkable powers of observation to match!' continued the voice from below, at which point, over the general hubbub, she noticed that Ken had indeed found the party and Boo had found Ken, for they already appeared to be immersed in hilarious confabulation. Ken had been doing his usual trick of bringing his precious guitars indoors, for fear of theft or extreme temperature change (while leaving his Saab convertible unlocked) and Boo had picked him out immediately. Ken spotted Connie and he and Boo came over: the embrace that ensued between Connie and Ken was without the awkwardness each had dreaded, for already Boo seemed to have a subtle claim on his company and both Connie and Ken felt relief at the affirmation of their own re-continued platonic friendship. Ken began to tell Connie that he had received exciting news from a record company who had heard one of his demo tapes. This one featured a song which they were actually interested in recording, since they felt it had potential in the singles market: it was called 'Connie's Elegy' and he couldn't wait for her to hear it and give her opinion.

The vicarious pleasure with which Connie received Ken's news was heartfelt; but when Ken suggested he play it to her, she still remained distracted, apparently taking significant glances at the floor.

'I can't wait to hear it *in a moment*,' Connie answered, looking down purposefully again.

'One thing, Connie,' interrupted Boo, 'can you explain *why* you seemed to be talking to a table? It's a pretty poor ruse for sticking with the eats, I'd say!'

Connie waved her arms expansively in 'go away!' vigour, pointing at the floor by the table. Boo and Ken saw the brogues and finally took the hint as Boo continued smoothly, only her eyebrows arching mischievously: 'And, of course, why *shouldn't* one talk to a table? I know I often do!'

'Me too,' responded Ken gallantly, 'regularly! After meals!' And he took Boo's arm as though he had known her a lifetime and steered her away towards the back of the room. Connie felt the tiniest pang at this sight, but overriding it was a joy at seeing the evident frisson which two of her best people were finding in one another. Meanwhile there was a table to attend to, after all, for friendship was blossoming also for Tramp beneath the tablecloth, as he responded to the resonant voice with some of his most expansive snorts and grunts, each of which were being expertly returned in kind.

'I wonder,' Connie asked provocatively, in the table direction, 'how it can be possible to form an opinion on the wearer of the unremarkable boots when the rest of him, or indeed her, is, as yet, an unknown quantity?'

'Because she is *not* entirely unknown to me and I do believe she is mistress to the VID with whom I am keeping company!' At this point curiosity got the better of Connie. She lifted the edge of the far side of the tablecloth and there saw a large man, his legs inelegantly hunched up beneath him, dressed in a dark-blue cabled jersey and jeans. His head was a tasteful combination of baldness and a 'Caeser number one', tanned to a Mediterranean polish, while a definite hint of designer stubble coarsened his smiling face. His eyes, which were directed amiably upon her, reminded her of chocolate Minstrels, for they were huge, round and shining – and to Connie's befuddled mind they appeared to be spinning like a merry-go-round!

'Do I know you?' asked Connie, thinking that there could possibly be something familiar about him, but that surely she would have remembered this unusual and endearing face.

'Well, I'm not surprised you don't remember me – I think you may have been feeling a little preoccupied at the time – and I was wearing a hat – however, I did have quite a conversation with my furry friend under here. I'm just so pleased it's been possible to renew the acquaintance!' He was scratching Tramp expertly behind the ears and Tramp's back foot had begun, absurdly and irrepressibly to tattoo its delighted response.

'I'm sorry…' Connie was chiding herself, 'I know I *do* get a little preoccupied sometimes. I can't think…'

'And you drive a "dingy, dirt-coloured old Discovery, with an even older dog in the back?" *Old dog indeed! How d'you like that?*' She mused, the dull thump of Tramp's tail just audible from his world beneath the table: his description did sound familiarly like her own.

'Oh, I know: the airport car park! What a nightmare! And you were so helpful. I think I would still have been there searching for the car, if it hadn't been for you! Did you find your green BMW?'

'Eventually!' he laughed. 'It was lurking with intent around a most disagreeable pillar and took some time to detect!'

'I'm sorry I wasn't very helpful though…'

'Oh, but you were! I was going ape, until you gave me the chance to become acquainted with this venerable old stager,' he smiled down at Tramp, who was contentedly scratching his left ear with his back foot, 'for which I am most grateful, for he gave me much-needed perspective!'

Connie suddenly felt the desire to confide, to explain why she had indeed been so very 'preoccupied' (*utterly stressed, actually!*) when he had seen her. She wanted him to understand and think better of her and wondered why it should matter? However, here they were again, by the strangest of coincidences, and this being a social occasion and Connie knowing no one other than Ken and Boo (who had whisked away so readily) – and this man, seemingly completely taken with her heraldic animal – what greater opportunity than this?

They remained locked in conversation therefore, while the party swirled around them. Ken had been easily persuaded by the hosts of the party to play his guitar as his fee for gate-crashing. He was in his element, the centre of attention, perched on a kitchen stool, with Boo at his feet looking admiringly up at him. He was playing all the trusty, rabble-rousing, party stompers, causing the company to dance around him, applauding loudly, adoring him for his presence, his eminence, his undoubted skill, as his lean fingers ran effortlessly over the strings. Connie would normally have been unable to resist jigging beside him, singing and adding harmonies – indeed Ken would have insisted on it. She might have put up a show of reluctance, but once there, the music would have burned within her and she would have come alive, from shyness to extroversion in one bound.

Those were some of the events that *would* typically have happened in the normal run of events, but Connie, although happy at Ken's obvious success, was not tempted either to sing or to dance and Ken knew her well enough to sense this and not suggest it. Indeed, she was barely conscious of the music at all, so absorbed was she in her animated conversation with Sebastian. (*Sebastian*!) His slightly 'off the wall' perspective on everyday trivia seemed to coincide very much with her own and she found herself effortlessly singing the same metaphorical tune.

Just now they had returned to the theme of attitude towards the canine species: he was telling her, with that scrunchy, deep voice of his, about his abhorrence of what he called 'the entrenched Sunday suburban smuggies', to whom a dog without a pedigree was simply not a dog. If it were up to him, he said, warming to his diatribe encouraged by Connie's obvious enthusiasm, there would be classes at Crufts displaying and heralding the individuality and uniqueness of the Mongrel.

The room gradually emptied of revellers, as the guests retrieved their shoes and called their heartfelt thanks and farewells. Those who remained formed a ragged gathering around Ken, before a dwindling fire. He was playing more gently and melodiously now, and a particularly haunting, melancholic melody caused Connie to listen with half an ear, for she had caught the sound of her own name. It was 'Connie's Elegy', and indeed from what she could tell, it seemed more arresting and compelling than Ken's other more *up-tempo* work. She smiled across at Ken and gave him the 'thumbs up', before returning to further repartee with Sebastian, this time on the implications on the countryside surrounding the issue of the 'right to roam'.

The hosts had begun to hand out mugs of coffee to the remaining diehards, a sure hint that the party was over and they were hoping to regain the house for themselves so they could get it straight again, fill the dishwasher and go to bed. Boo's head was resting on Ken's knee as she sprawled comfortably and voluptuously across the sofa. Ken was obviously quite taken with her, to which she pretended to be wholly oblivious. Connie was dismayed at how quickly the time had flown, realising, with sadness, that the delight she had taken in the energising *rapport* between herself and this new intriguing acquaintance must inevitably come to a close. She felt torn and cheated by time, for she had rediscovered her lively, vivacious self, who, she now realised, had been missing in essence for some while; perhaps ever since Stuart? She wondered if Sebastian might have been someone with whom she could have unburdened about those times that she had locked away. Perhaps she would have spilled it all out, dealing with it *today* and not tomorrow. Well, she had better get the farewells out of the way, for it had been an unexpectedly wonderful evening and she didn't want to tarnish it by outstaying her welcome.

Connie turned brightly to Sebastian, searching for a parting cliché, but most of him remained beneath the table still and was facing Tramp.

'Now, I'm wondering, old fellah,' he was saying to Tramp, 'if you'd care to come out for a bit of a bone tomorrow lunchtime – and you can bring your mistress along of course, if she'd like…'

Connie became seized with a mixture of elation and panic. She swallowed to gain time, while willing herself to get this right. 'Actually, he doesn't have a mistress…' (Beneath the table Sebastian's brow furrowed in bemusement.) 'He has five!' There it was, better out than in, and Connie began to buffet herself for the inevitable rain of excuses.

'Five mistresses! Lucky chap! May I ask if they're all related?' He didn't seem remotely knocked back at the prospect.

'They are indeed, four of them being daughters of Big Mistress here!' *Spell it out, and give him a last chance to withdraw*, thought Connie.

'Even luckier chap! Well, what d'you think? Would they *all* like to come along – or would they find the bones too gristly?' Sebastian had unfolded himself a little from the confines of the table and his warm brown eyes kindled anxiously upon her.

'Well, I think they might like to, but they're all with their father until Monday – I'm missing them.' For some reason it was important to her that he understood this – she also needed to play for time and not seem too eager; but her heart was leaping absurdly.

'I see – I can fully understand that.' He considered Tramp a little longer, then spoke slowly in a low voice. 'Well, I wonder, could the *big mistress* be persuaded to accompany us?' (*Yes!*) All the while Tramp was relishing the caressing fingers in his fur. It was so delicious he couldn't contain himself any longer and gave out the loudest of snorts, reserved as his clearest indication of delight.

'Cshhhhooooooo!'

'May I take that as a yes?' asked the voice, a slight tremor giving away the lack of confidence: anxiety and hope were evidently playing their part here too. Connie answered slowly, willing herself to sound calm over the trumpets in her ears.

'I think, perhaps, you may!' she answered throatily, feeling her cheeks suffuse uncomfortably pink and diving, too, for Tramp's cover beneath the tablecloth

.

Printed in the United Kingdom
by Lightning Source UK Ltd.
115656UKS00001B/10-21